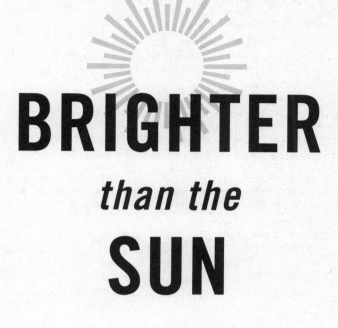

BRIGHTER
than the
SUN

Daniel Aleman

LITTLE, BROWN AND COMPANY
New York   Boston

Copyright © 2023 by Daniel Aleman

Cover art copyright © 2023 by David Curtis. Cover design by Sasha Illingworth and Patrick Hulse. Cover copyright © 2023 by Hachette Book Group, Inc.
Interior design by Carla Weise.

Little, Brown and Company
Hachette Book Group
1290 Avenue of the Americas, New York, NY 10104
Visit us at LBYR.com

First Edition: March 2023

Little, Brown and Company is a division of Hachette Book Group, Inc. The Little, Brown name and logo are trademarks of Hachette Book Group, Inc.

The publisher is not responsible for websites (or their content) that are not owned by the publisher.

Little, Brown and Company books may be purchased in bulk for business, educational, or promotional use. For information, please contact your local bookseller or the Hachette Book Group Special Markets Department at special.markets@hbgusa.com.

Library of Congress Cataloging-in-Publication Data

Names: Aleman, Daniel, author.
Title: Brighter than the sun / Daniel Aleman.
Description: First edition. | New York : Little, Brown and Company, 2023. | Audience: Ages 14 & up | Summary: "After the loss of her mother, high school junior Soledad finds herself struggling to balance classes and her new job in California to support her family in Tijuana, Mexico, in this thoughtful story about identity, immigration, and family." —Provided by publisher.
Identifiers: LCCN 2022011505 | ISBN 9780316704472 (hardcover) | ISBN 9780316704519 (ebook)
Subjects: CYAC: Family life—Fiction. | Grief—Fiction. | Mexicans—Fiction. | High schools—Fiction. | Schools—Fiction.
Classification: LCC PZ7.1.A4344 Br 2023 | DDC [Fic]—dc23
LC record available at https://lccn.loc.gov/2022011505

ISBNs: 978-0-316-70447-2 (hardcover), 978-0-316-70451-9 (ebook)

Printed in the United States of America

LSC-C

Printing 1, 2022

To Luis Ernesto Guerra,
who believed in me before anyone else did

PART ONE

CHAPTER ONE

WHEN MY PARENTS PICKED OUT MY NAME, I DON'T think it even crossed their minds that they would be cursing me for life. Soledad—*solitude*. Or, to give them some credit, María de la Soledad, because I was unlucky enough to be born on December 18, the feast of Our Lady of Solitude.

No matter how hard I've tried, I have never been able to let go of the burden that comes with my name. My loneliness has a way of following me everywhere I go. I used to try to run away from it—I even tried to convince people to call me Marisol, but the nickname didn't stick, so I had to try with Sol instead. It was then, once people stopped calling me *solitude* and started calling me *sun*, that I almost fooled myself into believing I would become a different person.

Now, even though almost everyone calls me Sol, most of the time I feel like a Soledad. That is especially true today, while I sit at the breakfast table next to Papi, breaking off bits from a piece of pan dulce.

Sitting here in silence has become part of our daily routine, much like getting up at the crack of dawn, or rushing out the door before the clock strikes five thirty. This is one of the few moments of peace I get to have each day, so I usually try to make the most of it. I like to breathe in the stillness of the silence, taste the sweetness of the bread, feel the warmth of my hot chocolate as it makes its way down my throat.

Today, however, there's something about the silence that's making me deeply uneasy. The bread tastes like nothing, and my hot chocolate may as well be cold, for the lack of comfort it's bringing me. Since I opened my eyes this morning, I haven't been able to stop thinking about all the ways everything's about to change. I haven't been able to shake off the realization that today will be our last day of normality, and come Monday, life will be a lot different.

From the corner of my eye, I catch Papi staring at me. He does this sometimes. It's as if he's trying to read me, as if he's trying to figure out what's going through my mind, even though it's been a long time since either of us has spoken during breakfast.

"You don't have to do it," he says suddenly. His voice is loud, as though it came out stronger than he'd intended it to—as though he had been holding back what he wanted to say for a while, until it finally burst out of him in a near-shout.

"You could stay," Papi adds, and this time, his voice comes out weak. In the muted glow of the kitchen lights, it's impossible to ignore that there's a lot more gray in his black hair and mustache than there used to be, or that the lines on his face are now deeper, as if they've been carved into his skin.

I turn to the window, and my eyes fall on the lime tree that Mami planted years ago, when she and Papi first moved into our house. On sunnier mornings, its leaves look bright green, but the days have been getting shorter lately, and today the sunlight is nothing but a soft gleam far off in the horizon. The tree is just a dark shape silhouetted against the sky, but still, I stare at it, trying to make sense of this loneliness that's swirling around inside of me—loneliness because I wish more than anything that I could take him up on his offer, loneliness because I'm terrified of leaving home and starting a new life somewhere else, loneliness because even though Papi is sitting right next to me, there is distance between us that I don't know how to bridge.

"We don't have to talk about this, Papi," I say finally. "Not now."

I swallow hard, and a dull pain hits the back of my throat—the kind of pain that comes with holding back tears, with not being able to say the things that I actually wanted to say. Right when the tears start burning my eyes, I push my plate aside, looking up at the clock on the wall. It's almost five thirty.

"We should get going."

The morning air is crisp as we walk out of the house and toward our old Volkswagen. I get in the passenger seat, and Papi hops in a second later, slamming his door shut with a loud bang.

Tijuana looks bleak at this time of day. Even though those of us who cross the border every morning are already awake, the rest of the city doesn't come to life until much later. It's when the sun is shining high in the sky that you can see the bright facades of the houses along the street and hear the sounds of the city—the cars beeping, the music blasting from speakers at storefronts, the street vendors yelling to attract customers. Right now, all I can really see are the red lights of cars braking ahead of us.

Papi has always insisted on driving me to the border— ever since I started going to school across the bridge, back in the ninth grade. That's the reason he wakes up at the crack of dawn and sits beside me at the kitchen table every morning. He says he wants to make sure I get to school on time, but I know he just doesn't like the idea of leaving me to have breakfast on my own while the rest of the family sleeps, or of me walking through the city alone while it's still dark out.

The streets become more alive as we approach El Chaparral. Finding a spot to pull over is near impossible some days, with all the traffic, and taxis dropping off people, and pedestrians moving between the cars. There are times when Papi has to slow down just long enough for me to jump out, but today we get lucky. A car pulls out ahead of us, and Papi takes its spot.

"Are you okay?" he asks as I unbuckle my seat belt.

I freeze, trying not to look directly at him. I don't want to make him feel any more guilty than he already does, so I choose to lie.

"Yeah," I answer. "I'm fine."

Papi presses his lips together, nodding slowly. I know none of this has been easy for him, either. I know how badly he wishes things were different, how hard he's tried to figure out alternatives, how long it took him to accept that this was the only way—that me taking a job on the US side of the border was the only remaining option we had to keep the family afloat.

I reach for my bag. With one hand wrapped around the strap and the other on the door handle, I try my best to give him a small smile. "I'll see you tonight, okay?"

Without waiting for his answer, I step out of the car and start walking across the esplanade, toward the big sign that says PUERTO FRONTERIZO EL CHAPARRAL. This is as far as people who won't be crossing the border can go— where parents wish their children a good day at school, and where people say goodbye to loved ones who are leaving for a while. I walk past the small crowd to get onto the ramp—a long, zigzagging structure that leads up to a bridge—and hold on to the straps of my backpack as I tighten my pace.

There are countless people rushing up the ramp all around me, many of them students wearing backpacks. There's a good amount of workers, too, some of them in plain clothes, others in uniforms, and even a few dressed in suits and high heels. Nearly everyone here knows exactly what they're doing. They know that you have to walk as quickly as you can, because for every person you pass, you'll end up saving a few minutes.

The pedestrian bridge begins where the ramp ends. In the two years I've been doing this commute, I've heard some people say it makes them feel claustrophobic, and it's not hard to understand why: It's an iron and glass enclosure that seems to go on for miles. I walk quickly, twisting and turning with the bridge, until I see people slowing down ahead, where the line begins. It isn't too bad today. Judging by where I'm standing, I'd say it'll be about an hour, an hour and fifteen minutes at most.

While I move slowly with the line, watching the sun rising through the metal grating walls of the bridge, I can't help but think about my brothers. A part of me suspects Luis is still asleep. Lately, his schedule seems to be the exact opposite of mine: He goes to bed late and sleeps in, but Diego might be getting up soon. He might open his eyes and begin his day without fully understanding that this will be the last normal Friday we'll get to have in a long time.

"Sol!"

I turn around to find a familiar face staring at me. Bruno Rodríguez is one of the kids at Orangeville High who also commutes from Tijuana every day. He's a year older than I am, so we never really hang out at school, but he always joins me whenever he spots me on the bridge.

"What's up?" he asks as he comes to stand next to me. There are at least ten people who have lined up behind me since I got here, but no one protests. Joining friends in line is considered fair game.

"Not much," I reply. "Just tired."

Bruno nods once, as if to point out the obvious—that he's tired, too. He has jet-black hair, which he rarely ever combs, and round features that make him look like an overgrown child—round eyes, round chin, round nose. Most importantly, though, he has a way of reading me that nobody else does. When I'm not in the mood to talk, he stands quietly beside me, keeping me company while we move slowly with the line. Other days, when I'm feeling more lively, he keeps us both entertained by telling stories—about his dog, a rescue bulldog who's the laziest being on the planet; about his younger sister, who's a year away from starting high school; and about his obsession with a Santa Monica–based rock band. He usually does most of the talking while I just listen, but I've also shared a few stories with him over the years—about my family's restaurant, which has been around longer than any of us can remember; about my younger brother, whom I worry about every second of my life; and about what everything used to be like before Mami died.

Today, he seems to understand that I'm not in the mood to talk, so we wait in silence while my throat gets tighter and tighter. I've always resented the long hours of waiting at the border, but now that I know I won't be doing this any longer, I'm almost nostalgic. I almost miss standing in line next to Bruno, even though we're both still here, and even though I won't be officially moving to Chula Vista until Monday.

The line moves slowly while the sun keeps rising, and it's at least an hour before we reach the end of the bridge, which spirals down into a large room with shiny white floors, where the crowd breaks up into several smaller lines.

By now, I know most of the border officers by name—or by last name, at least, because that's all that is printed on the front of their uniform. I get Johnson today. He is very different from officers like López or Harris, who some-times joke around with the students. He takes a quick look at my passport, scans it, and hands it back to me, barely even looking into my eyes.

"Welcome to the United States," he says.

I look over my shoulder to check if Bruno is coming up behind me, but he's nowhere to be seen. He must still be stuck in line, so I keep walking toward the exit, knowing he wouldn't expect me to wait for him anyway.

I swing my bag over my shoulder and follow the crowd toward the MTS station. When I get on the trolley, I look down at the time. It'll take me about fifteen minutes to travel a couple of stops and another ten to walk to school, which means I'll be early today. It's just as well. I have found myself running breathlessly into school too many times, so I've learned that it's much better to be early than late.

A bell rings softly overhead, and a woman's voice comes from the speakers.

"This is a blue line trolley, bound for America Plaza in downtown San Diego. All passengers must have a valid fare. There is no smoking or eating permitted on the trolley and—"

Leaning my head back against the window, I allow my eyes to shut just for a little while. The commute is never exactly easy, but today has felt particularly difficult. Even with the short line at the border, I'm exhausted already, and my day hasn't even started yet.

⁀⁄⁄⁄‿

There are a few things about Orangeville High that surprised me when I first started coming here a couple of years ago. The first was how massive the school is—three times as big as the middle school I went to back in Mexico, where almost everyone knew each other. The second was the fact that the walls were freshly painted, the desks in classrooms undamaged, the equipment in the laboratory

9

relatively new. The third was how lonely this place can be, even when I'm surrounded by people at all times.

"No inventes. She couldn't have said that."

"Eso fue lo que me dijo, I swear!"

"—don't think I got the answer right, porque—"

"He asked me que si quería ir a ver una movie after school, pero of course I said no."

"Well, why did he even—"

The voices that fill the hallways are always a mix of Spanish and English. At least half of the students at Orangeville are Latino, which means that if you don't have even a basic understanding of Spanglish, you might be feeling a little left out. Not that that's a problem for me— I speak both languages, but there just aren't many people I talk to on a regular basis, regardless of the language. The only person I ever really hang out with is Ari, but we aren't in any of the same classes this semester, so I mostly see her at lunch.

When I walk into the cafeteria, a feeling of dread invades my stomach. It may be easy to blend into the crowd when I'm walking down the hallways, but here, where there's lots of open space, I can almost feel a dozen different pairs of eyes falling on me the second I walk in.

"No one's looking at you, Sol. I promise," Ari said to me last year, when I told her about the way I feel exposed sometimes. "You could walk into the cafeteria in your underwear, and no one would bat an eye."

That didn't help much. If anything, the image of me

standing in my underwear in front of all these people haunted me for weeks.

Once I've gotten a slice of pizza and an apple, I hold on tight to the edges of my tray and turn around to face the rows of tables. I can see Ari from here, already sitting at our usual spot and laughing at something that one of her new friends must've said.

She and I have known each other since we were both in diapers. She's tiny, probably well under five feet, but she has a loud voice, which she's always been unafraid to use—especially when I can't use my own. When we were in elementary school and a kid on the playground pulled my hair, she made sure one of the teachers found out. When a guy made a mean comment about my shoes in freshman year, she snapped back at him before I could even open my mouth. And when I've told her about all the things I can't quite understand, like the fear that people are watching me, or the loneliness that follows me everywhere I go, she's always been there to listen to me, to reassure me, to make me feel a bit more like Sol even when I'm feeling most like Soledad.

"Hey!" she says when she sees me approaching the table. In a quick movement, she takes her bag off the chair she saved for me and places it on the floor beside her.

"Hi," I say. No one else looks at me as I put my tray down. The conversation keeps going, which isn't all that unexpected. Even though we've been sitting at this table for almost two years, I still have a hard time thinking of any of these people as my friends. To me, they've always been Ari's new friends, even though they're not at all new anymore.

"Congratulations again," Ari says to me, her smile widening. "Did you do anything last night to celebrate the job offer?"

"Uh ... not really," I say. "My dad and my abuela were a little shocked that it's all happening so quickly, so ..."

Ari presses her lips together in a way that tells me she doesn't need any more explanation than that—she gets it.

She's the one who helped me find a job. For weeks, I sat in front of our family computer, applying to every single opening I could find, but the furthest I ever got was with a movie theater chain in Imperial Beach, which sent me a generic email where they spelled my name as "Sole" and blandly explained I was not right for the position at that time.

When I told Ari that I needed to find an after-school job to help my family, though, she jumped into action. She spoke to one of the managers at the department store she works at, got me an interview, and then helped me prepare for it, cheering for me every step of the way—up until yesterday, when I got a call saying that I'd gotten the job.

"No way," Tony says suddenly from the other end of the table, his eyes widening. *"No way."*

Ana María nods, her her mouth twisting into a smile. I've never understood what she sees in Tony. She's the kind of pretty that makes people do double takes, whereas Tony is just… Tony. A bit snarky at times, a bit funny at others, entirely obnoxious always.

On my other side, Camila and Olivia are talking about this influencer that I've never heard of before.

"Oh, her eyebrow game is so strong."

"I know, but it's not like I have hundreds of dollars to spend on that shit."

Before I can open my mouth to ask who they're talking about, Ari whispers into my ear again.

"My mom told me to ask you whether you prefer a soft or a firm pillow."

"I don't—"

"She's gonna freak out if I don't come back to her with an answer."

I can't help but smile at Ari. I love it when we're able to do this—when we're able to have our own private conversations even though we're sitting at a table full of people. If it wasn't because of these whispered chats, I wouldn't normally say much during lunch.

"I guess… soft, maybe?" That's the way my pillow is at home, but it's only because I've had the same one since I was little. For all I know, firm pillows could be so much better, but I don't wanna cause Nancy any more trouble than I already am. Because Ari didn't just talk to her manager at the store. She talked to her mom, too, and convinced her to let me move in with them so I'll be able to make it to my early-morning and late-night shifts.

Ari nods once. "Soft it is."

"Are you sure your mom is okay with everything?" I ask. "I don't wanna be—"

"She is *more* than okay," she interrupts me. "And, you know... I was thinking. Once you move in, we'll be able to do fun stuff after school—when we're not working, of course."

"Yeah," I say, nodding slowly to myself. "Totally."

It feels like a lifetime ago that this used to be my main concern—finding time to hang out with Ari after school, not missing out on fun plans, trying to fit in with her new friends.

The truth is, I used to try a lot harder, but I stopped at some point. I just can't remember when that was. It might've been when my mom first got sick, and I had to take on bigger responsibilities at home. It might've been last year, when Mami died and everything came crumbling down around us. Or perhaps it was much sooner than that, when I started realizing that making it back to Tijuana before sundown was more important than whatever after-school plans Ari invited me to—when I started to feel like I couldn't fully be a part of her new friend group, no matter how badly I wanted to.

"Wait, wait, wait," Tony says. "You gotta start from the beginning."

Ari and I turn back toward the rest of the table, and while we listen to Ana María telling the story of how she got free tickets to a concert tomorrow, I can't help but realize something: Things won't just be different back home starting next week. They'll be different around here, too, and maybe the change won't be all bad.

Maybe leaving home won't only mean missing my family, and worrying about my little brother, and stressing about making money to help Papi. Maybe Ari and I will be able to spend more time together, just as we used to before her family moved away from Tijuana. Maybe I'll be able to join in on after-school and weekend plans, and get to know all her friends better, and start to feel as though I'm part of something on this side of the border for a change.

Maybe.

CHAPTER TWO

WHEN I WALK INTO MY HOUSE LATER IN THE DAY, I find Diego sitting in the living room with his hands over his lap.

"I'm sorry," I say as I close the door behind me. "Sorry it took me so long to get here."

The commute back into Tijuana is never as bad as the commute out. I just have to go a couple of stops on the trolley, get off at San Ysidro, and walk through the tunnel toward Mexican customs, which is usually a quick line. Some days, the officers don't even check my passport. I just flash it at them, they nod once, and then I'm on my way. The issue today was the bus. I typically take the Azul y Blanco, which drops me off a few blocks away from home, but as soon as I got to the stop, I heard people complaining about a service disruption.

I figured that waiting for the bus to come would be better than the hour-long walk home, so I stood there with the hot September sun in my eyes, until a blue-and-white van finally pulled up in front of me.

"You said you'd be home early," Diego says. I know he doesn't mean to make me feel guilty, but he can't keep the disappointment out of his voice.

"I know," I say, sitting on the couch next to him. "But we still have time. The ice cream shop won't close for another hour."

I texted him earlier, promising I'd take him out for ice cream as soon as I made it home. I figured that would be the best way to break the news to him that I'm leaving, because he's the only one who doesn't know yet—the only person I haven't had a chance to talk to one-on-one since I got the job offer yesterday.

Diego nods slowly. "Okay."

While my brother and I walk down the uneven side-walk in the direction of Don Ignacio's ice cream shop, I think about Mami. Among all the memories of her that fill my mind every day, there's one that has felt particularly vivid today: the time she tried to teach me and Luis how to make homemade ice cream and gave up halfway through the process, which ended with a creamy mess in the trash can and a trip to Don Ignacio's.

Something warm fills my chest when I remember the way we all laughed as we walked back home holding ice cream cones that day, and the way trips to Don Ignacio's

DANIEL ALEMAN

became much more common after that. Mami started taking us every other day, and when she had to stay at the restaurant late and couldn't come along, she'd make sure there were three ten-peso coins on the little table by the door, so that Luis, Diego, and I could go get ice cream ourselves.

"Oye, ¿Diego?" I say, breaking the silence that has filled the air between us since we left the house.

My brother looks up at me, and for a moment, I'm shocked at how much he looks like Papi. Everyone's always said that Diego's a carbon copy of our dad, but I've never been able to see it, just as I've never been fully convinced when people tell me I look just like our mom. Today, though, it feels so obvious: They have the same thick eyebrows, the same sharp nose. If you added a mustache, gray hair, and thirty-five years of age, Diego would be an exact clone of our father.

"I, uh... I need to tell you something."

"What is it?"

I clear my throat. "You... you know Papi's been struggling with money, right?"

Diego frowns slightly, which tells me he knows exactly what I'm talking about—how Papi sits at the dining room table sometimes, sorting through endless stacks of papers and sighing loudly to himself every few seconds. The fact that our fridge and cupboards have been getting emptier lately, so the only option we've had for dinner is whatever leftover food Papi brings from the restaurant. The way

18

trips to the movies, and the hair salon, and even to Don Ignacio's have become all but nonexistent over the past few months.

"Well... we've been trying to figure out what to do," I say. "You know, to get everything back on track."

Suddenly, Diego stops walking. "Is he gonna close down the restaurant?"

"No," I say quickly. It may be true that the restaurant is costing us more money than it's bringing in, but the thought of it closing down brings a deep fear to my stomach. "Of course not. But we need extra money to pay the bills, and to keep the restaurant running, and..." *And to put food on the table*, I almost say, but I stop myself in time.

"So how's Papi gonna get the extra money?" Diego asks me.

"That's the thing—I'm gonna help him. I'm gonna go work in San Diego for a while."

"You're leaving?" My brother's frown deepens, and all of a sudden he looks much younger, much more innocent than he did a second ago.

"Yeah," I answer. "I'm gonna stay at Ari's house for a while. But I'll be back most weekends. It'll be—"

"Don't go," he says, wrapping his arms around my waist. "Please, Sol."

"I have to," I answer, hugging him back. "But I promise I'll be back—as soon as I've made enough money, I'll quit my job so I can come back home for good."

"You can't leave me alone."

I swallow hard, realizing exactly what all of this means for Diego. I don't like admitting it—not even to myself—but sometimes it's impossible to deny that I've become the closest thing he has to a mom. And now he's losing me. He's losing a companion, losing the one person who has the time and patience to help him with his homework, losing what little stability he's started to feel since Mami died.

"Look at me," I say. "Diego, you have to listen."

He steps back, and I lean down slightly to level with him. He only meets my eyes for a second before looking away, but in his gaze, I can see all the things he's trying to hide—the loneliness he's felt over the past year, the struggles he's had to face with kids picking on him at school, the distance he feels from our father. I have no idea how he does it—how he manages to deal with all of that at his young age. All I know is, some days, I feel like I'm about to crumble under all the pressure. I can't even begin to understand how his tiny shoulders are able to withstand it.

"I'm always here," I say, trying to keep my voice from shaking. "Even if I'm far away, you will always have me. You know that, don't you?"

The corners of his mouth twist downward. He blinks quickly to keep the tears at bay, and then he starts nodding.

"Come on," I say. "We gotta make it to Don Ignacio's before closing time."

Diego clears his throat, and we keep walking in the direction of the ice cream shop. Just as we turn at a corner, the sun disappears behind the houses along the street, which makes the light turn softer and yellower.

The shop is completely empty when we walk in. There's music playing from a speaker in the corner, and I'm pretty sure I hear movement coming from the back, but there is no one in sight.

I hit the bell at the counter softly, and Don Ignacio stomps out from a curtained entryway a moment later, wearing the same old stained apron he always does. When he sees me and Diego, he presses his lips into something that looks almost like a smile.

"What can I do for you kids today?"

"Can I get a scoop of mango?" Diego says.

Don Ignacio shakes his head. "Can't help you there, buddy. We have chocolate, vanilla, and strawberry."

"But I thought mango was still in season," I say.

"You know what else mango is? Freaking expensive these days," Don Ignacio replies bitterly.

"Can I get lime instead?" Diego asks.

"Chocolate, vanilla, or strawberry only."

"But you always have lime."

"Not today, we don't."

I narrow my eyes a little. "Don Ignacio, is everything okay?"

"You tell me," he says. "I haven't seen you kids around here all summer, and suddenly you show up asking to see all the flavors."

"But we—"

I'm interrupted by Samuel, who sticks his head out from behind the curtain. "Señor Ignacio, can I get your help back here? The blender's stuck again."

Don Ignacio lets out his breath in a groan. "Leave it to me. You take care of these kids."

Samuel holds the curtain open so Don Ignacio can walk through, and then he steps forward to come stand behind the counter.

"Hey," he says with his usual shy smile. "How are you?"

"Good," I say, my voice several octaves too high. I'm hoping we'll get our ice cream and be on our way as soon as possible, but Samuel leans his elbows over the counter and looks down at Diego.

"And you?" he asks. "How's it going?"

Diego mumbles something, but I'm not sure what it is. My throat tightens all of a sudden, and I decide to intervene before Samuel has a chance to ask my brother any more questions.

"So... you've cut back on flavors, huh?"

His eyes flicker back to mine. "Yeah," he says. "I heard Don Ignacio giving you a hard time just now."

"It's fine. He just—"

"It's been a slow summer. I've heard a few people say that tourism was down this season," Samuel says, lowering his voice. "And with fall right around the corner, he's losing hope that business is gonna pick back up."

"Oh." I think about the restaurant. On the one hand, it

22

makes me feel better to know that we're not the only ones who have been going through a rough period—that the lack of customers might not be entirely our fault. But on the other, I can't help but worry, because if this is true— if tourism has been down and other businesses are also struggling—it might be a lot harder for us to bounce back.

"I mean, it's not just us," Samuel adds, almost as if he can read my mind. "The coffee shop I worked at before was also cutting back—on staff, not on the menu, but you know."

Samuel was a waiter at my parents' restaurant a couple of years ago, back when the business was doing so well that we needed to hire extra help. Ever since we had to let him go, he's worked all kinds of odd jobs, even while studying full time.

"Anyway," he says, with that same shy smile, "what can I get for you?"

"I, uh... I think I'll go with vanilla," I say. "Diego? Have you decided?"

He gets chocolate in the end, and then we're on our way back home.

I keep trying to sneak glances at him the whole time, trying to figure out what's going through his mind. I almost ask him if he's okay, but I stop myself when I realize that maybe I don't want to hear the answer. He has every reason to be mad—mad that I'm leaving, mad that I waited until now to tell him the news, mad about all the ways I won't be there for him anymore.

But when he looks up at me, it is not anger I see reflected on his face. Instead, there is gentle curiosity.

"You're not eating your ice cream," he says.

I look down to realize he's right. My ice cream has started to melt, making my hand wet and sticky.

"There's just... a lot on my mind, I guess."

"Yeah," he replies. "Mine too."

There's something in his voice that makes my heart break—something that tells me he's growing up too quickly, that he's no longer the child he should be.

While I clean up my sticky hand with a napkin, I try to keep my face hidden from Diego. I don't want him to see the sadness in my eyes. Sadness because I won't be able to take him to Don Ignacio's for ice cream anymore, because I'll no longer get to walk into the house every day to find him waiting for me in the living room, because we won't get to sit next to each other doing homework every afternoon. But, mostly, sadness because I can't stop thinking about how Diego has already lost a big part of his childhood, and now that I'm leaving, there'll be no way to get it back.

Papi brings home a seafood paella that he served at the restaurant earlier.

"There's plenty for all of us," he says as he sets down a big casserole at the center of the dinner table, but there's something grim about his tone. It's no secret that the less he sells at the restaurant, the more food he has to bring home at the end of each day.

We all sit around the table—Papi, Abuela, Diego, and me—waiting for Luis to get home, but even as the paella gets colder and the clock on the wall keeps ticking, there's still no sign of him, and he's not even answering his phone.

"I thought Luis was working at the restaurant today," I say softly.

"He was," Papi answers with a small shrug, which tells me Luis ran off the second they turned the sign at the door from OPEN to CLOSED. My brother's been doing this a lot since the start of last summer—disappearing to go who-knows-where. I'm pretty sure he has a girlfriend he hasn't told us about, but I haven't dared to ask.

"Well," Abuela says, leaning forward in her chair. "We should probably start eating."

We've only just filled our plates with rice when the front door swings open and Luis steps into the house, wearing his old leather jacket and a white t-shirt.

"You didn't wait for me?" he says as he approaches the dinner table. It's been a few days since he last shaved, and even though he can't really grow a beard, the scruff makes him look a lot older than nineteen.

"We waited for as long as we could," Abuela says, nodding toward her left, where an empty chair is waiting for Luis.

"Not long enough," he mumbles as he walks around the table to go sit at his spot.

Luis reaches for the spoon and starts serving himself some paella, which I've noticed is all rice and no shrimp. Mami would've rather switched up the entire menu at the restaurant than serve something like this, but my dad's been trying to cut costs wherever he can, and I don't think any of us can blame him for it.

It's not every day that we get to go to bed feeling completely satisfied, so at first we eat quickly, eagerly. After a few minutes of sitting here in silence, however, Abuela looks up from her plate. Most days, it's she who carries the conversation at dinner. She's the one who makes comments about the food, or the temperature, or something that she saw on TV earlier, and who asks us all questions about our days.

She surveys us all carefully through her glasses, as if trying to decide who to interrogate first. But before she's had a chance to make up her mind, Luis clears his throat.

"I've been thinking," he says, and we all turn toward him at the same time.

"Thinking?" Papi asks, lifting his eyebrows.

"About my future."

Ever since he graduated high school over a year ago, Luis hasn't been willing to talk much about the future. The idea of going to college had always been in the back of his mind, but when Mami got sick, it all went out the window. He had to put everything on pause so he could help out at the restaurant, but now there isn't much to show for it. The business isn't doing well, Luis hasn't been able to go back to school, and with every day that goes by, the dreams he once talked about seem more and more distant.

"I—I want to apply to college."

"That's good," Abuela says. "Very good, mijo."

"It's not *good*," Luis replies. "We don't even have money to pay for the application fees."

A heavy silence falls around the table, because there's nothing any of us can say—no way for us to convince Luis that what he's saying isn't true.

"I think I should get a job, save up some money," he adds.

Papi frowns. "You already have a job."

"A different one."

We played around with this idea at some point—the idea that if Luis got a job on the side, we'd be able to manage a lot better, and Diego and I would be able to keep focusing on school. But it didn't take long for us to realize that whatever job Luis could find around here wouldn't make much of a difference—not when the minimum wage for full-time workers in Tijuana is less than two hundred pesos, which comes to about ten dollars a day.

That was when we began doing a different kind of math: If I got a minimum-wage job in California, working after-school shifts, it would take me two or three months to make the same amount of money that Luis would make in a year. That was when I started looking for jobs, when I started getting used to the idea that I'd have to be the one to help the family.

"We need you," Papi says to Luis firmly. "*I* need you at the restaurant. I can't do it all on my own."

"The restaurant is a lost cause," Luis says, and suddenly, it's as if a dark shadow has fallen over the dining table.

I have no idea how he can do this—how Luis is capable of speaking our worst fears out loud. The restaurant is the one thing that has remained constant our whole lives. We may grow older, Mami may have gotten sick, and no matter how hard she tried to stay with us, in the end she may have lost her battle, but her restaurant remained. Her biggest pride, her biggest source of joy. If Luis is right—if the restaurant is truly a lost cause and we're left with no choice but to close it down—I don't know what any of us are gonna do with ourselves.

Papi is the first to find his voice. "We will get the restaurant back on track."

Luis shakes his head. "That's what you've been saying for over a year."

"I mean it this time."

"Why?" Luis says, leaning forward over the table slightly. "Because Sol is magically gonna save it?"

He throws me a quick, resentful glance, and I'm left frozen, unable to speak up, unable to move, unable to do anything at all.

"We are all doing our part," Abuela says. "And we will continue to do our part."

"Why does she get to leave, then? Why does she get to start over somewhere new?"

28

"I'm not *starting over*," I say, finally finding my voice. "It's not like I want to leave. I'd much rather—"

"You have *options*," Luis snaps back. "You always have."

I watch him for a moment, thinking about how we used to be close growing up. We used to run around the restaurant together, and play on the street outside our house until the sky turned dark, and laugh for hours at each other's jokes. I'm not sure when all of that changed, but I do know that right now, it feels almost as if there is a stranger sitting across the table from me, and I can't help but miss my brother. I miss the person he used to be.

"I didn't ask for any of this," I say.

I wish I could make him understand that I didn't choose to be born in the US, that Mami never wanted to be rushed across the border to give birth to me, but he's already heard this story a million times. Mami was eight and a half months pregnant when her doctor warned her that things were not looking good. There was a chance that neither of us would make it, and so she and Papi decided to try their luck across the border. She had to keep a straight face and her big belly hidden under a coat long enough to drive through the border crossing, and by the time she made it to a clinic in California, it was almost too late.

I wish I could make Luis understand that being the only American citizen in the family isn't what he thinks it is, because none of what I do is for myself. I cross the border every morning to go to school so I can become the first person in our family to go to college. I'll get a degree so I can get a good job. I'll work hard so I can take care of Papi and Abuela when they're older. And, come Monday, I'll move in with Ari so I can make enough money to keep the restaurant running, and so we can pay the bills. But if I could take all this responsibility off my shoulders, I would. If I could choose a life where I didn't have to look after everyone else, I'd take it, without a doubt.

"Your abuela is right," Papi says firmly. "We will all continue to do our part. For Sol, it means helping us with money. Luis, for you it means being at the restaurant. And that's the end of it."

Luis doesn't reply, and I don't, either. I notice the way he's twitching in his chair, eager to storm out, but he doesn't. He remains sitting at the table, eating slow bites of paella.

After a while, once the air around us has become a little less heavy and we are all getting full, I start to notice the way Diego is slumping in his chair. He's been so quiet all night, but I know he's been listening intently to what we've been saying, feeling more and more alone with each passing second.

I wish I could say something to make him feel better, but I just don't have the strength right now. Instead, I shift my gaze toward Abuela, only to find her staring right back at me. And in her eyes, I find comfort, and safety, and all the things that I haven't been able to find anywhere else today—all the things I wish I could bring with me when

I move to California, and the things that I wish I could make sure Diego won't ever have to go without.

✺

Abuela and I do the dishes like every other night. It's the only time of the day that truly belongs to just us—while Luis helps Diego get ready for bed, and Papi sneaks off into his bedroom.

This was something she used to always do with my mom, but I took over for Mami after she got sick. It used to feel weird, stepping into her shoes. I used to dream of the day when she would bounce back—when she'd be cancer-free and go back to managing her restaurant, and looking after us, and doing the dishes next to Abuela every night. As time went on, though, I started believing in that dream less and less, until I was forced to give up on it altogether.

"Mañana será otro día," Abuela whispers softly as she passes me the dish she was scrubbing.

I take it from her and start to rinse it, her words echoing inside my mind. *Tomorrow will be a new day.* I know that time usually has a way of making things better, but now I'm not so sure that it will. I can't see how life will get easier tomorrow, or the day after that, or even a year from now.

"What are you thinking?" she asks me when I don't respond after a few minutes.

"I just... I'm thinking about the restaurant."

"What about it?"

I let out a long sigh, trying to push myself to ask this question out loud—the question that was on my mind through most of dinner.

"Do you think Luis is right? Is the restaurant a lost cause?"

Abuela nods slowly to herself, frowning sightly while she dips the sponge into the dish soap.

"What I think," she says, "is that your brother is a little lost. And what he needs is not for us to push him away even more, but the exact opposite. He needs us to love him, and be patient with him, and try our best to understand him."

"But that doesn't answer my question."

"Your dad will find a way," she says. "He's always managed to find a way."

It makes me a little mad to think that Luis was right about at least one thing: the fact that our dad has been making empty promises for over a year. It was never Papi's intention to take over from Mami, but once she got too sick to do it all herself, he had no choice but to quit his own job and try his best to keep the business running. Because letting the restaurant fail would've been like allowing a piece of Mami to die even when she was still here, like giving up on the hope we once had that she would get better and jump back into it.

We've been waiting for what feels like the longest time for Papi to bring the restaurant back to its former glory, but now I can't help but wonder if this will end up being nothing but another dream that's meant to fall beyond our grasp.

"You don't need to worry, mija," Abuela says suddenly. "You're about to start a new job, a new routine. That should be enough for you to carry, without the added weight of worrying about what your brother said or didn't say during dinner."

I sometimes wish I could be a little more like Abuela— that I could think of my own worries in the same way she does, as though they were nothing but clouds drifting across a clear blue sky. As I take another dish from her and start rinsing it, I can't help but think that maybe she's right. Maybe by Monday I'll have to go back to worrying about the restaurant, and Diego being lonely, and Luis's resentment toward me, but for tonight, all I want is to wash the dishes silently next to my abuela. I want to let out my breath and just enjoy this small moment of togetherness.

CHAPTER THREE

Papi drops me off at the border on Monday morning. If we tried to pretend hard enough, this would feel almost like every other day, except that it's not. It's not, because my bags are packed and waiting on the back seat. It's not, because there's been a painful sensation in my chest all morning, as if someone were clenching my heart in their first. It's not, because the silence between me and Papi feels suffocating, even though we've been playing music during the entire drive.

We find a parking spot behind a big van, and Papi takes it before anyone else can beat him to it. When he turns off the engine, the music coming from the radio cuts off abruptly.

"Will you call us tonight?" he asks. This is the first thing he's said to me all morning, other than random observations about the time on the kitchen clock and the traffic on our way to the border.

"Of course," I say. "I'll call every night."

"And you'll be safe." This isn't a question.

"I'll be safe. You don't have to worry."

In the back of my mind, I can't help but remember freshman year, and the first few times I had to cross the border on my own to get to school. I remember how intimidating the whole process seemed back then, how I carried around written instructions from my mom on where to go, and what to do, and which numbers to call if I needed help.

Back then, at least I knew that I'd be coming back home at the end of the day, and having dinner with my family, and sleeping in my own bed. Now, all I have is the hope that I might be able to come back to Tijuana most weekends, although I can't fight off the feeling that I won't be coming back for years. I've never spent a night away from home, other than the occasional sleepover at Ari's when we were little. I've never been on the US side of the border on my own for longer than a school day, never been away from my dad and my brothers for more than twelve hours.

Papi loosens his tight grip on the steering wheel. When he turns toward me, there's sadness in his eyes that I haven't seen in a long time. If he aged a decade in the year since Mami died, then he may as well have aged another decade between yesterday and today.

35

"It's really come to this, hasn't it?" he whispers. "My daughter has to do all the things I'm not strong enough to do."

"You *are* strong," I say, leaning slightly toward him. "Stronger than anyone I know, Papi."

He shakes his head. "I should've been able to take care of the family. I should've been able to dig us out of this mess."

A dark, heavy feeling invades my stomach. I've known all along that he felt guilty about needing to accept my help, but he has never said these things out loud before. Sitting beside me is not the father who's always been so tough, the one who used to take so much pride in looking after all of us. Instead, there's the man I first caught a glimpse of when Mami got sick—the one who's capable of feeling uncertainty, and fear, and helplessness. The one who's trying desperately to do his best, and failing in the process.

"We'll fix things together, Papi," I manage to say. "You don't have to do it all on your own."

He nods slowly, looking down at his hands. "I called Rafael again last week."

"What did he say?"

"Same thing as last time—that he's fully staffed, but if one of his men leaves, I'll be the first to know."

I open my mouth to reply, but no words come out. Even if Papi was able to do shifts at the car shop where he used to work, we'd still need more money, but maybe he doesn't need to hear this right now. Maybe I can allow him to hold on to the hope that he'll be able to go back to the car shop soon and make some extra cash, because I can tell he needs something to hold on to.

Turning to look out the window, I notice that the crowd moving across the esplanade toward the ramp is becoming thicker. If I don't head up to the bridge soon, I'm gonna be late for school.

"I should get going," I say softly.

I lean over to grab my heavy bags from the back seat. I set them both over my lap and then turn toward Papi, waiting for him to say a few last words. I have a feeling that there are things left unsaid between us, that he's not quite done speaking, but even as the seconds stretch on and a car beeps somewhere nearby, he remains silent.

It isn't until I'm halfway out of the car that he clears his throat.

"Sol?" he says, which makes me stop suddenly. "Te amo, mija."

"I love you, too, Papi." I give him a small smile before swinging the passenger door shut.

As I turn around and start walking across the esplanade, I can feel his gaze following me. I know that if I looked back, I'd see our car still parked there, and that he's gonna wait until I've disappeared from view to start the engine and head back home.

For a moment, I almost turn around. I almost look over my shoulder to wave at him one last time, but there's something that stops me. And so I keep making my way toward the ramp decisively, with my school bag hanging from one shoulder and a heavy duffel bag hanging from the other.

The wait at the border feels extra long today. By the time I make it to school, my back and shoulders are sore from the added weight of the duffel bag, so I don't head straight to first period. I walk toward my locker instead, thinking that I'll be able to breathe a little easier once I've dropped off the bag and a few of my books.

No matter how many ways I try to make it fit, though, I just can't find a way for the locker door to close with the duffel bag inside it. In the end, I have no choice but to unload a couple of the heaviest items—a pair of shoes and a Ziploc full of toiletries—and then make my way toward my first class of the day.

"You look like you're in pain," Ari says to me when I run into her in the hallway right before lunch. There's a joking tone in her voice, but I can't manage to laugh.

"I am," I admit, readjusting the bag over my shoulder.

"Why don't you put that in your locker?" she asks.

"I tried, but I couldn't make it fit."

"Oh," Ari says. Her expression shifts, turning businesslike all of a sudden. "Come with me, then."

"Where are we going?"

"We'll run out and put it in my car."

Once the bag is safely stowed in the trunk of Ari's car, we make our way to the cafeteria. While we wait in the food line, Ari stares at me expectantly, almost as if she's waiting for me to say something, but the only thing on my mind right now is getting food.

When we show up at our usual table carrying our trays, Camila and Olivia are already sitting there. They both have salads and bottles of water in front of them, but it doesn't look like they've started eating yet.

"We were starting to think you weren't coming," Olivia says as we sit down across from them.

"Just had to run out to my car," Ari answers. "Where's everyone else?"

Camila shrugs, as if to say that she has no idea.

"So, is it true?" Olivia asks, leaning over the table toward me.

"Uh... is what true?" I ask.

"That you're moving into Ari's house?"

I sneak a quick glance at Ari, who smiles vaguely at me.

"Yeah," I say. "I'm gonna start working at Wallen's, so—"

"What's it like working there, Ari?" Camila interrupts me. "Do you like it?"

"Yeah," she answers. "They're pretty decent." Ari began working at the store last spring, right around the time when the career counselor at our school started spreading panic about college applications, and scholarships, and tuition costs. She doesn't talk much about it, but I know every penny she makes is going into her college fund.

"Maybe I should apply for a job there," Olivia says with a long sigh. "I'm sick of working at the café."

Camila turns sharply toward her. "I thought you liked the café."

"I've *never* liked the café," Olivia says. "Are you kidding me? I'm only in it cause the tips are good."

"Well, if you want a sales position, you're gonna have to wait until the holidays," says Ari. "They're only hiring for the warehouse right now."

"You're working in the warehouse, then?" Camila asks me.

"Yeah. I applied for a million other jobs, but in the end this was the only offer I got."

Olivia purses her lips. "I kinda envy you, actually. Customer service sucks. Like, *sucks*. So at least you won't have to deal with annoying customers."

"Yeah," I say. "That's true."

Before any of us can say anything else, Ana María, Tony, and Simon—Tony's best friend—approach our table, and we all turn toward them.

"What are we talking about?" Tony asks as he sits down on Ari's other side.

"After-school jobs."

"Oh." His face turns into a grimace. "I don't know how you guys do it. I can barely find time to do homework."

Ana María rolls her eyes at him. "Well, maybe if you

didn't play video games all afternoon, you'd have time for homework *and* a job."

"Nah, not worth it."

"Maybe *I* should get a job," Camila says. "You know, make some extra money for going out and stuff."

Olivia nods quickly. "My life *changed* when I stopped having to ask my parents for money to get my nails done."

I don't have to say anything else, because soon enough everyone is talking loudly, and the conversation quickly shifts to the house party they all went to on Saturday.

"So," Ari whispers to me after a while. "How was your weekend?"

"Weird," I reply. I can't bring myself to say any more than that—can't bring myself to tell Ari about the look on Diego's face when I broke the news to him that I was leaving, the bitterness in Luis's voice during dinner on Friday, or the conversation I had with Papi this morning.

Somehow, though, Ari seems to understand. Even without saying a single word, I know that she can see right through me.

"It'll all be okay, you know?" she says.

I try to smile at her, but my smile won't come out. The truth is, I can't stop thinking about the conversation we were all having barely a few minutes ago. I can't stop thinking about the fact that, even though Ari and I aren't the only ones who have after-school jobs, no one here is working to support their family. No one's had to leave home in order to start a job, and somehow, realizing that

41

makes me feel just a little more alone than usual, a little more separated from the rest of the table.

⁂

When the last bell of the day finally rings, I walk out of school to find Ari waiting for me right outside the front doors.

"Ready to go?" she asks me.

I nod, even as a wave of anxiety sweeps through me. There's something about meeting Ari out here that reminds me of the day she drove me to my interview at Wallen's a couple of weeks ago, back when I was terrified that I would wreck my chance at getting this job.

"How are you feeling?" she asks me once we get onto the highway and everything starts flashing past us as we speed up toward San Diego.

"Pretty nervous."

"That's how I felt before I started," she says. "But don't worry, you'll be great."

The drive doesn't take too long. Even with a bit of traffic, we make it downtown in less than thirty minutes, and Ari finds a spot in the underground parking lot.

"Will you be okay on your own?" she asks me as we step out into the soft afternoon sunshine.

"Of course," I say. "I'll just do homework."

"Maybe you could go to a coffee shop, or something."

Ari has afternoon shifts, but my training won't start until seven. Still, when she suggested driving up to San

Diego together after school, I agreed right away, thinking I'd find a useful way to kill time before heading into the store.

"Yeah," I answer. "Maybe I will."

Ari leans in to wrap her arms around me. "Good luck," she whispers into my ear.

For a moment, I'm frozen, but then I hug her back with all my strength. With my nose buried in her hair, my mind flashes back to when we were younger—to a time when it felt like Ari and I could conquer the world together, when nothing and no one could've torn us apart.

"Thank you, Ari," I say. "For everything."

"I'll see you tonight, okay?"

I watch as she turns around and disappears through the front doors of the store, and then I'm left standing all alone in the middle of the sidewalk. There's a coffee shop just across the street from Wallen's, but if I'll be making fifteen dollars an hour, I really shouldn't waste five of those dollars on a mediocre cappuccino.

I start walking down the street instead, trying to think of somewhere I could wait for a few hours that won't require spending much money. Back home, I'd be able to find an heladería or a cafetería where I could grab an ice cream or a coffee for less than ten pesos, but one thing is for sure: This place is nothing like Tijuana.

Even though there's traffic and there are dozens of people walking quickly along the sidewalk, everything feels a little artificial—almost as if I were standing in the middle of a movie set. The sky is too blue, the facades of the buildings along the street too perfectly in harmony. In the back of my mind, I can't help but feel as though I'm the only thing that's out of place—the only person here who doesn't quite belong.

When I reach the corner, I see a park on the opposite side of the street—Horton Plaza Park. I've never been here before, but Camila and Olivia used it as the backdrop for a ton of TikTok videos last summer. I recognize the palm trees, the tall sculptures made of silver metal, the amphitheater-like stairs that lead down to an open area where there's a jet fountain that shoots water up from the ground.

I walk to the park and make my way down the steps. There are a few tables beneath bright green umbrellas, so I go sit at one of them and take out some of my books, eager to get started on all the schoolwork I avoided over the weekend.

The thing is, as hard as I try to focus, it's almost impossible. I attempt to solve a few problems for trigonometry, but I'm pretty sure all my answers are wrong. I try to read a few pages from the book we've been assigned for English this month, but I can't keep my mind off the anticipation of my first shift. After a while, a group of guys my age comes to sit on the steps behind me, smoking cigarettes and blasting loud music from a speaker, which doesn't help at all.

By the time 6:50 comes, the sunlight is already dimmer

and the air a little chillier. I pack up my schoolbooks and make my way back across the street, toward the entrance of the store.

The woman who interviewed me gave me pretty clear instructions on what to do: Take the escalator down to the basement, turn left, walk past the kitchen appliances department, and wait by the white door that says EMPLOY-EES ONLY. She didn't specify what would happen after I followed all those steps, but I suppose she's gonna meet me out here.

Sure enough, the instant the time on my phone changes from 6:59 to 7:00, the door swings open, and Helen appears.

"María," she says. "You're right on time. Come on in."

She holds the door open for me to walk through. I hesitate for a second, wondering if this would be a good time to say that my name is actually Sol, but it's probably too late. She's been calling me María ever since I sat down for my job interview a couple of weeks ago, and I can't find the confidence in me to correct her at this point.

Moving my heavy legs forward one at a time, I follow Helen and find myself inside a big room with tall walls that are painted a dull shade of gray. Stark white lights hang from cables in the ceiling, shining down on shelves upon shelves of clothes, each of which is stacked two levels high. Right in front of us is a massive table, around which at least a dozen people are working.

I can't help but be reminded of the school cafeteria—the

bright lights, the open space. The same old dread settles in the deepest part of my stomach, but as I look at the employees gathered around the table, I notice that none of them have even looked up since Helen and I walked in. They're all just moving their hands quickly, shoving clothes onto hangers, as if we weren't even here.

"Let me introduce you to Bill, the stockroom manager," Helen says, leading the way toward a well-built man who has his back to us.

"Make sure you put them in the A spot, but *don't* remove the long-sleeved shirts. Those are meant to stay up for another week, so—" He's speaking so quickly that I have no idea how anyone could keep up with what he's saying.

"Bill," Helen says firmly, and he and the two employees he was talking to turn sharply toward us. "This is María, the new hire."

Bill doesn't even look at me, but he does let his breath out in a loud sigh, as though he doesn't want there to be any doubt about how annoyed he is at this interruption. "Get her over to Nick."

He turns his back on us again and resumes his monologue right where he left off.

Nick turns out to be around my age—maybe just a year older than me. He's a full head taller than I am, with shaggy blond hair, broad shoulders, and what I can only describe as puppy eyes: big, brown, and kind.

"Nick, this is María," Helen says.

"Actually, my name is—"

"Nick has been with us for... how long has it been now?"

He smiles. His front teeth are a little cramped, in a way that tells me he never had braces as a kid. "Almost six months."

"Yes, very well. He knows exactly what needs to be done," Helen says offhandedly. "I'll leave you two to get started."

She walks away, and I'm left standing here awkwardly while Nick gives me an up-and-down stare, as though he's sizing me up.

"Have you clocked in yet?" is the first thing he asks me.

I rearrange my bag over my shoulder. "Uh... no."

"Let's do that first, then. You'll also need to leave your bag in a locker."

He turns around and leads the way out the door, across the kitchen appliances section, and toward the elevators.

"I, uh... I should mention something," I say as I follow him, trying to keep up with his long steps. "My name is not actually María. I go by Sol."

Nick turns over his shoulder to look at me with narrowed eyes. "Why did Helen call you María, then?"

"Well, my name is María de la Soledad." Even as I say the word—*Soledad*—I become aware of an instinct deep down that's telling me not to say the wrong thing, not to draw too much attention to myself, not to let my guard down.

"Fair enough." He stops as soon as we reach the elevators

and presses the button. The one farthest from us opens right away. "Have you ever worked in a stockroom before?" he asks as the doors close and we start going up.

"I haven't. But I have waitressing experience."

"Have you ever worked in retail?" There's no judgment in his voice. He sounds genuinely curious, and he listens to me intently while I reply, as though what I'm saying is actually interesting.

"Well, no," I say, remembering the advice Ari gave me before my interview—to always give my answers a positive spin. "But they're kinda similar, in a way. I . . . I mean, both jobs require being organized." I'm sure there were other, smarter things I said to Helen during the interview, but I just can't remember them right now.

"You already got the job, you know?" Nick says.

"I—I know."

"So you don't have to be nervous. I had no idea what I was doing when I first started, and I caught on pretty quickly. Besides," he says, "I'm your friend. I'm here to help you out."

He smiles at me, and all of a sudden my shoulders feel a lot looser. The fear in my stomach goes away, and for the first time since I stepped into the warehouse, I'm able to think a little clearer.

"Okay, then," I say, smiling back. "Friends it is."

When we get off the elevator on the fourth floor, Nick leads me into the staff room, and he helps me find an empty locker for my bag. Once it's stowed away, he teaches me how to enter my employee number into a small machine that's anchored on the wall.

"Rule number one: Never forget to clock in, and never forget to clock out," he says to me.

"Got it."

We leave the staff room and start making our way back down to the stockroom.

"What's rule number two?" I ask.

He purses his lips thoughtfully for a moment. "I haven't decided yet."

I let out a small laugh, and he laughs as well, the corners of his eyes crinkling slightly. I'm not sure what it is, but there is something comforting about Nick—something that makes me feel as though I've known him for a long time, even though we've barely just met.

Once we're back downstairs, his face turns serious again. "We're a high-volume store, so we get two shipments every day: one in the early morning, and one in the evening," he says as he keys in a code on the stockroom door and lets us in. "The evening one comes around six. There are people whose job it is to unload the trucks and bring everything in here." He points at a stack of plastic crates in the corner of the room, which is so big and tall I have a hard time understanding why the store could possibly need two of these deliveries every day. "The morning one comes at four a.m."

"Is that why I have shifts scheduled at five in the morning?"

"That is exactly it," Nick says, nodding once. "Now, our job begins by opening the crates. Each one of them is labeled by department. This one, for example, is men's sportswear."

He pops the lid open and waves me closer so I can look inside. There are clothes in it—more clothes than I can fit in my closet at home, probably. Nick sticks his arms deep into the crate, hugs the clothes tight against his chest, and carries them over to a corner of the large table where everyone is working—which, I now notice, is in fact made up of a bunch of smaller tables pushed together.

"First thing you gotta do is check the price tag," Nick says. "If the item's over twenty dollars—which most things are—you insert a security tag. Then, you place a size sticker on the bottom left corner, put it on a hanger, and sort it in the right rack. You got it?"

"I... I think so?" I hope he doesn't expect me to try doing all that right away, because I can barely even remember what he just said.

Nick laughs. "Let's do this crate together. You'll see what I mean soon enough."

I watch as he does all the steps, but his hands are moving too quickly for me to fully understand how it's done. It's not until after he's tagged, stickered, hung, and sorted a few items that I start to understand how the process works.

"Try with this shirt," he says. "Remember to put the tag near the lower hem."

While I follow his instructions, I sneak a glance up. There are about ten of us gathered around the table, and everyone else's hands are moving quickly, getting through two or three pieces of clothing in the time that it takes me to insert a single security tag. A few people are also talking animatedly while they work, which makes me wonder how long they've known each other, and how friendly they tend to be toward newcomers.

"Perfect! Now grab one of those," Nick says to me, pointing at a huge pile of hangers that's sitting at the center of the table.

In the end, the three hours go by more quickly than I expected. Nick is a patient teacher, and soon enough I start to get used to the repetitiveness—check price, insert security tag, hang, sort—even though I'm still hopelessly slow. We finish the first men's sportswear crate and have barely started on a second one when he tells me that we're done with training for the night.

"So?" he asks me after I've clocked out. "Have I scared you away, or will you be back again tomorrow?"

"Don't worry," I tell him. "I'll be back."

CHAPTER FOUR

ARI OFFERED TO STICK AROUND AFTER HER SHIFT ended so we could drive to her house together, but I insisted that she didn't need to. Abuela has always said: *Cuando alguien te da la mano, no le cojas el brazo*—or, *if someone offers a hand, don't grab them by the arm*—and I'm hoping to avoid that with Ari and her mom. They're already doing plenty by letting me stay at their house, so after I leave the store, I walk alone through the city streets and head straight to the MTS stop at Civic Center to hop on the blue line.

The trolley is pretty empty at this time of night. It's nothing like in the early mornings, when it's so full that you're lucky if you can find a seat. There's something eerie about the silence that surrounds me, about the tiredness on people's faces. Everyone who works normal hours went home long ago, so I know that the few of us riding the trolley right now must be feeling the same way: exhausted, hungry, ready for bed.

Looking out the window at the dark sky, I think of my family. I wonder how their first day without me went. They must've finished dinner by now, and Luis must be helping Diego get ready for bed. Abuela will be washing the dishes on her own, probably wondering about how my own day went. As for Papi... I'm not sure. Is he helping Abuela clean up the kitchen? Is he busy in front of the computer, looking for ways to make extra money as he said he would? Or has he gone off into his bedroom like he does most nights, not reappearing until the next morning?

A part of me wishes I could stay on the trolley the whole way to San Ysidro and cross back into Tijuana so I could sleep in my own bed and be with my family, if only for a little while, but I know it's impossible. I need to be back in San Diego by five a.m. tomorrow for my morning shift, and crossing the border in the middle of the night is never a good idea—especially not for a girl on her own.

I allow my eyes to shut, though I force myself to remain awake, repeating the words to myself every time the recording overhead announces we've made it to a new stop. *Barrio Logan... Pacific Fleet... E Street.* When we finally make it to Palomar Street, I pick up my bag and step out into the cool night air.

Hugging myself to keep warm, and feeling as though I might just pass out from exhaustion, I start walking in the direction of Ari's house.

Ari's mother and my own mom used to be friends. I don't mean they knew each other before Ari and I met at kindergarten, but they became friends *because* of us. I imagine it would've been hard not to start liking each other, seeing as Ari and I were inseparable. They began to enjoy chatting while Ari and I played, and soon enough they were relying on each other for all sorts of things—picking up the kids from school, and making sure we did our homework, and asking all kinds of random favors.

Things changed after Ari's family moved to Chula Vista. I don't even know when my mom and Ari's would've talked for the last time, but it might've been over a year before Mami died, and I can't say I've seen much of Ari's mom recently, either. I just hope she's as enthusiastic about having me over as Ari made it sound.

They live in a tiny single-story house about ten minutes away from the station. The streets are dark and quiet while I walk, but as I approach Ari's house, I find that the porch light is on, which casts a warm glow over the front lawn.

I climb up the steps and ring the bell. A second later, Ari opens the door with a frown on her face.

"Oh," she says. "I wasn't sure if that was you. Why did you ring the bell?"

"Was I... not supposed to?"

She smiles. "We'd left the door unlocked for you. Come in."

Their house is tinier on the inside than it looks from the outside. There's a small kitchen in the back, which is lined with old-fashioned wooden cabinets. The TV is on in the living room, and the smell of food lingers in the air, even though I can tell it's been at least a few hours since they were cooking.

"Sol!" Ari's mom says as she steps out of one of the bedrooms. "¿Cómo estás, mija? Cuánto tiempo sin verte."

"Hola, Nancy," I say. "Thank you so much for letting me stay here. I'm so—"

She waves me away, as if to say that it's nothing. "We saved you some food," she says. "But Ari will help you get settled in first. You can take Cecilia's room."

Ceci is Ari's older sister, who started college this year. Growing up, she was never our biggest fan. Even though she's only a couple of years older than Ari, she never really wanted to play with us, and she would always refuse to lend us any of her things. From what Ari has told me, though, she and Ceci grew closer after their parents separated.

"Here it is," Ari says as we walk into the room. "All yours."

I wasn't sure what to expect, but there's hardly any trace of Ceci left. She must've taken everything with her to San Francisco. The walls are bare except for an empty corkboard hanging above the bed. There's a square window, a tiny closet, and a desk with a lamp on it.

"Don't worry, we washed the sheets," Ari says to me.

"Oh, I wasn't even thinking of that."

"What are you thinking of, then? You're so quiet."

"I'm thinking that… this is perfect," I say, meeting her eyes. "Thank you."

"There's hangers in the closet for your clothes. And you can put your bag under the bed—or anywhere you want. This is your room now, so do whatever."

"Thank you," I say again.

After hanging clothes for three hours straight, though, the last thing I feel like doing is organizing the closet. I leave the bag in a corner for now and go straight to the bathroom to wash my hands.

Ari and her mom made flautas de pollo for dinner tonight, which Nancy heats up for me in the microwave. I smile a little to myself when I remember how much Ari used to love coming over to my house for meals when we were younger—mostly because Mami was a great cook, whereas Nancy… well, not so much. When I bite into my flautas, however, they may as well be the most delicious thing I've ever tasted. I'm just not sure if it's because I was starving, or because Nancy's cooking has gotten better over the years.

"Entonces, Sol," Nancy says to me. She and Ari insisted on sitting with me at the dinner table, even though I'm the only one eating. "How was your first day?"

I'm not sure how to answer. There's a feeling of lightness deep inside of me—one that feels a lot like satisfaction, because even after all the fear and anxiety of the past few days, I survived my first shift at Wallen's, and earned the equivalent of nearly nine hundred pesos in the process. But I'm also exhausted in a way that I can't even explain. Helping out at the restaurant never makes me feel as drained as I feel right now.

"It was good," I say in the end.

"It might take you a few weeks to feel settled in," Ari replies. "But you'll get the hang of it soon enough."

Nancy nods quickly. "Do you work at the same time tomorrow?"

"No," I say. "They put me on the morning shift on Tuesdays and Thursdays. I start at five a.m., so I'll have to figure out a way to get up to San Diego."

I wish I'd thought of something before. The first trolley of the day leaves from the Palomar Street station at four thirty, which would make me late for work. I could also take an Uber up to the store, but I'll have to check how much that would cost. I wouldn't want it to be more than what I'll be making for my entire shift.

"I'll drive you up there," Nancy says.

"You don't have to—"

"I *want* to. It's only Tuesdays and Thursdays, right?"

"Yeah," I say, feeling my face turning red.

"I'm an early riser anyway," Nancy replies. I don't know what time she normally wakes up, but I don't ask. I can't imagine she'd have any reason to be up at four in the morning.

After I finish eating, I thank Nancy and Ari a million

57

times for saving me food and sitting at the table with me, while they insist that it's great to have me here. There's something about the way they stared at me all through dinner—as though they were eager to hear what I was going to say next—that makes it easy for me to believe them. As I head off into Ceci's bedroom, it occurs to me that maybe they're happy to have three people in the house again.

I pull my phone out of my pocket, thinking that I'll take a shower before bed. From the corner of my eye, I see a notification waiting on the screen—a text from Diego: **How was your day?**

I sit on the bed, clutching my chest. I don't think I'd realized how worried I am about him until now. It's as though my heart has been ripped apart, because I can feel the loneliness behind those four words, the longing he feels to have me home, for things to be normal again.

It was okay, I write back, typing as fast as my fingers will allow me. **How about yours? Are you okay? How was dinner?**

I hold the phone in front of my nose for a few seconds, waiting for his response, until I realize that it won't come. It's already past eleven, so he'll be asleep by now. My heart aches again when I think of the disappointment he must've felt when I didn't write back, the loneliness he must've gone to bed with.

My fingers linger over the phone screen while I debate whether I should call my dad, as I said I would. He and Abuela must still be up, but I'm not sure if I can do it.

Hearing their voices right now would only make me miss them more, so all I do is write a text to Papi.

First day went well. I'll tell you about it tomorrow.

I throw my phone aside, search my bag for my pajamas, and head for the shower.

With the hot water falling over me, this whole thing starts to seem much bigger than it did before—the job at Wallen's, the commute to San Diego, the idea of living at Ari's. I can't understand how I managed to convince Papi, Abuela, and even myself that I could handle it all, because now that I'm here, and now that I know what I actually signed up for, a part of me feels more scared than ever. Making it through the first day is one thing, but doing this for weeks and months, well… I'm not sure I'll be able to survive it.

"Good night," I say to Ari and Nancy when I step out of the bathroom with my hair wrapped in a towel.

"Don't you want to watch TV with us?" Ari says, turning to look at me over her shoulder. They're both sitting in the living room with a late-night talk show playing on the television.

"Not tonight," I say. "Thank you, though."

"Sleep well, honey," Nancy says, also turning to look at me. "I'll set my alarm for four a.m. tomorrow."

"Thanks, Nancy."

Closing the bedroom door comes as a relief. In the cool darkness, I can almost imagine I'm in my own room back home. I can let out my breath and remind myself of what Abuela would say if I'd told her about everything that happened today—that tomorrow will be a new day.

I was pretty certain my exhaustion would be enough to knock me out as soon as my head hit the pillow, but once I'm lying in bed, I find it hard to fall asleep. Even though this place felt like my own room a minute ago, all of a sudden I'm too aware of all the ways in which it's different. The bed is too soft, the curtains too thin. The moonlight filters gently through them, so that I can make out the shapes of the room around me.

There's also the fact that the street outside the window is silent—too silent. Back home, the sounds of Tijuana are there at night, like a lullaby that puts me to sleep. We don't even live on a busy street, but I can always hear a soft murmur in the distance that reminds me there are things happening out there, that I am not alone.

I'm not sure how long I've been lying in bed by the time I hear the door next to Ceci's bedroom opening and closing, which tells me Ari has also gone to sleep. My body and my eyelids feel heavy, but I just can't bring myself to relax. Turning to lie on my other side, I stare at the window, thinking about Tijuana.

There's longing in my chest, and I'm not entirely sure why—if I'm aching for the life I had only last week, or for the one I used to have long ago, before Mami died. All I know is that I've never felt so far away from home. Even though Tijuana is only ten miles away, tonight it feels like it may as well be on the other side of the world.

CHAPTER FIVE

When morning comes, I lift my head up from the pillow feeling as though it's about to explode. I must've slept for less than three hours, and now I feel even weaker than I did last night.

Still, I get dressed, brush my hair, pick up my school-bag, and then I step out of Ceci's room to find Nancy already awake and waiting at the kitchen table. There are dark circles under her eyes and her hair is a tangled mess, but she smiles gently when she sees me.

"Ready to go, mija?" she asks.

The drive up to San Diego isn't bad at all. We speed up the near-empty highway, the lights on the sides of the road flashing past us in a blur, and we arrive in about twenty minutes.

"Here we go. Have a good day," Nancy says as she

pulls over right in front of Wallen's. I don't know what
it is—if it's the fact that she woke up early just for me,
or the way she's staring into my eyes, or the softness in
her voice—but all of a sudden I get a knot in my throat.
There's something so maternal about Nancy. Something
that I've grown unused to.

"Thank you," I say. "I'll see you tonight."

I follow the instructions Nick gave me yesterday. I go
around to the back entrance, where a security guard lets
me in. I then make my way through the empty store up to
the fourth floor, shove my bag into a locker, clock in, and
head straight down to the basement.

After I key in the code to open the door of the stockroom, I search for Nick's smiling face somewhere near
the table. Instead, I lock eyes with Bill, the manager, who
stares back at me with his lips pressed into a thin line.

"You're late," he says.

"I'm sorry," I answer quickly. I clocked in right at five,
like Nick told me to. If I'm late, it must be because of
the couple minutes it took me to get down here from the
fourth floor, but I'm not brave enough to say that. "Won't
happen again."

"Go on, then," he says, gesturing toward the pile of
crates in the corner of the room. "Get to work."

I sneak past him to go join Nick at the big table. The
two people working beside him—an older man with a
thick mustache and a thin woman with dark brown hair—
scurry sideways to make room for me.

"Thank you," I whisper to them. "Thanks so much."

They don't say anything back, but they both give me kind smiles before returning their attention to what they were doing.

"You're back!" Nick says to me.

"Yeah," I answer. "I'm back."

"You see, I wasn't sure if you were lying or not when you said I didn't scare you off."

I let out a small laugh, just as I catch Bill's judgmental gaze pointed at us from across the stockroom.

"What is there to do?" I ask Nick, trying to look more serious.

"I just started working on this crate of women's casual wear," he says. "We can go through it together."

Unlike yesterday, when Bill seemed too preoccupied with other things to care much about what the rest of us were doing, today he paces around the stockroom. And whenever he passes near me and Nick, he wastes no opportunity to tell me that I'm doing things wrong—the security tag should be placed lower. No, that's not the right hanger. You wrinkled those pants, go get the steamer.

"I'm sorry," I say to Nick as I come back with the steamer for the second time. The last thing I want is to make him look bad—I wouldn't want anyone to think he's doing a poor job at showing me the ropes.

"You don't have to be," he whispers back to me. "It's not a big deal."

He gives me a smile from the corner of his mouth, and

just like that, I'm able to let my breath out. I'm quickly realizing that around Nick, I don't need to be afraid of making mistakes. I can just be myself, because that is exactly what he is doing—being himself. He's not trying to impress me, or Bill, or anyone in the stockroom. He's not concerned with anything except being kind and getting his job done, which reminds me that if I try to focus on those same things, I might find it easier to get through the rest of the week.

"Do you always do this?" I ask him while I run the steamer up and down a long skirt.

"Do what?"

"Train the new people."

"No, I don't," he says, smiling a little. "We take turns doing it. You're actually my very first trainee."

"Oh. Well... I hope I'm not a terrible one."

"Impossible," he replies. "You're doing great."

In the end, my shift feels much longer than yesterday's. When the clock on the wall finally marks seven o'clock, I can't help but feel relieved.

"See you tomorrow?" Nick asks, lifting his eyebrows hopefully at me.

"Definitely," I say, trying and failing to suppress a smile.

I'm halfway toward the door, thinking that I'll need to grab my bag and clock out as fast as possible if I want to make it to school on time, when I hear Bill's voice behind me.

"Heading out?"

I turn around to face him so quickly that I feel dizzy for a moment. "Uh, yeah…" I reply. "I—I would stay, but I need to head to school, and—"

"I know, I know. I just wanted to ask one quick thing before you leave," he says, and I take a step forward, eager to hear his question. "Has anyone told you about the employee discount?"

His eyes travel down to stare at my clothes, and I suddenly become all too aware of what I'm wearing: my old, faded jeans and a loose t-shirt, which is how I always dress to go to school. Ari told me this was fine to wear at the store—that they weren't too strict with the dress code for people in the stockroom—but now I feel so underdressed, I may as well be wearing pajamas.

"I… I think someone mentioned it," I answer in a small voice.

"Good." The corners of Bill's mouth twist upward slightly. "Everyone is strongly encouraged to use it."

I head to the trolley with a hole in my stomach. I wonder what Bill will do if I keep showing up in the same clothes. I don't think he can force me to spend money on new ones, but I should've probably read my contract more carefully before signing it and returning it to Helen.

While I stare at the road flashing past the windows of the trolley, I tell myself that I should hold on to the good things that have happened today—the way Nancy woke up early just to make sure I'd get to work on time, and the look on Nick's face when he saw that I'd returned for my second shift, and all the patience he showed me during my entire shift. But no matter how hard I try to focus on that, all I can think about are Bill's words.

I'm not sure why it has to be like this—why the good things have a way of slipping through my fingers, but the bad things stick with me like a bad song that keeps playing over and over again inside my head. Maybe it's the curse that my parents gave me when I was born. Because even when I try my hardest to be Sol, Soledad has a way of winning every single time.

When I walk into Ari's house after school, I feel almost like an intruder. With Nancy still at work and Ari up in San Diego for her afternoon shift at Wallen's, the house feels dark and quiet, almost like a museum after hours.

I head straight into Ceci's room, thinking this might be a good opportunity to make it feel more like home.

I unpack all my clothes and hang them in the closet. Then, I shove the duffel bag under the bed and place a photo of me and Diego on the desk. This frame used to hang on my wall back in Tijuana, but I decided to bring it along at the last minute. The picture was taken at the restaurant years ago, and it's always been one my favorites. I look much younger, much more relaxed. My long hair is tied back in a braid, and Diego's smile has a big gap from losing a couple of his baby teeth. This photo also reminds me of what people have said my whole life—that I look just like Mami. I may not always feel like that's true, but staring at this image, it's pretty hard to deny that I inherited her thin frame, her high cheekbones, her deep brown eyes.

There are a few other things I brought from my room: a scented candle that I've never wanted to light because I love the smell too much; a rosary Abuela gave me when I was younger, which I've never used to pray but I felt guilty leaving behind; and a newspaper clipping I've kept inside a drawer of my bedside table for years. The corners are frayed and the paper is starting to turn yellow, but the image is still perfectly clear. It shows Ellen Ochoa, the first Mexican American woman to go to space, smiling in front of the American flag.

I remember the day this article was printed in *El Sol de Tijuana*, and how Mami's eyes sparkled as she read it at the kitchen table.

"What is it?" I asked her. She didn't say anything; she just stretched out the newspaper so I could see, and I could feel her gaze on me as I stared at the image, as though she didn't want to miss a second of my reaction.

Later that day, when the newspaper lay abandoned on the kitchen counter, I picked it up and cut out the article. I didn't tell anyone about it—not even Mami. It's not that I want to become an astronaut or anything, but there was something about Ellen Ochoa's story that made me feel a closeness to her that I couldn't explain. She was born in

California, like me. Her grandparents were from Sonora. She went to San Diego State University, and later on to Stanford, which suddenly became my answers when people asked me where I wanted to go to college. And now, as I pin the newspaper clipping on the empty corkboard above the bed, her photo is a small reminder that if she could do something as wild as go to space, perhaps I'll be able to survive living away from home, and the crazy work hours, and the pressure of getting my first paycheck over to Papi as soon as possible.

Once I'm done unpacking, I take my books out of my school bag and set them neatly on Ceci's desk. After getting almost no homework done yesterday, I have a lot to catch up on, but there's one last thing I need to do before I can focus on school. Lowering myself to sit on the desk chair, I dial Diego's number and press the phone hard against my ear.

"Why haven't you called?" he asks when he picks up.

"I'm sorry," I answer quickly. "I've been busy with work, and school, and—" I let out a long sigh. All the excuses in the world won't make any difference, so instead, I ask my brother a question. "How is everything at home?"

"Different," he says.

"Different how?"

He breathes quietly into the phone for a few seconds. "It feels like you're just out—like you're at school, or at the restaurant, and you're gonna get back home any minute.

But then I remember you won't... and that's when things feel different."

I nod slowly to myself. I wish I could say something to comfort him, but there's a knot in my throat that makes me feel like I wouldn't be able to get the words out, even if I tried.

It takes me an extraordinary amount of effort to swallow hard and say, "How was school today?"

Diego doesn't like talking about it much, but he's told me bits and pieces about how he's struggled since the end of last year, if not earlier than that. Turning ten didn't just make him more perceptive—it made all the other boys in his class more perceptive, too, and they've also started to pick up on things that they didn't see before: the fact that my brother is sensitive, that he shies away from sports, that he's happier playing in a corner with a small group of people or drawing in his sketchbook.

"Same as always," he says, which tells me everything I need to know.

"Has Abuela been helping with your homework?"

"Sort of," he says. "I mean, she tries, but she gets tired quickly."

"Just do your best," I say. "Don't stop doing your schoolwork, okay?"

I can almost hear Mami in my voice. This is the kind of thing she used to always say to me, because she knew just how important getting an education is, just how many doors it could open for me and my brothers. Even though she didn't even get the chance to finish high school, she used to talk about the dreams she once had of going to college—dreams that she had to give up on in order to start working at her parents' restaurant full time. Dreams that she had to pass on to Luis, Diego, and me, because they were far too impossible for her.

"Yeah," he says. "I'll try."

"Are Papi and Abuela there?" I ask.

"Yeah, they're here. I think they wanna talk to you."

"Put them on."

A second later, Abuela's voice comes through the phone. Diego must've put me on speakerphone, because I can also hear Papi clearly.

"¡Mija! ¿Cómo estás?"

"Sol, why didn't you call us last night?"

"I'm okay," I say. "I've just... been busy."

"How's the job?"

"It's all right. I'm trying to get the hang of it."

For a moment, all three of them speak at the same time—Papi, Abuela, and Diego—so I can't hear what any of them are saying.

I clear my throat. "How are things at the restaurant, Papi?"

"Good," he says. "We closed up a bit early today. A big group came around lunch, so the special menu nearly sold out."

"That's great," I reply, even though I can't help but

wonder what they're gonna have for dinner tonight if there weren't enough leftovers to bring home from the restaurant.

Maybe they're wondering that same thing, because for a moment, we all fall silent. I can hear Diego, Papi, and Abuela breathing through the phone, but none of us says anything.

"And Luis?" I ask.

"He, uh... he's not here right now," Papi says. He must've gone out again without telling anyone where he was going.

"Don't worry about us," Abuela says firmly. "We're all doing just fine. Focus on yourself, mija. Focus on doing well in school and at work."

I nod slowly to myself, realizing just how impossible Abuela's instructions are. I will always worry about them—no matter how busy I may be, or how hard I may try to focus on other things.

"I'll try my best," I say to Abuela, because there's nothing else for me to say. Nothing for me to do except stay here on the line, trying my best to breathe through the knot that has settled in my throat.

CHAPTER SIX

GETTING READY ON FRIDAY MORNING IS ONE OF THE hardest things I've had to do all week. While I look at myself in the bathroom mirror, I see all the ways in which the early mornings and late nights have taken their toll. My skin looks dry, my lips are cracked. There are dark circles under my eyes, and my hair keeps breaking as I braid it, so that by the time I tie a band at the bottom, the sink and the floor around my feet are covered in loose strands of hair that have fallen out.

I wrap a bunch of toilet paper around my hand, wet it a bit at the sink, and start picking up the hair. I'm half-way done, trying my hardest to get all of it, when I hear knocking on the bathroom door.

"Sol? Are you in there?"

I throw the toilet paper in the bin and rush to open the door. Ari is standing there, still wearing the t-shirt and shorts she wears to sleep.

"Hey," I say. "Sorry, I was just—"

"No, no. It's okay," she says, sneaking into the bathroom. "I just really have to pee."

I step out into the hallway, and she closes the door right away. Remembering that I forgot to pack up my books after doing homework last night, I go into Ceci's room to gather everything before it's time to head out.

School drags on. Friday has always been the toughest day of the week, but today is particularly difficult. I can't think, can't read, can't even see the blackboard clearly. When Miss Acevedo, the trigonometry teacher, calls on me for an answer, I have no idea what to say.

"I, uh . . . I don't know the answer. I'm sorry."

I'm afraid she's going to give me a hard time, that she's going to tell me I need to pay attention. Instead, she narrows her eyes at me.

"Are you feeling all right, Sol?" she asks. "You don't look too good."

"I'm fine."

"You can step out for a minute if you need to."

"No, no. I'll be okay."

The truth is, even if she doesn't force me to pay attention, I have to force myself. And so I take a deep breath, straighten my back, and blink repeatedly, trying to make sense of the problems written on the blackboard and telling myself that if I start falling behind in school, life will only get harder.

At lunch, everyone seems to be in a particularly good mood, and it doesn't take me long to find out why.

"Who's coming tomorrow?" Simon says loudly. He's sitting at the end of the table, staring down at the rest of us as if he were our boss. "Olivia, Camila, you coming? Ari, you coming?"

They all nod quickly, and I lean toward Ari, trying to speak softly enough that no one else will hear. "Coming where?"

"Imperial Beach," she says. "We're gonna head over around noon."

"Oh."

"What time do you have to go home tomorrow? Maybe you could come, at least for a little while—you know, before you head back to Tijuana."

"Yeah," I say. "Yeah, maybe I could."

The thing is, I already know I can't. When I spoke to Diego on the phone last night, I promised him I'd make it back as early as possible—maybe even before he woke up, I said. My shift at the store goes until midnight tonight, but that doesn't even matter. I'll shove my exhaustion aside, set my alarm for early in the morning, and make the trip across the border so I can spend as much time as possible with my family this weekend.

Still, I imagine what it would be like to be able to join

Ari and her friends tomorrow—to just drop everything and head to the beach.

That's what gets me through the rest of the day at school—the image of myself by the ocean, sitting on a towel and laughing next to Ari. I daydream about the warmth of the sun on my skin, the sound of the waves, and the feeling of the wind in my hair, telling myself that maybe next time—maybe next week, maybe sometime soon—I'll get to just be a regular girl doing regular things with her friends on a Saturday.

Ari doesn't have Friday shifts, so we head straight back to her house after school. During the drive, I stare fixedly out the passenger window, watching as rays of yellow sunlight break their way through a few scattered clouds.

"You've almost made it through week one," she says once it's started to feel like we've been silent for too long.

"Yeah," I reply. "Almost."

"And?" Ari takes her eyes off the road for a second, turning toward me with a half-smile on her face. "How has it been?"

I consider saying the same as I've been telling her all week—that it's been good, that the people in the warehouse are nice. But then, letting out a long breath through my mouth, I say, "It's been hard."

She turns toward me again, but this time she isn't smiling. "What do you mean?"

"It's just… I thought I was exhausted before, when I had to wake up early to cross the border. But now I'm a whole other kind of exhausted. It's like…"

"Like what?"

"I don't know. Like I haven't even been able to breathe. There's been too much on my mind this week, with work, and learning everything, and trying not to mess up cause I can't get fired. And then there's my family, and the restaurant, and school. I mean, I already feel like I'm falling behind on some of my classes, and I'm just so—"

Ari shakes her head. "You've always worried too much about some things. Especially school."

"Well, that's because—"

"I know—because you gotta make your family proud, and get into college, and be a good Mexican daughter. I feel all that, too. But what I'm saying is, I've known you since we were in kindergarten, and I still remember the time you cried because our teacher put a smiley face on your art project instead of a star."

"It probably deserved a star."

"You're too hard on yourself," Ari says. "And maybe I'm too easy on myself. That's why we're best friends— we're opposites. And, as your opposite *and* your best friend, it is my job to tell you: Sometimes letting go is much better than trying to be in control."

"It's not that easy."

"Just try. You could—"

"Sometimes, I just feel like… like I'm drowning," I

say. I turn back to stare out the window, not wanting to see the look on Ari's face as I tell her this. "It's like there's this version of me that manages to wake up, and do all the things she's meant to do, and put on a straight face long enough to get through the day, but… but the real me is buried deep down, and she can't even breathe. She's stuck under all the pressure, and the loneliness, and I just… I don't know how to allow her to come out. I don't know how to save her from drowning."

For a moment, I'm frozen in my seat. I've never admitted this to anybody—not in plain words, at least— and now that I've said it to Ari, I have no idea what she's meant to do with all the baggage I just unloaded onto her lap.

"It sounds like a lot," she says softly. When I finally meet her gaze again, she's staring at me with her face scrunched up into a grimace, as though she's trying hard not to look sad but failing. "It hasn't been an easy couple of years for you, has it?"

I think of Mami. I think of the restaurant, and I think of the five of us—of Papi, Luis, Diego, Abuela, and me— sitting around the dinner table, taking slow bites of food while we sneak glances at the chair where my mother used to sit.

"No," I say, swallowing hard. "No, it hasn't."

"So maybe it'll take some time to help her—you know, the side of you that feels like she's drowning."

Slowly, I nod, leaning my head back against the seat.

Maybe Ari is right. Maybe that's exactly what I need—time. I'm always in such a rush to get out of the water, always so desperate to reach the surface, that I forget I need time to learn how to swim, time to heal, time to become someone other than who I am.

"I'm here for you," Ari adds suddenly. "You know that, right?"

"I know that."

"Good," she says, pressing softly on the brakes as we turn onto her street. "As long as you're sure of it."

As we step out of the car and make our way toward the front door, I hear my abuela's voice inside my mind: *Desgracia compartida, menos sentida—shared misfortune hurts less*. Perhaps it's true. Perhaps I should be less scared to let Ari in on what's going through my mind, because even now, I feel as though a huge weight has been lifted off my shoulders.

I try my hardest to hold on to this feeling. It even helps me focus on my homework, and for at least a couple of hours, I'm actually able to get stuff done—until I hear soft knocking on the bedroom door, and Nancy slowly peeks in.

"Ready to eat?" she asks. It's only five, but she offered to cook dinner early. It was her idea that we should all eat before I head out for my seven o'clock shift, so that I won't have to go to work on an empty stomach.

"Yeah," I say. "Thanks, Nancy."

Once we sit around the table, my stomach gives a loud

grumble. For the past few days, I've been a lot hungrier than usual, which might have something to do with the fact that at Ari's, we don't have to be careful about splitting the portions evenly, or worry about what we will do if we're still hungry at the end of the meal. There's always enough food for the three of us, and then some.

"How was your first week of work, mija?" Nancy asks me, cutting into her enchiladas.

I meet Ari's eyes. Now that she knows the truth about how overwhelmed I've been feeling, I find it much easier to smile at Nancy and say, "Longer than I expected."

Nancy shakes her head. "I swear to God, they're trying to kill you with these schedules."

"Yeah," I say. "But... the more hours, the better." During my training yesterday, I had the courage to ask Bill if he could schedule me for longer shifts. I did the math earlier this week, and the truth is, two- and three-hour shifts just won't cut it—not if I want to make enough money to save the restaurant anytime soon.

I would've thought that Bill would see that as a good thing—as a sign that I'm willing to work hard. Instead, I had to listen to him going off about how he's not legally allowed to schedule a minor before five a.m. or after ten p.m. on school nights. The latest I'm allowed to work is midnight, and only on weekends. Since the roster was already full for this Saturday and Sunday, I had to settle for a long Friday shift, which will at least mean five hours' worth of wages in my pocket.

"I don't like the idea of you taking the trolley after midnight," Nancy says. "Do you want me to pick you up tonight?"

"You don't have to," I reply. "I'll be fine." She's already woken up at four in the morning twice this week. The last thing I want is to cause more trouble for her.

"If you change your mind, just let me know."

"Thanks, Nancy. You don't have to worry about me."

"Of course I worry, mija," she says. "*Of course* I worry."

And just like that, the feeling of lightness returns, spreading to every inch of my body. Because no matter how much time has passed since Ari and I first became friends, and no matter how much things have changed since then, she and Nancy have managed to remind me of something that has become too easy to forget lately: That I don't have to feel lonely all the time. That Soledad doesn't have to always take over. That Sol is still here, and that maybe she's not as buried within me as she sometimes seems to be.

CHAPTER SEVEN

THE NEXT MORNING, I SNEAK OUT OF THE HOUSE right before seven. The sun is already shining and the sky is a deep shade of blue, but there's a still silence around me as I walk toward Palomar Street station. There are no cars, no people. It seems as though even the birds have decided to sleep in today.

I left a note on the kitchen table for Ari and Nancy to find: *I'll see you on Monday. Thank you for everything.* I wish I could've left something more—flowers, or a small gift, or an envelope with money for all the extra expenses they've had to cover with me living at their house this week. Perhaps I'll be able to do that once I've gotten my first paycheck, but for now, I hope the note is enough.

I make it through Mexican customs quickly, to find that on this side of the border, the city is already awake.

Street vendors move around in circles, selling candy, and necklaces, and chicharrones, keeping their eyes peeled for tourists. There are also taxi drivers waiting at the bottom of the ramp, leaning against the hoods of cars and talking casually to each other while they wait for customers to arrive.

I'm walking toward the Azul y Blanco bus stop when I realize something: There's a light-blue Volkswagen parked on the side of the road, just behind the taxis. I mentioned to Papi that I'd be getting home around eight, but I never asked him to pick me up.

Ignoring a taxi driver who's gesturing toward his car, I approach the Volkswagen. Sure enough, I spot a familiar scratch on the back door, and when I lean over to look through the window, he's there—Papi, sitting in the driver's seat with his arms crossed over his chest and his eyes closed.

"Papi?" I ask, knocking on the window.

He jolts awake and looks around quickly, as though he's trying to remember where he is. When he sees me, he smiles and unlocks the doors.

"You didn't have to pick me up," I say as I jump into the car.

"I thought you might be tired. I didn't want you to have to make your way home on your own."

I smile back at him. I can picture him waking up this morning, and leaving the house, and getting here extra early just to make sure he'd be waiting for me by the time I made it across the border.

"Why didn't you text?"

Papi shrugs as he turns on the engine. "I, uh... I switched to a cheaper phone plan, so now I have to be careful with how many texts I send a month."

I'm about to say something—that having a cell phone is too important, that he should keep his same old plan because he needs it for the restaurant and to stay in touch with the rest of the family—but I stop myself. I suppose we all need to make sacrifices.

While we drive through my city, I can't help but feel as though I'm seeing these streets for the very first time. And after feeling like I couldn't breathe for an entire week, I am finally able to draw in a deep breath and let the air out.

My heart starts beating fast as we enter our neighborhood. I don't think I've ever been happier to see my house—not even when we'd come back from a trip to visit extended family in Mexico City, or when I would get home after a long day at school. It's not much bigger than Ari's, and way older, but it's always been so *ours*. The facade, which was once bright orange, has been in need of a paint job for many years. The windows are tiny and curtained, with cracked panes here and there, and the wooden front door is worn and faded from standing in the direct sunlight for decades.

When I walk in, the smell of fresh coffee and eggs hits me immediately. For the briefest moment, I imagine Mami in the kitchen. A part of me is certain that as soon as I walk in, I'll find her wearing her apron, holding a spatula and humming to herself while she cooks, but instead, I find Abuela.

"Sol," she says the instant she sees me, letting out a long sigh. "How are you, mi amor?"

Before I can answer, she wraps her arms around me and plants a kiss on my forehead.

"You're just in time." Her gaze shifts toward the stove, where the eggs are starting to look cooked. "We're almost ready to eat."

Even though I'm exhausted, I head straight for the sink to wash my hands, and then I try to find small ways to help—by setting forks and knives on the table, by taking the salsa out of the refrigerator, by pouring cups of coffee for Papi and Abuela.

I'm about to go wake Diego up, eager to see him and tell him that breakfast is ready, when he appears at the kitchen door, wearing his pajamas. My first instinct is to run toward him and give him a hug, but something stops me, keeping me frozen on the spot: There's a purple bruise on his face, right under his left eye.

"What happened?" is the first thing I say to him.

"He got into a fight at school, that's what happened," Papi says bitterly as he walks into the kitchen, throwing my brother a disapproving look.

"Is that true?"

Slowly, Diego nods. We stare at each other in silence for a moment, while I think of the reunion I had wished we'd have. It didn't involve this sad look on his face, or the lingering bitterness that Papi brought into the kitchen. Deciding that I'll ask him about the fight and the bruise later, I smile at Diego, gesturing at him to come sit next to me at the table.

"Is Luis awake yet?" Abuela asks.

"I don't think so," Diego replies.

Abuela moved in with us many years ago, right after Abuelo passed away, and my two brothers have had to share a room ever since. It used to be the source of many conflicts and complaints—mostly from Luis, who resented not having his own space. Over time, though, they've found a way to coexist. Luis has learned how to help Diego brush his teeth and get into bed every night, and Diego has learned to sleep through the noise that Luis makes when he finally goes to sleep after midnight. Over the past week, though, Diego has been staying in my room, which might just be one of the few good changes that have come from my absence.

"I'll set aside his breakfast, then," Abuela says, lifting up the pan to split the scrambled eggs onto different plates.

I'm hoping for something more—toast, or chorizo, or bacon—but when Abuela sets a plate on the table in front of me, I realize this is truly all there is: A scoopful of plain scrambled eggs for each of us. Meals have been getting smaller for months, but the food Abuela made today would barely be enough for two people, let alone five.

While we eat, I notice certain things about Papi and Abuela. Even though they don't have bruises beneath their eyes like Diego does, there are other signs on their faces that reveal how this past week went. Abuela's wrinkles look more pronounced. She seems tired, worn out, as though her energy levels have been turned down really low. From the way she's staring at Diego, who's barely even touched his food, I can tell there are words hanging from her lips. She must want to tell him to finish his breakfast, that he needs to eat, but she just can't bring herself to do it. I imagine she's had to repeat the same things to him all week—and that he hasn't been very willing to cooperate.

Papi, on the other hand, looks wide awake. He eats his eggs loudly, slurping coffee after every few bites. He doesn't stare at anything or anyone in particular, but I'm pretty sure that his mind is hard at work. I wonder what he's thinking—if he's keeping track of the time he has left before he needs to head to the restaurant, or if he's dreaming of receiving my first paycheck from the store next week, or if he's trying to figure out what to do about Diego.

And then I start to wonder what stories my face would tell if any of them looked closely. I wonder if they would see the longing I've felt for this exact moment—for the moment when I'd be back in my own house, eating breakfast next to them. I wonder if they'd see any signs of the exhaustion of the early mornings and the late nights, or of the kindness Ari and Nancy have shown me.

"I'd better get going," Papi says suddenly. He's already finished his breakfast, even though the rest of us are eating slowly, trying to make our eggs last as long as possible.

"I wanna come," I say. "Can you wait for me?"

"Está bien. Be ready in five minutes," he says to me before walking out of the kitchen.

I wish I could stick around to help Abuela clean up after breakfast, but there is no time. I'm barely able to finish eating before Papi reappears, wearing a jacket and holding the car keys.

"I'll see you tonight," I say to Diego and Abuela as I push my chair back.

"Can I also come?" my brother asks in a small voice.

There's something in his eyes that makes my heart melt. Without saying anything, he begs me not to leave him alone for the rest of the day. Abuela, on the other hand, nods from behind him. She may be thinking the exact opposite: That she could really use some alone time, especially after all the extra work she's had to do this week.

I nod at my brother. "Bring your homework," I say. "Come on, let's hurry."

When we walk into the restaurant, I feel as though I've finally arrived at the one place where I'm absolutely certain I belong. This is my favorite place in the world—the safest one I know. I love its warmth, its smells, its noise. Mostly, I love the fact that Mami's presence still lingers here. She may as well be hiding behind the counter, or back in the kitchen. It's as if she never truly left.

It was her parents who first opened this place, long

before El Arco de Tijuana was installed right around the corner. I'm not sure what the area was like back then, but the location is nothing short of perfect now—just off the street from Revolución, the main tourist street, but not *right* on Revolución, which means that most of our clientele are locals, but we're also in the way of tourists who wander off the main street and decide to try a more authentic Mexican restaurant.

I've seen photos that Mami salvaged from the old days, and the place hasn't changed one bit—the tile on the walls, the wooden tables, even the ugly tapestry on the chairs. Mami kept it all the same, except for the menu, which she expanded over the years. At first, my grandparents mostly served Mexican antojitos—sopes, molletes, quesadillas, and tostadas—but Mami wanted more. She wanted to offer comida corrida—a special menu with a starter, a main dish, a drink, and a dessert, all for an affordable price and a short preparation time. Coming up with each day's menu was Mami's favorite thing to do, and now it hurts to see Papi's scribbles on the chalkboard above the counter: sopa de tortilla, milanesa de pollo, agua de horchata, and flan—one of the old, boring combinations he came up with last year, which he hasn't been willing to change despite the fact that all of our regular customers have gotten tired of it.

Once Diego is sitting in a corner with his books spread open in front of him, I do a quick lap around the place. From what I can tell, Luis and Papi have been doing a decent job at keeping the restaurant clean, but I figure it wouldn't hurt for me to sweep and mop, just in case.

Papi stays busy in the kitchen while I grab cleaning supplies and get to work. After a while, I start thinking about the fact that no one has walked in the door, even though my dad turned the sign to OPEN as soon as we got here. My throat tightens when I think of the good times—when the restaurant would get so crowded that Mami had to hire more waiters, when she spent her days and nights dreaming up ideas on how to keep growing the business. I wish I could find a way to bring all that back, but there's nothing I can do—nothing but sweep, mop, and hope that keeping the restaurant extra clean will make some sort of difference.

I'm almost done by the time the front door swings open, and I turn toward it expectantly, thinking we're finally getting our first customers of the day. Instead, Luis walks in.

"Hey," he says, putting his hands in his pockets.

"Hey," I say back.

We stand awkwardly in front of each other, and it takes me a moment to make sense of the look on his face. It's as if he's wary of me. He's probably wondering if I'm about to give him a hard time for showing up this late, but I don't have the energy to have that conversation.

I press my lips into a smile, and he nods vaguely at me before turning away to walk into the kitchen.

"What's the menu of the day?" I ask Papi once I'm done cleaning and have put everything back in the closet.

"Sopa de tortilla y milanesa de pollo," he says.

"Again?"

I linger for a few seconds, but he doesn't look up from the cutting board where he's chopping an onion. In the back, Luis is stirring a big pot that's sitting over the stove.

When neither of them says anything, I turn around and walk out of the kitchen, eager to sit with Diego for a while and hopefully get some homework done.

"So," I say to my brother as I take a seat in front of him, staring at the bruise on his face. "What happened?"

He looks back at me with pursed lips. For a moment, it looks as though he's about to cry, but he manages to stop the tears from coming.

"It doesn't matter," he says in a whisper.

"It matters to me." I lean over the table to look closely into his eyes. "Was it those kids at school? The ones who have been... *saying things*?"

The thought of kids calling him names just because he's sensitive makes my blood boil. It makes me want to throw this table aside, just to reach out and wrap my arms around him.

"It didn't happen the way you think, though," he says, avoiding my gaze.

"What do you mean?"

"They didn't start it. Or, I—I mean, they did. They were laughing, and I knew they'd just said something about me, and I couldn't keep it in."

I let out a long sigh, slowly making sense of what he's saying. "So you threw the first punch?"

"Not a punch," Diego says. "I pushed one of them, but one of his friends got to me, and well..."

"Did you get in trouble?" I ask.

Diego looks down. "Not at school—not really. But Papi's mad at me."

"Well, he's probably just—"

"He said I shouldn't be weak—that I should've done a better job at defending myself."

Something burns deep inside of me. Papi used to be much softer, but there is a bitterness inside him that has only grown stronger over the years. It must've appeared when Mami first got sick, because the old Papi—the one I remember from my childhood—would've never said something like that.

Staring into my brother's eyes, though, I realize just how unfair this is, because it shouldn't be up to him to deal with Papi's harshness. Diego already has plenty to worry about with those kids giving him a hard time at school. The last thing he needs is to face pressure at home, too.

"How about Luis and Abuela?" I ask. "What did they say?"

"Luis took me to the ice cream shop on the day that it happened. I think he was trying to make me feel better, but then Papi found out, and it all got so much worse," Diego says. "He kept telling Luis that he shouldn't be rewarding me with ice cream right after I'd gotten into trouble. Abuela just tried to heal the bruise. She put ice, and ointments, and even bags of chamomile tea on my face, but none of it helped much."

I nod slowly to myself, wondering what Mami would've done if she'd been around to deal with this. She would've probably found a solution that none of us can even think of. She would've found a way to comfort Diego, to help him feel more confident, to protect him.

"Don't worry about Papi," I say. "I'll deal with him."

Diego's expression softens, and I feel it again—the desperate need to hug him.

"You're not weak, you know?" I say, marking my words carefully. "You're strong—stronger than anyone who tries to tear you down."

Diego nods quickly, but he doesn't say anything. I'm not sure how long we sit here in silence, but eventually we both remember that we have homework to do, and so we turn our attention to our books.

A few customers start flowing into and out of the restaurant a while later. I get up from my chair right away and go greet them, making sure they're seated quickly, that they feel looked after, with the hope that they'll want to come back to the restaurant soon enough.

Ana Sánchez, one of our oldest customers, shows up with her family. At first, I'm thrilled to see them, but then, when they start asking for items that are no longer on the menu, I get a little nervous.

"What about quesadillas fritas?" Ana's youngest daughter asks me after I've already told them we're not serving paella, or fish, or shrimp cocktails. "Can you make those?"

"Let me find out," I say. Quesadillas fritas were one of Mami's specialties, one of the old favorites that survived from the original menu that her own parents created. I'm just not sure if Papi has the ingredients we'd need to make them, or if they now fall in the same category as seafood—stuff that we can't afford to buy anymore. "I'll be back in a second."

I step into the kitchen to find Papi standing in front of the grill.

"Can we make quesadillas fritas?" I ask him.

"No, we can't," Papi barks at me, leaning away as he sets down a piece of raw chicken over the fire, where it starts sizzling and smoking.

"It's for Ana Sánchez and her family."

He lets out a loud breath. "Está bien. Yes, tell her I'll make them. But I can't promise anything other than cheese and mushrooms."

I go back out and tell Ana's daughter that we can make quesadillas after all. Everyone is so excited about this last-minute addition to the menu that they all decide to order them. And later, while they're eating, turning toward me every few minutes to ask for extra salsa, and more napkins, and another round of drinks, I start to feel longing for what this place once was—and for what I know it can become once we've rescued it.

CHAPTER EIGHT

THE SIGHT OF THE SETTING SUN ON SUNDAY EVENING brings deep sadness to my chest. No matter how hard I've tried to slow down time, my weekend in Tijuana is nearly over.

"What are you thinking?" Diego asks me suddenly. He and I are in the living room, watching an old Pixar movie. Neither of us has said much since we sat down an hour ago, but he must've noticed the way I've turned away from the TV—the way I'm staring at the orange sky through the window.

"Nothing," I answer quickly. "Just wondering when Papi and Luis will be home."

Diego nods. He turns his attention back toward the movie, but barely a moment later, he clears his throat and says, "Can I ask you something?"

"Of course."

"Where would you rather be? Here or there?"

Many people have asked me this question over the past couple of years, but I don't think anyone in my family ever had. They haven't really seen the point, I guess—not when we've all known from the moment I was born that I was destined to live in the United States when I got older. Even though Mami and Papi didn't plan for me to be an American citizen, they knew from the start that this would open doors for me that they never even dreamed of themselves—the opportunity to build something for myself beyond anything anyone in our family has ever built.

"Here," I answer, just as I have every other time I've been asked about this.

The truth is, I don't think this is the answer anyone expects to hear. For many people, Tijuana is a halfway point, a place of waiting, a gateway between two worlds. For as long as I can remember, we've heard the stories of people coming here from all over Mexico and Central America, hoping to cross into the United States. Stories of asylum-seeking families who have been through hell and back only to get to this point in their journey and be told that this is as far as they can go. Stories of those who have been deported from the US, who are forced to settle in Tijuana temporarily while they wait to find out if they'll be able to go back to the lives they've had to give up. Stories of people who, if asked the same question, would always answer "there."

To me, though, Tijuana is home. And it doesn't matter how much time I may spend away from here. There will always be something about its streets, and its sounds, and its colors that will make me feel safe in a way that no other place ever could.

"Good," Diego says, crossing his arms.

I keep waiting for him to ask me something else, but he doesn't. Maybe this is all he needed to know—that, when given the choice in a few months, I will pick Tijuana over San Diego. That I will come back as soon as I've made enough money to help Papi and the restaurant, just as I promised I would.

After a while, I reach out and squeeze his arm, trying to remind him that I'm here, even if I can't be with him in the same way I used to be.

He turns toward me and smiles, which brings warmth to my heart. My biggest hope is that, by the time I return to San Diego tomorrow, at least some of the loneliness he's felt over the past week will have vanished. If I can just accomplish that, then this weekend will have been a success.

Abuela and I do the dishes after dinner. At first, we work in peaceful silence, and it's almost easy to pretend that nothing has changed—that tonight is just a regular Sunday night. But then, suddenly, she looks up from the sink to stare at me through her glasses.

"You look different," she says.

My first instinct is to lift a hand up to my hair. I'm not sure what she could possibly mean, because I haven't changed a single thing about my looks.

"I don't mean it that way," Abuela says. "There's something different in your eyes."

Maybe she's right. It's only been a week since I left, but I already feel like a different person. Who that person is, well... I have no idea. I don't even want to find out what it is that Abuela can see in my eyes, so I just look away, staring down at the cloth I've been using to wipe the kitchen counter.

"I'm worried about Diego," I say. "Papi is too harsh on him."

Abuela lets out a long sigh. "Tu papá y él son como el agua y el aceite," she says. *He and Papi are like oil and water.*

We've known this all along. Diego and I have always been more similar to Mami—more sensitive, more aware of our feelings—whereas Papi and Luis... well, they're the opposite. They're used to bottling it all up, and letting it out only when it starts to reach a boiling point.

"Can you promise me something?" I ask, squeezing the cloth tightly in my hand. "If Papi ever says anything harsh to him again, can you just... can you step in? Diego told me some of the things Papi said after he got in trouble at school, and—"

"I will," Abuela answers as she rinses a dish. "You know I will, mija."

97

I hold her gaze for a moment. I know she means well, that she will try her best to keep her promise, but I just hope she'll actually be able to do it. I hope she'll find a way to give Diego the comfort he needs, that she'll manage to stand up to Papi in the moments when it matters the most.

Abuela places the clean dish on the rack. "I understand why you're worried."

"You do?"

"Of course I do, mija. Diego needs your mom more than any of us do. And, as hard as you or I may try . . . we're not her."

"No," I answer. "We're not."

"But that doesn't mean we'll stop trying."

"Yeah," I say. "I just . . . I keep thinking about how much he's changed since Mami died. He's growing up so quickly, and if he starts going off in the wrong direction . . ."

Papi has always worried about Luis. He used to tell him to be careful who he hung out with, and what he did after school, because he's seen how easy it can be to take a wrong turn. Despite the things that show up on the news, most people in Tijuana know that trouble doesn't usually come unless you go looking for it. But for a boy like Diego, the opposite can be true—sometimes, trouble *does* come looking for kids who are feeling a little lost, who aren't quite sure where they fit in, who are looking for a place to belong.

"That's why we're here," Abuela says slowly. "We're all here to make sure that doesn't happen."

Again, I know she means well, though I can't help but

worry that we're already on the wrong track—that my brother is starting to slip between our fingers.

"How are *you*, mija?" Abuela asks me after a moment of silence.

"I'm good."

"How are you really?"

"I'm not sure," I say. "This week was so . . . *long*. I can't believe it was only five days. And now the weekend's over, and tomorrow . . ."

"You'll have to do it all over again."

"Exactly."

Abuela smiles at me. "It'll get easier," she says. "Life will start feeling normal before you know it."

"I hope so," I say, even though I don't really mean it. In the back of my mind, I don't want this life to ever feel normal. I don't want to ever give up on the idea of coming back home for good, because that is one of the few things I have left to hold on to.

"Have you all been eating well?" I ask. Tonight's dinner was small, but at least we each got a few strips of chicken and some soup. I'm not really hungry, but I'm not full, either.

"We've been eating enough," she replies. This might be another good thing about me not being here during the week—with one less mouth to feed, they must all be getting a bit more food than usual during dinner.

"Papi told me he's cutting back on some expenses."

Abuela nods. "He changed the phone plans. He also

wanted to cancel the Netflix subscription, but Diego and Luis begged him not to."

"That must've been an interesting conversation."

Abuela raises her eyebrows at me, making me laugh.

"I'm not sure what else he's gonna change, or cancel, or cut back on, but I'm certain there are many things he just hasn't thought of yet," Abuela says.

"I'll get my first paycheck at the end of this week. Once I get that money, maybe we can—"

"It's like I told you last week, Sol," Abuela interrupts me softly. "Focus on what matters—going to school, and doing a good job at the store, and getting that paycheck. Whether we cut back on things here and there... well, that's your father's problem."

I nod slowly at her. I want to say that what goes on at home when I'm not here matters way too much for me to shut my eyes and ears to it. But it's also true that I'm tired, and I still have some homework to do before I go to bed, and I need to be up early tomorrow to return to California.

And so I go back to wiping the counter, scrubbing on something sticky that won't come off, doing my best to remind myself of what Ari said to me on Friday—that sometimes, letting go is much better than trying to be in control.

"Great job," Nick says to me during my shift on Monday evening.

"Thanks," I say, trying not to blush as I lift up one last sparkly dress and hang it on the rack. It took me over an hour to work through just one crate of women's evening wear, but there's no judgment in his voice.

We turn back toward the big table, and I help Nick pop the lid off a crate full of children's clothes. Now that I've started my second week of work, my training is technically completed, so he's no longer responsible for showing me the ropes. Still, we've been working side by side, and I've been asking him questions every time I'm unsure about something, which he's been more than willing to answer.

"Do you remember what I mentioned last week?" he asks. "About how the hangers and tags are different in the children's department?"

I nod quickly.

"So... you up for the challenge?"

"I think so," I answer, feeling myself smiling.

I've only just started tagging a pair of pants when Bill's voice booms across the warehouse, and everyone turns toward him at the same time.

"Who put this here?"

Looking over my shoulder, I find Bill standing by the racks, holding one of the dresses I just sorted.

"It might've been me," Nick says immediately, even though we both know that's not true.

Bill's eyes travel toward me, as if he can see right through Nick's lie. "I expect better from you, Nick.

Donna Karan *always* goes in modern. I don't want ever to find it in the classic rack again."

"I hear you. Won't happen again."

When we both turn back around, Nick shoots me a quick glance from the corner of his eye.

"Don't worry about him too much," he says in a whisper as he inserts a tag into a coat. "Bill's just... Bill."

"Is he always this awful to be around?" I ask. The second the words leave my mouth, I fear I've overstepped, but then Nick's face crumples up into a thoughtful frown.

"Yeah," he says.

I let out a small laugh, which I quickly try to pass off as a cough. I wouldn't want Bill to hear me laughing after what just happened.

"He's worked here for over ten years," Nick says. "It's taken him a very long time to become a manager, and you know how it is... when someone's had a tough time making it to the top, they either try to make it a little easier for the people who come after them, or they try to make sure everyone pays for it as much as they did."

"That's what it is, then? He just wants newer employees to have a hard time because he had a hard time?"

Nick hunches his shoulders slightly. "Pretty much, yeah."

"I'm glad you're not like that."

"Well, I'm glad you *think* I'm not like that." He smiles at me.

The children's clothes turn out to be simple enough to

work on. After dealing with the long gowns and the delicate fabrics from the last crate, I find the small pants and shirts way easier to handle. I've gotten through nearly half of this crate when Nick clears his throat loudly.

"So, what's your story?" he asks.

"Huh?"

"Your story," he says. "I was thinking over the weekend about how we trained together all of last week, but I still don't know much about you."

Nick lifts his eyebrows hopefully at me, and something starts fluttering around in my stomach as I realize two things. The first is that he just admitted to thinking of me outside of work. The second is that he seems genuinely interested in learning more about me.

"Uh... I'm from Tijuana," I reply, blurting out the first thing that comes to my mind. "Well, not *from* there. I was born in California, but I grew up in Tijuana."

"Interesting," he says.

"How about you?"

"Me?" he asks, almost as if he didn't think himself worthy of my curiosity. "San Diego born and raised. Same as my parents and grandparents."

"That's nice."

"That's what most people say," Nick answers. "That San Diego is a *nice* city. I'm just not sure I believe them. I guess I'd need to compare it to other places to really know."

"You've never been outside of San Diego?"

"I mean... I've been to LA a few times. But I'm sure there are way nicer places."

"Yeah," I say. Even though I'm used to traveling across an international border every day, I've wondered about this a few times before—about what other parts of the world might be like. The only other place I've seen is Mexico City, which is where Papi is from, so we would spend a week or two there during the summer when we were younger. I always enjoyed seeing our family—all the tíos and tías and primos whose names we'd heard before but whose faces we'd never quite learned to recognize. When it came to the city itself, though, I've never really understood how anyone could be comfortable living in the middle of all that noise, all that traffic, all that movement.

"And why Wallen's?" Nick asks me.

"Why I got a job here, you mean?"

"Yeah."

A part of me doesn't want to admit the truth. It might be easier to brush off his question and tell him my best friend referred me because I just wanted to find an after-school job to get some extra cash. But then, when I meet his big brown eyes, I can't help but feel as though he wants to hear the real answer—as though I can be honest with him.

"My family's going through a rough time," I say. "We need the money."

"I get that," he says, his eyes focused on the t-shirt he's stickering.

"You do?"

He nods, still staring down at his hands. "It's the same for me, kinda. My mom got sick earlier this year, so she's had to take some time off work. That's why I took the job here."

"Is she... okay?" I ask, my voice coming out a lot weaker than I intended it to. Suddenly, I feel what other people must've felt when I told them Mami had cancer—the awkwardness, the pity, the uncertainty about what to say next.

"She needs a transplant," he says. "Kidney transplant. But the doctor says she should be okay once she gets it."

"I hope she's able to get it soon."

"Thanks," he answers. "Me too. We'd been waiting to see if she could get it before the school year started, but the call didn't come. So I had to skip senior year so I could pick up extra work hours."

"You had to drop out of school?" I ask, feeling a little breathless all of a sudden. That has always been one of my biggest fears—not being able to finish high school, not getting into college. After all the dreaming Mami did on my behalf, and after everything I've done to get the education she so desperately wanted me to have, I can't even picture the idea of not getting my degrees.

"Without my mom's job, I didn't have much of a choice. It's been just the two of us ever since I was little," he says. He must notice the way my eyes have turned sad, because he clears his throat. "On the bright side, though, I've gotten to meet cool people around here."

"Really?" I ask.

"You're one of them," he adds. "You're pretty fun to be around, you know?"

When I look up, he's smiling at me, and so I smile back, thinking about what he said on the elevator during my very first day of work: *I'm your friend.*

I don't think I believed him then—not entirely—but I do now. I'm just not used to making friends this quickly, this easily. I'm not used to being described as fun, or to anyone trying to get to know me better.

As I finish up the crate of children's clothes and move on to another, it occurs to me that maybe the best types of friendships happen like this—quickly, effortlessly. And when they do, there's no point in questioning them. Maybe we're just meant to jump in headfirst and trust that the other person can feel the same connection, and that they're also a little less alone because of it.

CHAPTER NINE

THERE'S SOMETHING ABOUT KNOWING THAT I HAVE A new friend at work that makes my week much brighter and easier than the last. With Nick standing by my side, the hours in the stockroom go by quicker, the lights hanging overhead seem softer. Even the walls seem to have come just a bit closer together, so that the place feels smaller and warmer than it did before.

While I walk through school on Thursday, I realize that something has also changed around here. The hallways feel less suffocating, the loud voices speaking in Spanglish friendlier than they ever have.

When I walk into the cafeteria, I head straight for the food line without thinking about the open space or the fear that people might be watching me. I'm daydreaming of making it to the end of the week so I can head back to

Tijuana and see my family, when I hear a voice that brings warmth to my chest—a voice that reminds me of home.

"Where have you been hiding?"

I turn around to find Bruno Rodríguez standing behind me. I'm so unused to talking to him at school that for a moment, my mind transports me to the line at the border. It's as if Bruno and I were standing on the bridge as we did most mornings, and the cafeteria, and the noise, and all the people around us had simply vanished.

"I haven't seen you on the bridge at all," he says, taking a step closer to me.

"Yeah," I answer. "I haven't been crossing the border lately."

"Oh."

I mentioned to him that I was looking for a job weeks ago, but I must've not told him the rest—how I finally got one at Wallen's, how I've had to move in with Ari, so I fill him in while we move slowly with the line.

"But I thought you were looking for jobs near the border," he says to me as we reach the pizza station.

"That was the original plan," I reply, placing a slice over my tray. "You know, doing after-school shifts closer to home so I could head back to Tijuana every day. I sent out a ton of applications, but Wallen's was the only offer I got."

"Well, I know a couple of people who work at Las Americas Outlets," Bruno says. "If I hear of any openings, I'll let you know."

"Gracias, Bruno. I—"

"The line's moving, can't you see?" someone interrupts me from behind.

Looking up, I find that the people who were standing in front of me have disappeared, and now there's a big gap between me and the cashier counter.

"Sorry," I say over my shoulder, reaching into my pocket for my student card. Before I can wrap my fingers around it, someone pushes past me, nearly knocking my tray over.

"Hey," Bruno says. "No puedes hacer eso. ¿Qué te pasa?"

"Bruno, it's okay. I—"

The guy who just stepped ahead of me in line turns around to face us. He's tall, with reddish brown hair and a square jaw, and there is something about the way he's looking at Bruno that makes my heart skip a beat.

"What?" he asks Bruno. "Can you say that again? I don't speak Spanish."

I'm pretty sure he's a senior. I've heard people calling out his name in the hallways a few times before—Josh, I think. Or maybe it's Jack.

Bruno clenches his jaw, staring back at him with the same kind of spite. "I said, move aside so my friend can pay for her food."

"See? That wasn't so hard," Jack says. "Least you could do is ask for things in English, don't you think? This isn't Mexico."

My heart stops beating altogether. There must be people standing in line behind the three of us, but no one dares to pass us. Whether they heard what Jack said or not, I have no idea. All I can think about is the fact that the air around us has started to feel really hot, as though the temperature had suddenly gone up by a hundred degrees.

"Apologize to Sol," Bruno says to Jack.

"What?"

"You almost knocked over her food. Apologize to her."

"I don't mind," I say quickly, but neither of them seems to have heard me. They stare into each other's eyes without blinking, as the temperature continues to rise more and more.

"Apologize," Bruno says again.

"What are you gonna do if I don't? Stab me?" Jack replies. "I hear that's what they do where you come from."

Bruno's face turns red. He takes a step closer to Jack, who lifts his chin menacingly. For a moment, I'm hoping that we will all let out our breaths and go our own separate ways, but then Jack lifts up a hand to push Bruno on the shoulder, and Bruno pushes back.

"Wait," I say. "We really don't need to—"

Jack says something else to Bruno, but I don't even make out what it is. They lunge at each other, knocking me aside as they do. My tray flies out of my hands, landing on the floor with a loud crash, but before I can even look down at my spilled food, Bruno and Jack have both fallen to the ground, wrestling with each other.

"No!" I yell. "Bruno, stop!"

Jack throws a punch, hitting Bruno on the side of the head. Bruno's neck jerks sideways, but after taking barely a second to recover, he throws himself back on top of Jack, trying to pin him to the ground.

Everyone in the cafeteria seems to be looking our way. People start pulling their phones out to record, but I'm unable to move, unable to even blink. All I can think about as I watch is that my lungs feel heavy, as if there wasn't enough air around me to fill them.

"*Shut up*," Bruno yells.

The doors of the cafeteria swing open and Mr. Vázquez, the bio teacher, walks in. Before he can get too close to where we are, Bruno throws a punch of his own, and the sound his fist makes as it hits Jack's face echoes throughout the cafeteria.

"Stop that," Mr. Vázquez says, pulling Bruno from behind. "Come on, break it off."

Bruno gets to his feet, but the damage is done. Jack is bleeding freely from an open wound near his jaw.

"Don't you *ever* say that again," Bruno yells, his face red and his finger pointed furiously at Jack.

"That's enough, Rodríguez," Mr. Vázquez says. "We're going to the principal's office. Both of you."

I watch frozen as Mr. Vázquez helps Jack onto his feet, and the three of them walk out of the cafeteria at the same time that loud voices explode all around me.

I'm not sure if it's the exhaustion from waking up early this morning, or the shock of what just happened, but I'm completely numb. My tray is still lying at my feet, and there's spilled food all around me, but I can't seem to be able to move, can't seem to remember why I'm here or what I was supposed to be doing before Bruno and Jack were dragged out of the cafeteria.

It isn't until I feel a hand squeezing my shoulder that I come back to my senses.

"Come on," Ari whispers into my ear. I have no idea where she came from, but I'm grateful she's here. "Let's go sit."

She leads me across the cafeteria, all the way to our table. As we lower ourselves into our seats, everyone—Olivia, Camila, Ana María, Tony, and Simon—watches me intently. I wish they would just ignore me, that they would go back to their conversations, but I can tell there's an endless number of questions hanging from their lips.

"That was crazy," Ana María says, frowning deeply.

"What happened?" Simon asks.

I turn toward Ari, silently begging her to help me—to deflect the attention away from me, because the last thing I want to do is talk about this. But in her eyes, I find the same kind of curiosity that is on everyone else's faces.

"I'm not sure," I answer. "It . . . it happened so quickly."

"Well, who pushed who first?" Olivia asks, at the same time that Camila says, "What were they fighting about?"

"I—I'm not sure," I say again. Suddenly, I feel as though it was someone else who was standing there and not me—as though everything that happened in the food line was nothing but a bad dream that I've just woken up from.

"I've heard things about Jack Akers," Ari says to the table. "And none of them are good."

Camila nods quickly. "I bet he's the one who started it. He must've said something to Bruno."

Simon raises his eyebrows. "Must've been something bad, for them to fight like that."

While everyone speculates about what may have happened, all I can think about is that none of it was worth it. We should've just let Jack skip the line, and say those mean things, and walk away. I have no idea what got into Bruno's head, but I wish I could've done something. Maybe I could've found a way to stop all this before it even happened.

"I just hope Bruno doesn't get in trouble," I say in a small voice.

Simon shakes his head at me. "Probably a bit late for that."

From the moment I get to school the next day, I can tell something is going on. There's a group of kids standing near my locker, whispering among themselves and staring down at something that I can't see.

While I take books out of my bag, a girl lifts a hand up to her mouth in shock, and one of the guys who's facing away from me starts shaking his head. Whatever's going on with them, it can't be good, because they're talking in low, worried voices that don't carry over to where I'm standing, even though I'm only a few feet away.

Throughout the day, I keep noticing similar things happening all around me—groups of people talking in whispers, gasping, heads shaking. As I pack up my things after English, I notice a guy holding up his phone while a couple of his friends watch something, but before I can catch a glimpse of what's playing on the screen, they huddle together, blocking my view.

It isn't until I run into Ari at lunchtime that I'm able to confirm my suspicions about what's going on.

"Hey," she says to me as she joins me in line for food. "Did you hear about the video?"

"What are you talking about?" I reply, relieved to finally be able to ask the question that's been on my mind all day.

"Someone posted a video on YouTube of Bruno punching that kid, and people are losing their minds over it."

When we get to our table, we find Olivia holding her phone up for Tony and Ana María to see. Approaching them slowly, Ari and I sneak a glance over their shoulders.

"Shut up!" Bruno's voice comes from the speaker. Whoever filmed this was sitting close to the food line, so it's easy to notice things that I missed from my angle—like the anger in Bruno's eyes, just how red his cheeks were as he struggled with Jack on the floor. Meanwhile, I'm standing in the background looking pale, my hands hanging helplessly by my sides as I watch.

The sound of Bruno's punch is even worse in the video than it was in person. It makes my stomach churn.

"Stop that," Mr. Vázquez says. I don't linger long enough to watch him pull Bruno off the other guy. I've seen enough.

"I don't get it," I say as I set my tray down on the table. "Why is everyone obsessing over this?"

"It's not just the video," Olivia says, her eyes still glued to the screen.

Ari nods at Olivia. "Show her."

"Show me what?"

Olivia puts her phone down. Clearing her throat, she slides it across the table toward me so I can read the comments.

I don't know, seems fake to me.

This is WILD!

I go to this school, and it's 100% real.

WHAM!

Heard Jack is still in the hospital. His jaw is completely screwed up.

And then there's one that makes me stop scrolling: **The kid who did this didn't even get in trouble. Only got a five-day suspension.**

Below that, there's a response that has almost two hundred likes, and the number keeps going up even as I stare at the screen. **I'm friends with Jack's brother**, it says. **His family is pressing charges. That Bruno kid won't be around much longer.**

"Did you get to the comment from the brother's friend?" Olivia asks me.

I try to answer, but I can't. I'm frozen in my chair, unable even to breathe properly.

"Sol?"

"They won't actually press charges, though, will they?" Ari asks as she sits down next to me.

Olivia, Tony, and Ana María all start talking at the same time. While they discuss the likelihood that the police will get involved, and what that will mean for Bruno, I tune out their voices.

I don't get why Bruno had to go and do this, why he chose to hit Jack back. I try to remember what we talked about while we were standing in line, but not much comes to me. All I can really remember is that I was more relaxed than usual, and that running into him made me feel as though I had found a small piece of home. Maybe Bruno was having a bad day. Maybe he needed someone to listen to him. Maybe I should've asked how he was doing, or not talked about myself so much, or found the right thing to say to keep Jack's words from getting to him.

"Anyways," Olivia says, reaching for her phone. "What does everyone have planned for this weekend?"

Her words make me feel like I've had the air knocked out of me, and it takes me a moment to realize why that is. While everyone around me starts eating, I can't bring myself to pick up my fork.

Because to everyone else, whatever happens to Bruno must feel distant, unimportant, like something you watch on TV from the safety of your own couch. They don't understand what it could mean for him. They don't get that after years of waking up at the crack of dawn, and crossing the border, and trying his best to keep his head down and his grades up, his entire future could be ruined. He could lose the chance to graduate from Orangeville, and get into a good college, and make something happen for himself.

He could lose everything.

CHAPTER TEN

I WALK DOWN THE RAMP ON SATURDAY MORNING FEELING victorious. My shoulders are heavy under the weight of my backpack, and I am exhausted from getting up early after a late night shift, but my first paycheck is inside the pocket of my jeans, and that is the only thing that matters.

It is crisp, and bright white, and it has my name on it, along with the amount of money I've earned: $327. At first, when Helen handed it to me, I thought there might be a mistake, but then she explained the store has to take out some money for taxes and other stuff I don't really understand. When I pulled out my phone and did the math, though, I realized this comes out to $6,540 pesos, which sounded a lot better.

I can't wait to hand it to Papi. I want to see the look on his face and witness the glimmer of hope that this money will bring to him, to the restaurant, to the whole family.

Just like last week, I find him parked behind the taxis, resting his eyes while he waits for me. I hop into the car, swing the door shut, and turn toward him immediately.

"Here," I say breathlessly, handing him the check.

I remain still for an instant, waiting for his reaction. I'm half-expecting him to smile, or let out a sigh of relief, or say something. Instead, he nods slowly, not looking directly into my eyes, and places the check in the center console of the car.

"Thank you, mija," he says softly as he turns the key to start the engine. "How was your week?"

I open my mouth to answer, but I choke on my own words. I've always known that Papi is a proud man. I just wish I could find a way to erase the shame he feels over having to accept money from me—that I could get through to the soft-hearted person I know exists deep within him.

I'd say that I have no idea where that man has gone, but I think I do. He's buried under the grief, under the failure, under the stress. If I was braver, I would try to talk to him about it—I'd try to tell him about how sometimes I feel buried, too, but I don't know if I'd be able to break through his hard exterior anyway.

The air in the kitchen is sizzling with the smell and sound of bacon in the frying pan when I walk in. Diego and Luis are already awake and sitting at the table, and Abuela is standing in front of the stove wearing her apron, just as I knew she would be.

"Did you get it?" she asks, turning to look at me through her thick glasses.

"What do you—"

"The check."

I smile at her, nodding. "I did. I already gave it to Papi."

She smiles back, and we both seem to let out a long sigh at the same time.

I have no idea where the bacon came from, but I don't ask. Maybe it's a treat—something Abuela saved for today's breakfast because I was coming home. Or maybe my dad found it inside the refrigerator at the restaurant and decided to put it to good use before it expired.

While Abuela flips it, making sure it's perfectly crispy as she always does, Diego and Luis set the table, and I watch over the eggs.

"Well?" Abuela asks once breakfast is ready. "How was the second week?"

I look down at my food, thinking carefully about my answer.

"Better," I say. I haven't been able to get the thought of Bruno out of my head since Thursday, but I've been trying my best—trying not to forget the good things that happened this week, to focus on the thought of dinners with Ari and Nancy, to make the most of the hours spent next to Nick in the stockroom.

"How about you?" I ask, looking around the table at my family's faces. "How was your week?"

Staring at Diego, I notice the bruise on his face has changed colors, so that it's now a yellowish shade of green.

I talked to him on the phone a couple of times over the past few days, but he didn't seem to have much to say.

Luis looks tired while he lifts his fork up to his mouth. I can't even think of the last time he was awake before ten a.m., and it couldn't be any more obvious that mornings don't agree with him. I can almost make out the shape of his pillow on his thick black hair, and he keeps blinking nonstop, almost as if the sunlight coming through the window is too harsh on his eyes. For a moment, I wonder what could've possibly made him get out of bed early today, but then I think about the smell of bacon, and the fact that even he must've been unable to resist it.

Meanwhile, Papi seems to be in even more of a rush to head out than he was last week. He's slurping down his food, not even looking at the rest of us.

Suddenly, Diego leans in closer to me. "How much money did you get?" he whispers into my ear.

"Almost seven thousand pesos," I answer, and his eyes widen slightly, as if he'd never even heard of such a big amount.

"What are you gonna do with it?" Luis asks Papi.

"We have bills we need to pay," Papi answers. "But first, I'm gonna go buy ingredients for pozole."

With everything that has been on my mind lately, I haven't given much thought to Mexican Independence Day. Even though the actual holiday was yesterday, on September 16, most of the celebrations would've happened the night before, on the fifteenth. That's when most people have parties, and family gatherings, and watch El

Grito de la Independencia on television. I'm pretty sure I know what Papi is thinking—that the festive spirit might just carry over into the weekend, and if it does, people will be in the mood for pozole, or chiles en nogada, or mole.

"Was the restaurant busy this week?" I ask.

Papi nods once. "Busier than usual."

"A ton of people came in asking for pozole, but we had to turn them away," Luis says.

"Well, that won't be a problem anymore," Papi says. "Who wants to come with me to get the ingredients?"

I look into Luis's eyes, and then Diego's. Without saying anything at all, the three of us smile at each other, the way we used to when we were younger and Mami or Papi would ask if we wanted to go with them to run errands around the city, or when we walked into the house after school to find that Mami had left us money for ice cream on the side table.

"Can we all come?" Diego asks.

"Está bien," Papi answers, reaching for his cup of coffee. "I might need all of your help carrying stuff."

There's something about having a busy restaurant that makes my heart feel bigger, my shoulders feel more relaxed. It's as if there's a little light shining inside of me—one that was extinguished long ago, but now that it has returned, everything just makes a lot more sense.

From what I can tell, I'm not the only one who feels different, either. Papi seems focused and content as he prepares the dishes, pressing his lips together into a small smile every time a new order for pozole comes in. Luis looks wide awake as he and I step into and out of the kitchen carrying trays, and plates of food, and drinks, and even Diego is more alert, more cheerful than he has been lately.

It was Luis's idea that we should set a sign outside announcing that we're serving pozole as part of our Independence Day menu, and it worked much better than any of us could've anticipated. People haven't stopped coming in the door since we first opened, and with the arrival of lunchtime has come an influx of customers that's unlike anything we've seen in at least a year.

I lead a group of college-aged students to one of the few empty tables we have left—a spot by the corner that I haven't seen occupied in a while—and then turn toward the family of four I sat a few minutes ago, who seem ready to order.

"Can I get three bowls of pozole and an order of tacos de asada for table seven?" I say to Papi as I walk into the kitchen.

"*Three* bowls?" he asks, lifting his eyebrows at me even as he pours a large spoonful of soup into a bowl.

"Yeah," I answer. "Why? Is everything okay?"

"We're going through the pozole much faster than I thought," he says, frowning deeply.

"Well, can't we make another batch?"

Papi looks over his shoulder at Luis. "What do you think?"

"We'll need more meat," my brother answers. "But we might be able to work with what we have left of the other ingredients."

"Go get more meat, then. You can grab the money from the cash register."

Luis quickly undoes his apron, and while he runs out of the restaurant to head to the butcher, Diego helps me look after the customers. It is then, while my younger brother and I are rushing through the gaps between the tables, bumping into each other every now and then as we make our way into the kitchen, that I start to feel Mami's presence around me, stronger than ever before.

I can feel her watching us, can almost picture her smiling. I'm not sure I believe in some of the things Abuela talks about—souls, and heaven, and eternal life—but if any of it is true, then Mami must be thinking about us right now, and she must know we're trying our hardest. Trying to make the most of today, trying to save her restaurant, trying to hold on to the hope that this weekend might lead to the beginning of something new for all of us.

≈⁂

By the time our last customers of the night step out of the restaurant and Papi locks the door behind them, we are all exhausted. Even though the crowd slowed down a bit after lunchtime, we managed to run through nearly two additional pots of pozole.

Now, all there's left to do is clean. While Luis and Papi stay busy in the kitchen, I grab a cloth and some spray cleaner and start wiping down the tabletops, with the sound of two dozen voices still ringing in my ears.

I'm almost done with the tables and about to move on to mopping the floors when a soft tapping noise starts filling the air around me—one that sounds a lot like knocking. I drop the cloth and turn toward the entrance, my heart beating fast. I can't think of why anyone could be knocking on our door past closing time.

But then, when I spot Abuela and Diego staring back at me through the glass, I almost laugh to myself.

"What are you doing here?" I ask as I open the door for them.

"Your dad called earlier and said how busy you all were," Abuela says, holding Diego's shoulders as they both step into the restaurant. "So we figured we'd come here for dinner instead of having you bring food back to the house."

"Sol?" Papi calls out from the kitchen. "Is someone there?"

"It's just us!" Abuela yells back. "And we're hungry," she adds in a whisper, smiling down at Diego.

My brother stuck around at the restaurant for as long as he could, but all the movement from today quickly became tiring for him. He decided to walk back home on his own just so he could relax for a while and get some homework done, but now that he's back with Abuela, he looks wide awake.

"Is there any pozole left?" he asks.

"Why don't you go ask Papi?" I say. "Abuela and I will set everything up around here."

He runs off into the kitchen, and Abuela helps me

push two tables together. We've barely started setting down the cutlery before Papi, Luis, and Diego step out of the kitchen, carrying big bowls of soup just like the ones we've been serving to our customers all day.

"I hope you all like it," Papi says. "Luis and I tried to follow your mother's recipe as closely as we could."

We all take our first spoonful at the same time, and as I swallow the hot liquid, I sneak a glance up at Papi, who's staring at all of us expectantly.

"It tastes just like the one she used to make," Diego says.

I nod quickly. "Even better, maybe."

"Your mother really did have the best pozole recipe, didn't she?" Abuela says, sinking her spoon right back into her bowl.

When Diego and Luis ask if we're allowed to have seconds, Papi quickly pushes his chair back and goes into the kitchen to refill our bowls. And later, while I'm finishing my second bowl of pozole, I can't help but think about the fact that the late nights and early mornings in the stockroom have been for something—and this is it.

Because, as long as I keep bringing back checks, maybe nights like tonight could become normal again. Maybe we could all get used to a busy restaurant, and full stomachs before bed, and to being a family once more.

Maybe life could go back to being just a little bit more like it was before Mami died, and we could all figure out a way to become the people we saw a glimpse of today.

CHAPTER ELEVEN

DURING THE HOURS I SPEND IN THE STOCKROOM BESIDE Nick over the next few days, he and I start paying attention to the conversations that happen around the table, trying to keep our minds busy while our hands work fast.

It doesn't take me long to learn the names and stories of some of the people I've been bumping shoulders with every day for the past couple of weeks. Lina, for example, has been working here almost four years. She lives with her older sister and her niece, and she's a big fan of true crime. We haven't been formally introduced, but I pick up on all that just from hearing her talk about a new TV show she's been watching, and how mad she was at her niece for watching an episode without her the other day.

There's also Marcos, a man with a big mustache who mentioned he has a wife and three kids, and Kelly, a woman with a bright, round face who gently points out to me during my late shift on Wednesday that I'm using the wrong hanger for a pair of men's jeans.

"It's okay, hun," she says to me when she notices I'm blushing. "You're doing much better a few weeks into the job than most people after two full months."

Lina nods quickly while she places a gray coat on a hanger.

"She's one of the good ones," she says.

They both smile at me, and I smile back, all too aware of the fact that now I'm blushing even more.

"How are your legs?" Lina asks, leaning closer to me.

"Uh... sorry?"

"Your legs. Have they been sore from standing during your shifts?"

"Oh... not really," I answer. "But I'm used to being on my feet a lot. I've helped out at my parents' restaurant since I was young."

"You're lucky," Nick says beside me. "I used to get the worst leg and back pain when I first started working here."

Kelly and Lina nod in agreement, and an instant later, they launch into a million questions—about where I go to school, about my family, about life in Tijuana. Even though I've already told most of this to Nick, he listens along with Lina, Kelly, and Marcos, and all four of them stare at me as if I was the most fascinating person to have passed through this stockroom in a long time.

"He'd get along with my son," Marcos says after I tell

127

them about how much Diego loves sketching. "But he's probably too young to be friends with your brother—he only turned seven in August."

"Give it a few years," Kelly replies. "Age differences stop mattering after a certain point."

It's so easy to talk to them that time seems to go by twice as fast. After a while, Lina says she needs to go get the steamer to remove creases from a pair of pants, and Kelly and Marcos turn around to go grab new crates, leaving me alone with Nick.

"You're popular around here," he whispers into my ear.

I let out a small laugh. I'm not sure if I'll ever be what you could call popular, but there's something about the last few days that has made me feel different.

I'm not sure how to explain this new feeling, but I've been aware of it at school, too. It's been easier to pay attention in class, to follow along with what my teachers are saying, and to keep up with the conversations that happen around me while I'm sitting in the cafeteria during lunch.

Mostly, though, I've been aware of it when I'm at Ari's. I feel it in the way she and Nancy smile at me when I walk into the house, in the way we all sit together at the dinner table every night, in the way they've been asking me to join them on the couch to watch the talk shows they both love so much.

"How are you doing with your homework, mija?" Nancy asks me after we finish eating on Thursday night. "Do you think you can squeeze in some TV time?"

The truth is, I have plenty of homework to catch up on, but I just can't find a way to say no.

"Sure," I answer. "I have some time."

"Mom, I think we should let Sol decide what we're gonna watch tonight," Ari says, pushing her chair back to take her plate to the sink. "We've forced her to sit through our shows three nights in a row."

"No, no," I say quickly. "I'm happy to watch whatever you two want."

"Are you sure?" Nancy asks, leaning her head to one side. "We could put on a movie, or something."

"I'm sure. Your usual shows are more than perfect."

Nancy stretches out a hand to grab my empty plate. "If you change your mind, do let us know, mija."

It is while I'm sitting in the cool darkness of the living room, with Ari on one side and Nancy on the other, that this new feeling reappears in the deepest part of me, spreading to every inch of my body like a beam of light.

And while the two of them laugh out loud at jokes that I can barely understand, I finally realize what this feeling is all about. Because I'm suddenly finding it a lot harder to remember what it's like to be lonely.

⁂

Despite all the ways life has felt brighter over the past few days, when the end of the week comes, it's impossible to deny that I'm every bit as exhausted as last week, or the one before. For the most part, I've gotten used to sleeping in Ceci's room, but I can't say I've been getting much rest. It's as if the hours speed up between the moment I close my eyes every night and the moment my alarm goes off the next morning, so that I'm always tired and groggy by the time I need to get up from bed.

I'm standing in front of my locker on Friday morning, taking books out of my bag sleepily and wishing for a nap, when I hear a husky voice calling my name.

"Sol!"

I turn around, feeling wide awake all of a sudden. Bruno is walking toward me with a small smile on his face. For a second, it's easy to forget about all the things that have changed since I last saw him. It's easy to pretend that the video of him fighting with Jack Akers hasn't gotten thousands of views, or that he's never gotten suspended.

"How have you been?" he asks me, and that's when I remember just how different things are now. It's mostly in his voice—a hoarseness that had never been there before.

"I've been okay," I say quickly. "How about you?"

"Things have been kinda rough."

"Is today your first day back?"

"Yeah," he says, looking down at his feet. "I'm not sure what's worse—being under suspension, or having to come back and face everything and everyone."

"Bruno, what happened that day? Why did you—"

"I don't know," he answers. "The second it was over, I wished I hadn't let Jack get into my head. But... I guess

I was fed up. It wasn't the first time he or his friends have said things like that, and I just..."

I nod slowly, because I know exactly what he's talking about. Even though we go to a school where most people couldn't care less about where we come from, the fact that there are people like Jack can have a way of getting under our skin, of making us feel like we will never fully belong.

"I'm not proud of it, but... I can't take it back. No matter how much I wish I could."

"What's gonna happen now?" I ask. From the corner of my eye, I see people looking at us as they make their way down the hallway, but no one lingers for long.

"They're not pressing charges—Jack's family, I mean. The principal convinced them not to."

"Well, that's good," I say, but Bruno's expression doesn't change. "Isn't it?"

"There's something else," he answers, letting out a long sigh. "Principal Flores agreed to take this to the school board instead... so there's gonna be a disciplinary hearing."

"A what?"

"They're trying to get me kicked out of school," Bruno says. "They didn't think the suspension was enough."

"But you didn't even throw the first punch."

"I know. It's just that Jack's parents are saying I caused long-lasting damage to his jaw."

"Well, did you?"

"I don't think I did. They're trying to make it sound a lot worse than it was." Bruno shrugs. "If anything, he might've done something to my ear, cause I haven't been able to hear the same since I took that hit. I just haven't been able to see a doctor, but he has. He got X-rays, and all, but his parents won't even share them with the principal, and I think it's because they know what they'll show—that Jack's jaw is fine, and all he got was a bruise."

"Why is Principal Flores taking their side, then? Did you tell him your version of the story? Did you—"

Bruno frowns in a way that tells me he has—that he's already tried everything I was about to suggest.

I shake my head slightly, thinking of Principal Flores. I've never even been in his office, but I've heard a lot about him—good things, for the most part. It's no secret to anyone that there are kids like me and Bruno—kids who live in Mexico and go to school here. But it is people like Principal Flores who make it all possible for us, because he understands that American kids should be able to have an American education. He understands that most of us will end up living on this side of the border, and that denying us a spot in this school wouldn't make things better for anyone—because if we're able to go to an American high school, we'll find it easier to get into an American college. And if we're able to get into an American college, we'll be able to find good jobs in the future. And if we're able to get good jobs, we'll be able to pay the taxes that will allow other kids to get the opportunities they need.

I wonder why he hasn't been willing to hear Bruno's side of the story—why he's found it so easy to listen to Jack's parents instead. Perhaps it's simply because Mr. and Mrs. Akers are right here, putting pressure on him, whereas Bruno's parents are on the other side of the border, unable to speak up for their son.

"When's the hearing?" I ask.

"They haven't set a date yet."

There are so many other things I want to ask him— what his parents have said, or what he's doing to defend his case, or whether there is anything I can do to help—but then I remember the way he's always been able to read my mood, the way he always stood peacefully in silence next to me whenever I didn't feel like talking.

Maybe there'll be a better time to ask all these questions, but for right now, I just smile at Bruno, hoping he can somehow feel that I'm here for him, and that I am on his side.

"It's gonna be okay," I tell him. "You're gonna be okay."

"Thanks, Sol," he replies, but I can tell he doesn't believe me.

CHAPTER TWELVE

BREAKFAST WITH MY FAMILY ON SATURDAY MORNING is both similar and different from last week. It's similar because Abuela made bacon again, because some of the hope that my first paycheck brought still lingers in the air. It's different because Luis didn't get up early today, because Diego and my grandmother are much quieter than usual, and because Papi doesn't seem to be in a rush to head out. He eats slowly, sipping coffee between bites, and turning every now and then to stare out the window at the lime tree in our backyard.

By the time we get to the restaurant, things feel different around here, too. There's none of the excitement from last week, none of the noise and movement. Now that Independence Day has passed, the place is every bit as quiet as it has been over the past few months.

"Do you need any help?" I ask Papi when I step into the kitchen. After dinner last Saturday, when we all helped him clean up, the place was left spotless, but now I can see some of the signs of disarray that have become normal lately. The sink is filled with dirty dishes, pots, and pans. The floors are in desperate need of sweeping and mopping, and there's a smoky smell in the air that I recognize—the lingering stench of burnt meat.

"I'm good here," he says. "You can help with the dining area."

I go to the closet to grab cleaning supplies. Taking a quick lap around the place, I notice that things in this part of the restaurant have also taken a turn for the worse. The floor is every bit as dirty as it was in the kitchen, and there are salsa stains on tables three and four that look several days old.

I've barely started wiping the tables when Diego looks up from his homework and asks if there's anything he can do, so I hand him the broom.

"How was everything around here this week?" I ask him while we work.

"All right, I guess," he says. The broom is normal-sized, but it looks big in his small arms. "Papi was in a better mood."

"How about you? How have you been feeling lately?" I ask.

Diego shrugs. The bruise beneath his eye may be all but gone by now, but there's still something in his gaze that reminds me of the day I got back home to find out that he'd gotten into a fight—something that tells me there are things happening deep inside him that he's unable to speak out loud.

Before he can answer, Papi's loud voice comes from the kitchen.

"¡No me jodas!" he shouts. He used to curse a lot less—mostly because Mami didn't like it—but he's been slowly going back to his old ways.

Diego stops sweeping, turning to look over his shoulder at the entrance of the kitchen.

"Should we go check on him?" he asks in a whisper.

"No," I say quickly. "Let's leave him."

I drop the cloth on top of another table to start wiping it, but a second later we hear it again: a curse, even worse than the previous one. And then, suddenly, a hissing sound comes from the back, followed by two loud bangs.

"I'll go," I say to Diego.

The second I step into the kitchen, Papi curses again.

"What's wrong?" I ask him.

"This damn fridge," he says, giving it a small kick with the tip of his foot.

I use a hand to cover my mouth and nose while the refrigerator—the big, industrial one we've had for as long as I can remember—makes a sputtering sound. There's smoke coming from the back, which seems to be turning thicker and darker with each passing second.

"Can you fix it?" I ask, even as another coughing sound comes from the refrigerator.

"That's what I was trying to do," Papi says, leaning forward to get a look at the back of the fridge. "It's been acting up for weeks, but I don't know what's gotten into it today."

Before I can say that the fridge has had a long life—that it's probably not meant to last more than fifteen or twenty years—Diego's voice comes from behind me.

"Some customers just walked in," he says. "What should I tell them?"

Papi turns sharply toward him. "To take a seat! What else is there to say?"

"But can we even make food right now? The entire restaurant smells like—"

"Sol, you go take care of the customers!" Papi growls at me while he sticks a hand behind the refrigerator.

I don't argue. I don't say that what he's doing probably isn't safe, that it's not Diego's or my fault the refrigerator is not working. I turn around, and as I walk out of the kitchen, I squeeze my brother's shoulder, trying my best to remind him that I'm here for him, and that we should leave Papi alone when he's in this type of mood.

"Bienvenidos," I say to the new customers, a family of tourists. "The menu of the day is milanesa de pollo with—"

"Is everything okay back there?" the mom interrupts me in heavily accented Spanish, staring at the back of the restaurant with wide eyes.

"Yeah, yeah. Everything's fine."

The dad crinkles his nose. "Are you sure? Cause it smells as if—"

"I'll just, uh... crack the door open to let some air in."

In the end, they take a quick look at the menu and leave, saying they weren't too hungry after all, and then the restaurant is as empty as it was a few minutes ago.

I keep sneaking glances at the door, wondering if the smell of smoke has filtered out, scaring any potential customers away. Because, even as the clock keeps ticking, there's no one. No one except for me and Diego, who keep sweeping, and mopping, and wiping while smoke continues to swirl out of the kitchen.

※

"I'd say it's a goner," Luis says, sneaking out from the gap between the fridge and the wall. The corner of his lip twists downward in a way that makes him look sad, but it disappears so quickly that I'm left wondering if I only imagined it.

"Are you sure?"

"Pretty sure."

My dad's face crumples into a frown. "No puede ser," he says. "Your abuelos installed this refrigerator themselves. It's worked perfectly for decades!"

Luis shakes his head.

"*So how can it not be working all of a sudden?*" Papi hisses, throwing his hands up.

"Well, maybe because it's been here for decades," Luis says with a shrug.

Papi remains silent for a long time, staring at the refrigerator with a frown on his face. "We should ask someone else. Maybe there's a way to fix it."

There's only one person he can think of—that is, only one person who won't charge him for coming to take a look: Samuel. Among his many odd jobs, he once worked as a helper to a property manager, so during the months he spent as a waiter at the restaurant, he helped us fix a few things here and there.

"It's the compressor, Mr. Martínez," he says.

"Can you fix it?"

Samuel lets out a long sigh, running a hand through his hair and leaving a dark spot on his forehead without noticing. "I think so. I know a shop that sells used parts. I'll have to run out and find a replacement, but even if I manage to fix it, it might not last long."

"How much time, do you think?"

"It's hard to say," Samuel answers. "Maybe a few weeks, maybe a few months. You'll most likely have to buy a new refrigerator in the end."

"How much would that cost?" I ask Papi, but he doesn't reply. I guess we all know the answer already: more money than we can afford right now.

"Muy bien," Papi says, nodding slowly to himself. "Samuel, how long will it take you to find the compressor?"

"If I go look for it right now, I could be back in a couple of hours."

"Okay," Papi says after a long silence, nodding to himself. "Okay. Thank you, Samuel."

"Anytime, Mr. Martínez."

Samuel gives me a small smile as he walks out of the kitchen, and then it's just us—Papi, Luis, Diego, and me. It's strange, the way the kitchen remains silent long after Samuel has left. Papi keeps staring at the fridge, rubbing his forehead and shaking his head to himself, as if praying for a miracle. Luis crosses his arms, frowning deeply, and Diego looks right at me.

For a while, it's as if we're in mourning. And maybe we are, because this is the last thing we need right now. Staring at my father's and my brothers' faces, I can tell they're all thinking it—that this might be the moment we've feared all along. From the day Mami stepped down, we've been afraid that the restaurant would fail without her. And now, with an empty dining room, a broken fridge, and no food cooking on the stove, it feels as though it has finally happened, and none of us is quite sure what to do or say.

"I'm gonna need your help," Papi says all of a sudden, rolling up his sleeves. "All of you."

He asks Luis to go buy a bag of ice from the convenience store down the street. Meanwhile, Diego and I go back to the dining room to finish our cleanup, and Papi remains in the kitchen, trying to air out the smoke and carry on with preparing the menu of the day.

When an older couple walks into the restaurant, I sit them at the table that's farthest from the kitchen, with the hope that they won't catch the lingering smell of smoke. They take an extremely long time looking through the menu, and then they ask me to bring them two Coronas and a guacamole, which is at least a simple enough order.

A few more customers come and go, and I have to make a few last-minute corrections to the menu as people order things we can't make right now. For the most part, though, we're able to manage until Samuel returns to the restaurant a couple of hours later with a triumphant look on his face.

"Well?" Papi asks when he sees him.

"I found the compressor, Mr. Martínez," he says, nodding at a big box that he's carrying in his arms.

"Samuel, I don't know how to thank you. We're so—"

"I'm happy to help."

While he works on the refrigerator, the rest of us try our best to remain focused. I look after the tables, sneaking my head into the kitchen every now and then to place orders with Papi and Luis—a menu of the day for table two, quesadillas fritas and tostadas for table four. But the entire time, I can't stop thinking about how different things were barely a week ago. I can't help but feel stupid for being hopeful then, because a broken fridge is something that a paycheck from Wallen's and a few batches of pozole simply can't fix.

The people at table four pay their bill, and the ones

at table two follow soon after. Once the dining room is empty again, I start to worry about it more and more: the fact that our dream of saving the restaurant might end up being just that—a dream. An unachievable illusion that is meant to fall just beyond our reach.

"What are we gonna do?" Luis asks during dinner that night.

"About what?" Papi answers.

"Are you gonna buy a new fridge?"

Papi brings a piece of chicken up to his mouth. "Not right now."

"When, then?"

"Whenever it becomes necessary."

Luis lets out his breath in a way that seems to fill the entire house, but he doesn't say anything else. Samuel was able to fix the compressor in the end, but before he left, he gave Papi about a million warnings—not to overstuff the refrigerator, not to keep the door open for too long, not to push it too close against the wall. His final warning was what he had already said: the fact that there's no way to know how long the compressor will last, and that buying a new refrigerator will end up being the only reliable solution.

Shortly before we closed the restaurant for the day, I did a quick search online of how much a new commercial fridge might be, and I couldn't find anything under four thousand dollars—or at least not anything that was similar in size to the one we currently have. That comes to around eighty thousand pesos. *Eighty thousand.* I can't even wrap my head around the idea that a fridge could cost that much money.

"I should start looking for other jobs," Luis says suddenly, and we all turn toward him.

I think about a few weeks ago, when he said the exact same thing. I'm waiting for Papi to tell Luis he can't—that he needs to be at the restaurant. I'm sure my dad is about to explain how he can't be chef, waiter, runner, dishwasher, and busser all by himself, and that if we ever hope to bring the restaurant back to its former glory, he's gonna need the extra pair of hands.

But as the silence stretches on, I realize Papi isn't going to say any of that. He's not gonna try to fight Luis this time, because we all know we could use an extra paycheck—now more than ever.

For the rest of dinner, we're mostly silent. After a while, I start noticing the way Diego's gaze keeps shifting to his right every few seconds, to the empty chair that belonged to Mami, and suddenly, I'm overcome with a million emotions that hit me like a train at full speed.

Because if she were still here, we wouldn't be in this situation. She would know what to do about the restaurant, and how to pay back our debts, and how to carry on whenever we're feeling most hopeless. But maybe her absence has really, truly broken us forever. And now that she's gone, there's nothing left for us to do but to accept this brokenness.

I put my fork down, pressing my lips together to stop myself from bursting into tears. Looking around the table, I can tell no one has noticed that I'm not breathing, that I'm struggling to hold it all in.

Everyone keeps eating, while I sit here missing Mami—missing her warmth, missing the safety we used to feel when she was with us, missing the way life used to be.

It's hard to believe that just yesterday, I was eager to get back home. Now, all I want to do is leave. I want to go back to California and eat dinner next to Ari and Nancy, and spend my mornings and evenings in the stockroom. I want to escape from this silence, from this uncertainty, from this grief.

CHAPTER THIRTEEN

I HEAD BACK TO CALIFORNIA RIGHT BEFORE SUNSET on Sunday evening. It isn't too hard to justify it to Papi—I tell him I'd much rather leave tonight than wake up early tomorrow morning, and that getting a good night's sleep at Ari's is exactly what I need before the start of the week.

It's also true that the wait at the border is much shorter on Sundays. I hurry through the bridge and make it to the end of the line quickly enough, where a US border agent greets me with a blank look on his face. He looks down at my passport, then back at me, and then at his computer screen.

"What were you doing in Mexico?" he asks me.

"I was visiting family."

"And what will you be doing in the United States?"

This isn't the first time this has happened—not the first time I've been asked questions about who I am, or what I'm doing, or what reasons I could possibly have to want to enter the United States. It's just the first time in a while. It doesn't matter that I have an American passport, that I was born on that side of the border. To some of these agents—especially the new ones, like Officer Coughlin seems to be—I'm just a Mexican girl, crossing over into a country that doesn't belong to her.

"I go to school here."

There's always been a deep fear in the back of my mind—the fear that I'll get sent to secondary revision, that they'll decide I could be carrying drugs, or suspect me of doing something wrong.

"Don't argue with them," Mami used to tell me when she warned me about all the things that might happen, back when I first started making the trip across the border. "And, whatever you do, don't let them see that you're nervous. That'll only make things worse."

I hold my breath as Officer Coughlin types something into his computer. When he finally hands back my passport, I wait until I've walked out the doors and into the soft twilight before letting all the air out. At least today wasn't the day when I'll be sent to secondary revision, when I'll have to explain myself even though I've done nothing wrong.

Once I'm on the trolley, the relief starts to turn into guilt. I should be having dinner with my family right now, and washing the dishes with Abuela afterward, and wishing Diego a good night before he goes to sleep. I just couldn't spend another minute inside my house, couldn't sit with the thought of the refrigerator, or Luis's job search, or the restaurant a second longer.

While I stare out the window at the road flashing past us, I wonder what Nancy will be cooking for dinner tonight. I can't wait to be sitting next to her and Ari at the table, or on the couch watching a show together, and to be able to just forget about everything that's going on at home, if only for tonight.

"Where's your mom?" I ask Ari the moment I walk into the house. I can't quite put my finger on how I know this, but there's a stillness in the air that tells me Nancy isn't here—not even inside one of the bedrooms. It's probably the fact that the TV is off, because Ari's mom likes to always have it on, even if it's just in the background.

"She's still at the salon. Sundays are usually busy days for her."

Nancy used to have her own shop back in Tijuana, but ever since they moved to Chula Vista, she's been working at a salon not too far from their house. You'd think that with Nancy being a stylist and all, she and her two daughters would have the most amazing hair, but they don't. Ari has always had the same blunt shoulder-length haircut, and Nancy usually just ties hers back into a ponytail.

"Should we make dinner for ourselves, then?" I ask. It looks as though Ari's been sitting at the kitchen table for a while, because she's surrounded by a big mess—open books, loose sheets of paper, empty cups of coffee, and plates filled with crumbs.

"I have a better idea." Ari's smile widens. "Let's bake a cake."

Baking was always her older sister's thing. Growing up, Ceci had one of those Easy-Bake Ovens that I always longed for, but she would refuse to share her creations with me and Ari. After a couple of years, Ceci moved on to baking in a real oven and Ari inherited the Easy-Bake, but we'd pretty much outgrown our obsession with it by then. Maybe the appeal was mostly in the fact that Ceci had it when we didn't.

"Before Ceci left for college, she and I used to bake all the time," Ari says to me once we're standing at the kitchen counter, the front of our shirts stained white from the flour.

"I don't think you'd ever told me that," I say. "Do you miss her?"

"Yeah. It's been weird without her. She called every day during the first couple of weeks, but now she only calls on Saturdays."

My stomach drops. I wonder if that'll ever happen with me—if there'll come a day when I'll start talking to my family less often, when Papi and Abuela will stop checking in on me every day, or when Diego will stop texting me regularly. Suddenly, I feel even more guilty about not being with them at home tonight, as I realize that I don't want that to happen—I don't want there to ever come a time when being away from each other is just part of our routine, when we feel comfortable with the distance.

"She's probably busy with school, and everything," I say.

"Yeah, that's true," Ari replies. "Could you get the milk from the fridge?"

I turn around to go grab the carton, and as she takes it from me, I look down at the bowl where she's mixing the batter.

"What are we making, exactly?"

"Pastel de tres leches," Ari answers, pouring milk into a measuring cup. "This is my dad's old recipe."

"Your dad's?" I ask, lifting my eyebrows. It's been a long time since she's mentioned him. I don't even know much about what happened when Ari's parents separated. I must've been too young to understand why or how they decided to go their own ways, so the only thing I remember clearly is the sadness I felt when I found out Nancy wanted to start a new life across the border, which meant Ari and I would no longer live right around the corner from each other.

"Well, not my dad's, exactly. But it comes from his side of the family," she says. "I've been craving it all weekend."

"Have you heard anything from him lately?"

Ari shakes her head. "Last thing we knew, he was living down in Ensenada. But that was years ago, so he could be anywhere by now."

149

"Do you ever... feel curious? About trying to find him again?"

"Sometimes," Ari answers with a shrug. "But then I remember that letting go is much easier than holding on—especially with people who don't put in any of the work themselves."

I nod slowly, thinking about what it must've been like for Nancy to move here with two young daughters, what it must've been like for Ceci and Ari to say goodbye to their life back in Tijuana. I'd never thought about it this way before, but I suppose Ari also knows what it's like to lose a parent, what it's like to leave the only home she's ever known.

She places the bowl on the mixer. While the whisk turns around in circles, she looks right into my eyes. "So... are you gonna tell me why you came back early?"

All I had to do was text her, asking if it would be okay for me to return to her house tonight, and she said yes right away. I'd hoped I could get away with not giving her an explanation, but as she stares at me expectantly, I can't bring myself to lie.

"It was just... too much," I say. "I needed to get away from everything."

"You were only there for one night."

"I know. But it was still a lot." Letting out my breath through my mouth, I start telling her about everything that happened this weekend, and while she keeps working on the cake, Ari listens intently.

"Your dad will figure it out, though, won't he?" she asks me. "I mean... he'll find a way to replace the fridge."

"I don't know," I answer. "That was part of the reason I needed to get away. I just couldn't stop thinking about how every time we take a step forward, we're forced to take two steps back. And if we ever get to a point where we have to close down the restaurant... well, there won't be much left at all."

"What do you mean?"

"There won't be much left of what my family used to be."

Ari remains very still for a moment, staring at me with a frown on her face.

"I mean... I *know* that saving the restaurant won't bring my mom back. But if we give up on it, then she'll be gone for good—all of her, and I'm just... I'm so scared of losing the only piece of her we have left. I'm terrified of what it would do to us."

I clear my throat. There's a salty taste in my mouth that seems to have come from out of nowhere.

"I'm sorry, Ari," I say. "Baking was supposed to be fun, and I've been—"

"It's okay," she replies. "You can talk to me about anything. Just don't forget what I said the other day—you gotta give yourself time. You don't have to give up on the restaurant just yet."

"Yeah," I answer, nodding to myself. "You're right."

"And if you ever feel like you're drowning, just... just

remember I'm here for you, no matter what. And my mom is, too."

Ari leans over to check on the temperature of the oven, and all of a sudden, I feel the urge to close the distance between us and wrap my arms around her.

"I couldn't do any of this without you, Ari," I say, trying my best to remain still. "You and your mom have been so—"

"Stop," she says. Even after all the times she saved me on the playground, or spoke up for me when I was too afraid to use my voice, she's always refused to hear me thanking her. "You know you're always welcome here."

I press my lips together really tight, forcing myself not to say something that will make her roll her eyes at me.

"Besides, my mom keeps telling me how much she likes having you around."

I smile at her. While we wait for the cake to be ready and start cleaning up the kitchen, the air around us feels lighter. Neither of us says much, but I feel a closeness to her that I can't fully understand, just as I used to when we were kids and we would spend hours playing next to each other. It's as if she's my sister, a piece of me. And even though she has a sister of her own, I'm pretty sure that she feels this way about me, too.

"You should change the Netflix password!" Kelly shouts at Lina during my shift on Tuesday morning.

"What's the point?" Lina squawks back. "She'll just guess it again!"

Nick looks at me with a smile on his face. We've been listening to Lina's problems for the past twenty minutes, which can be summed up in the fact that her niece continues to watch episodes of the show they both like without her.

"What's everyone been watching lately?" Kelly asks the table. "Any recommendations?"

Nick says he's been re-watching an old sitcom, and Marcos tells us about a gritty murder mystery, which—he warns us—gave his eldest daughter nightmares.

Kelly turns toward me. "Sol, how about you?"

"I, uh ... I don't watch much TV," I say, which is true. With my long commute to and from school, I used to always spend any free time I had at home either doing homework, or having dinner with my family, or helping Abuela clean up the kitchen. And now that I've been at Ari's, all I've been watching are late-night talk shows, which I don't have much to say about.

"Come on," Lina says. "There's gotta be something."

"Well, there is one show I used to like—a telenovela."

Kelly's face lights up. "Oh, I've seen a few telenovelas. Which one?"

"It's called *Pasiones de tu Corazón*. It's about this guy who survives a plane crash, and then finds out his best friend planned the crash to try to kill him."

"It sounds crazy," Nick says, letting out a small laugh.

"It *is* crazy," I answer. I used to watch it with Mami and Abuela long ago—before I started going to school in California, and before Mami fell ill. Somehow, the memory makes me a little sad.

Before any of us can say anything else, the stockroom door swings open, and Bill walks in.

"Too much talking, not enough working, people," he says, throwing us all a stern glance as he pushes a rolling rack toward the back of the warehouse. "It's already nine, and there are way too many crates left to unpack."

Lina looks over her shoulder at the pile of crates. "Doesn't seem like that many to me."

My hands freeze. I watch Bill intently, fearing that he might snap back at Lina, but he doesn't. Thinking back on what Nick said to me about Bill, I figure Lina has probably earned longevity privileges by now.

While Bill disappears among all the clothing racks, I let out a deep breath, getting ready for what I need to do. I've been preparing for this from the moment I walked into the stockroom earlier, trying to find the right time to go up to him and ask if he can schedule me for additional shifts this weekend. Because if there is anything more I can do to help Papi get things back on track, I need to do it.

As soon as Bill reappears from behind the racks, I wipe my sweaty hands on the back of my jeans and turn away from the table.

"Hey, Bill?" I say, my voice coming out a bit higher than I intended it to.

He turns toward me with his eyebrows raised. "Yes?"

"I, uh... I wanted to ask a question," I say. "I would really love to take extra shifts this weekend, you know, if... if there's space on the roster."

I fear he's gonna start yelling at me like he did last time I asked for longer hours. Instead, he narrows his eyes.

"Saturday and Sunday, eight a.m.," he says sharply.

"That's perfect," I answer quickly. "I'll be here."

"Good. Now get back to work."

I return to the table feeling a lot lighter. Even when I realize that the morning shifts will mean I won't be able to go back home at all this weekend, I tell myself it doesn't matter. Because, as long as I'm here, taking clothes out of crates, and tagging them, and hanging them in the right racks, I can at least be certain that I'm exactly where I need to be—that I am doing everything I can to help my family.

And later, when I run into Ari at school and tell her I'll be around this weekend, she lets out an excited squeal.

"Simon and Tony have been talking about going to the beach again this Saturday," she says. "It's gonna be so much fun, I promise."

The image I had a few weeks ago comes back—the one of myself sitting on the beach without a care in the world. As I head to class, I realize that might be exactly what I need. Maybe I could use a little distance from the emptiness of the restaurant, from the silence at dinner. Maybe I can fool myself into believing that my family doesn't need me to be around, at least for one full weekend.

CHAPTER FOURTEEN

THERE'S SOMETHING ABOUT THE CITY THAT FEELS OFF as I walk through the downtown streets toward Wallen's on Saturday morning. It's almost like an empty stadium after everyone's gone home. I thought there would be plenty of cars, and people walking around, and movement, but there is hardly any of that. Even though the sun is already shining, San Diego remains still and quiet.

When I push the door of the warehouse open, I see none of the people I usually work with—no one except for Nick, who's standing at a corner of the table surrounded by a bunch of new faces.

"Where is everyone?" I ask as I join him.

"Lina and Kelly usually work evenings on Saturdays. And Marcos doesn't have weekend shifts, so... I guess it's just you and me."

He smiles, and I smile back. As much as I've started to enjoy being around everyone else, there's something about my first few days working at Wallen's that I miss—back when I would spend entire shifts chatting with only Nick.

"Are you doing anything fun this weekend?" he asks me as he pops the lid off a crate.

"I am, actually. I'm meeting some friends at the beach after work today."

He lifts his eyebrows at me. "Which beach?"

"Imperial."

"Oh. I was hoping you would say Coronado. That's where some of my friends are going later."

In the back of my mind, I wonder what he would've said if I'd told him I was going to the same beach as he is—if he might've suggested meeting up outside of work. Before I can find out what he meant, though, he asks me a different question.

"Are you much of a beach person?"

"I used to be," I say. "When I was little, we would go to the beach in Tijuana all the time, but I haven't been in years. How about you?"

"Oh, I love the beach," he says. "Especially when surfing conditions are good."

"You surf?"

"Sure do."

While we work, I can't help but notice things about him that I'd never given much thought. Things like the golden chain he wears around his neck, which has left a vague tan line, or the scruff on the sides of his face, which makes his jaw look squarer than when he's freshly shaven. Mostly, though, I notice just how easy it is to talk to him, especially when it's just the two of us in our corner of the table.

"Really?" I ask him halfway through our shift. "New York?"

"Yup."

"If you could go anywhere in the *whole* world."

"There's gotta be a reason people say it's the greatest city in the world. I'd just like to see for myself," he says. "How about you? If you could go anywhere right now."

"I'm not sure," I say while I place a sticker on a pair of pants. "Maybe Paris."

"Paris?" he says, lifting his eyebrows. "Why?"

Mami used to talk about Paris sometimes. I'm not sure why—if she'd read about it, or if she'd seen it in a movie—but she always said she wanted to see it one day. "It's the city of love *and* the city of light," she used to say. "What could be better than those two things?"

"I don't know," I say to Nick in the end. "It just seems beautiful. I don't think I'll be going anywhere anytime soon, though."

He hunches his shoulders slightly. "You never know."

"Oh, I *do* know. I'll be either here or in Tijuana for the next few years—if not for the rest of my life."

"What about college, though?" he asks me. "Aren't you thinking of applying to schools anywhere else?"

"Not really. I mean... I'd love to go to Stanford, but even that's too far. So it'll probably end up being UCSD or San Diego State—if I'm able to get in, of course."

The corner of Nick's lips twists into a smile. "I've always wanted to go to San Diego State."

"Really?"

"Yeah," he says. "Both of my parents went there. It's where they met. But, you know... college applications have had to wait for now."

A part of me wants to ask about his mom—how she's doing, whether she's getting any closer to getting the transplant she needs—but I stop myself. If Nick wants to trust me with those details, I know he will.

Instead, I ask a different question. "What program do you wanna do?"

"Well..." I could be wrong, but I'm pretty sure he's blushing. "Do you promise not to laugh?"

"I promise."

Nick lets out a sigh. "I wanna go into music."

"Why would I laugh about that?"

"People have laughed before," he says, not looking at me. All of a sudden, he seems to be very busy with a security tag. "I've always loved singing and playing guitar. But, you know, it's hard to make it as an artist, and I've had people tell me all sorts of things—that I'm too tall, too clumsy, that I don't have the right voice, or the right smile."

"You shouldn't listen to those people."

"I try not to," he answers. He slips the tag he'd been fiddling with into a skirt, and then he turns toward me with a smile on his face. "How about you?"

I hesitate. I haven't given this much thought—not yet, anyway. I know the time to fill out college applications will be here before I know it, and that I'll have to choose a major that allows me to take care of Papi and Abuela when they're older, but I've never really spent much time thinking about what *I* want.

I clear my throat. "Do you know who Ellen Ochoa is?"

Nick frowns, so that his eyebrows come closer together. An instant later, he shakes his head.

"She's an astronaut," I say. "She was the first Latina astronaut to ever go to space."

"Wow," he says, staring at me with wide eyes. "You wanna be an astronaut?"

"Well, no..." I say, laughing a little. "Not really. But maybe I could be a physicist. Or a mathematician. Or an engineer. Or... I don't know. I've always been good with numbers, so one of those things might make sense for me."

He keeps staring at me, his eyes still as wide as they were a second ago. It's as if he's seeing something in me, as if there was something written on my face and he was taking his time reading it.

"I could see that," he says. "María de la Soledad Martínez—the first Latina director of NASA."

I can't help myself—I start laughing. "Really? Director of NASA?"

He nods. "You'd better hook me up with cheap space flight tickets once you've made it. You know, when space flights become a normal thing."

"You're crazy."

"I'm not," he says. "You're gonna go far. I can tell."

"Well," I say, "we both will. Nick Jones—Grammy Award–winning artist."

He laughs as his face turns a deep shade of red. "Yeah, well. Maybe one day."

In that moment, something happens. It comes as quickly and unexpectedly as a static shock or a streak of lightning—a spark that seems to be flying between us. I can feel it in the tips of my fingers, in the back of my neck, even though we're not moving, not touching, not doing anything at all—nothing but staring into each other's eyes. But then, an instant later, I blink, and the spark is gone.

"I, uh... I should go sort these," I say, nodding at all the clothes we've just finished tagging and hanging.

Nick nods quickly. "I'll help you."

I pick up a bunch of hangers, and he picks up the rest. We head to the back of the stockroom, to sort them on the women's business wear racks. Neither of us says anything while we work, but I can't stop thinking about what happened back at the table—about the spark. Maybe it was nothing.

But then, when Nick and I both try to place a hanger on the rack at the exact same time and cut the other off, I meet his eyes, and I can just tell right at that instant. He felt it, too.

The first thing I think about when Ari and I get to Imperial Beach later in the day is how different it is from el Malecón in Tijuana, where I used to go with my family when I was younger. This feels like an entirely different place, a different world, even though it's the same coast. We're just a few miles north, but this side seems quieter. It could just be because we only ever went to el Malecón on busy summer days, when it was filled with families, and loud music, and vendors trying to sell sliced fruit, necklaces, henna tattoos, and all kinds of other random stuff.

Ana María, Tony, and Simon are already there by the time we arrive. They've set up a few towels on the sand, and they brought along a big cooler.

"You can grab anything you want," Ana María says to us. "We've got more than enough drinks."

Ari reaches into the cooler and grabs a couple of beers. She cracks them open, hands me one, and says, "Cheers."

"Cheers," I reply, clinking my bottle against hers. I take a big swig, and I have to resist the urge to cough out all the liquid in my mouth. It's been a long time since I've had any beer, and the taste is a lot more bitter than I remember. Papi let me try sips of his beer once or twice when I was younger. It made me feel special, like it was a privilege that he was allowing me—a pact between the two of us—but now I can't understand what I used to find appealing about this taste.

I force myself to swallow my first sip, and then another. Before I know it, it stops tasting bitter, and I just sit back on a towel next to Ari, drinking slowly from my bottle. The sun is warm on my skin, the wind soft in my hair, and the ocean waves in front of us keep coming and going, filling the air around us with a gentle rhythmic sound.

"You guys started without us!" a voice comes from behind all of a sudden. We turn around to find Olivia and Camila walking in our direction, their feet sinking into the sand. They're both wearing bikini tops and sunglasses, and they're carrying big tote bags.

Beside me, Ari takes another sip from her beer bottle. "We've only had one," she says. "You can catch up."

Olivia and Camila set their towels down, and it takes them a while to unpack all the stuff they brought along— more drinks, about a dozen different types of sunblock, and a speaker that they set up in the middle of the group to play some music.

Once they're both sitting beside us holding bottles of beer, Camila turns toward me.

"Sol," she says, "you came!"

"Yeah," I reply. "I, uh... I'm not going back to Tijuana this weekend, so..."

"We were starting to think we weren't cool enough for you," Olivia says, her lips parted into a big smile.

"No, no," I reply, feeling myself blushing. "I just had to—"

"Be home on the weekends," Olivia completes my sentence for me. "We get it."

"How has it been?" Ana María asks, leaning closer to join our conversation.

"Huh?"

"Working at the store."

"Oh." I smile a little to myself, thinking about the warmth I've managed to find inside that big, cold stockroom. Thinking about Lina and the stories she tells about her niece. Thinking about Nick and what happened between us earlier.

Ana María gasps, pointing at me with her index finger. "There's a boy!"

"What?"

"Oh, I think you're right," Camila says, frowning slightly as she stares at me through narrowed eyes.

"How did you know?" I ask, even though it must be written all over my face.

"Sol!" Ari says beside me, her mouth falling open. "Why didn't you say anything before?"

"There's nothing to say. He's just... my coworker."

Ana María throws me a knowing look. "Hmmm. I'm sure he is."

"Well, who is it?" Ari asks, her eyes sparkling in the soft afternoon sun.

I don't think I should be talking about this. It feels

too soon, too dumb to turn it into anything bigger than it really is, but then I drink a small sip of beer and say, "His name is Nick."

Ari frowns. "I think I've seen him around the store. Tall guy, big smile?"

I nod.

"*Sol!*" she says. "Has he asked you out?"

"No," I answer quickly. "Nothing like that. He's just... nice."

I'm not sure what it is—if it's the fact that we're not in school, sitting around a loud cafeteria table, or that they all look so different in their beach clothes—but I'm suddenly finding it difficult to remember why I used to be intimidated by Ari's friends. I'm having a hard time understanding why I've always been so quiet around them, when they're so easy to talk to.

"How about the hours?" Olivia asks me. "Have they been crazy?"

"Yeah. But Ari and her mom have been pretty great. They always have dinner waiting for me when I get back after a late shift."

Ari snorts. "Well, it's not like we're gonna let you starve!"

I'm not sure how many beers it takes—maybe two or three—but after a while of sitting here with all of them, drinking, and laughing, and just being ourselves, I start to realize something. For the first time in a long time, the feeling of drowning is entirely gone.

I don't think I'd realized just how used I've become to the heaviness in my chest and the tightness in my throat, until now that I'm able to breathe normally again—to fill my lungs with warm, salty air, and let my breath out easily.

I wish I could feel this way all the time. I wish I could learn to break through the surface more often and let go of the person I've become over the past two years—the girl who feels lonely, who feels afraid. I wish I could fully escape from all the barriers that have kept me in the dark for so long—the grief, and the anxiety, and the walls I've built around myself.

All too soon, the sun starts setting in the distance, turning soft yellow and then the deepest, brightest shade of orange. As I stare out at the horizon, something stirs deep within me—a sadness that comes with knowing that once it gets dark, we'll have to pack up our things and leave. I don't want this night to end, but when I stare over at Ari, she smiles at me.

"We're going to Simon's house after," she says. "His parents are out."

I smile back at her, wishing I could figure out a way to leave Soledad behind on this beach and step into the shoes of Sol. But, as the sunshine keeps intensifying in the distance, casting its reflection over the surface of the water, I tell myself that for now, maybe this moment is enough. Maybe all that truly matters is that I'm still here, and the soft wind is still blowing in my hair, and there's still a feeling inside of me that seems to be spreading to every corner of my body—a feeling of warm light that is shining brighter than the sun.

Ari calls an Uber to get back to her house. We would've asked Nancy to pick us up, but it's almost one in the morning, and even though she's pretty open-minded about alcohol, it's probably a good idea not to let her see us after we've been drinking this much.

I cut myself off not long after we got to Simon's house, but I still haven't sobered up completely. Ari, on the other hand, kept opening beer after beer, but she must have a higher tolerance than I do, because she doesn't even seem that drunk.

For the first half of the way, we ride in silence, sitting in the back while the Uber driver leads us through quiet streets. But then, after a while, I notice Ari's staring at me.

"What?" I ask.

"Nothing," she says.

"It's something."

"It's just... you seemed different tonight."

I don't need to ask what she means. I'm just surprised that she noticed it, but I guess she knows me too well for me to be able to hide anything from her.

"They're so nice," I say. "All of them."

"They are."

I let out a small sigh, leaning back against the headrest. "Can I ask you something?"

"Sure."

"Was it me?"

"What do you mean?"

"When you met Camila, and Olivia, and them," I say, "I'm pretty sure everyone tried. I think they tried to make me feel like I was part of the group, and to invite me to come along to stuff, and I just... didn't."

Turning to meet Ari's eyes, I see that she's staring at me intently, not moving, not breathing. Her face comes into and out of the darkness as the car speeds through bubbles of light coming from the lampposts along the street.

"Every time I wanted to hang out with you guys, I knew I needed to make it back home before dark. I needed to be there for Diego, and to help out with the restaurant. But then, when I made it back home, all I could think about was that everyone was hanging out without me, and I'd tell myself that next time I'd make more of an effort to join, except... I never did."

"It wasn't your fault," Ari says to me softly. "You were doing what you needed to do."

I look down at my hands. "Yeah."

"I'm not sure if you know this already, but... when I became friends with all of them in freshman year, I didn't do it just because they were *nice*," Ari adds. "I became friends with them because not having you around outside of school always made me a little sad."

We both breathe silently for a moment, as I realize

what she's saying—that she never meant to push me away or replace me with her new friends. That she also had a way of feeling lonely, and she needed to figure out how to change that.

"But even then, I never blamed you for not being there for me. It wasn't up to you." She clears her throat. "And… I know it might seem like the rest of us hang out all the time without a care in the world, but… I've also had to say no to plans a million times so I could make it to my shifts at the store. And Olivia has long hours at the café, and Camila and Simon have younger siblings that they some-times look after. So… I think we all understood that you had places you needed to be. It's not like anyone resented you for it."

"It's funny, you know?" I say, my mind still foggy from the beers. "For the past two years, it's been like… when-ever I'm in the US, my heart is in Mexico. And when I'm in Mexico, my head is in the US. I've never been able to be in a single place fully. I've been neither here nor there."

"Well… you're here now," Ari says.

"Yeah," I reply, meeting her eyes again. "I guess I am."

The car starts slowing down, and the driver clears his throat.

"Thank you," Ari and I say at the same time, and then we hop out of the car, walking arm-in-arm up the front steps of the house to help each other stay balanced.

"My mom's probably sleeping," Ari says to me as she turns the key in the lock. "So try to be quiet."

I nod quickly, but when she pushes the door open, we don't step into complete darkness, as I thought we would. The TV is on in the living room, filling everything around us in a soft, bluish glow.

"You girls are home late," Nancy says from the couch, where she's curled up under a blanket.

Something pulls at my stomach. I can't help but hear my dad or my abuela in her tone—can't help but imagine what they'd say if I showed up home drunk at one in the morning.

"Yeah, uh…"

"Did you have fun?"

"We did," Ari answers quickly. "It was lots of fun."

Nancy smiles at us. "Good," she says, and then she turns her attention back toward the TV.

Letting my breath out through my nose, I follow Ari toward the bathroom so we can brush our teeth and get ready for bed.

Once I finally lay my head down on the pillow, I realize just how exhausted I am. For once, I don't think about the light seeping in through the curtains. I don't even think about Tijuana, or about the fact that I'll need to get up early tomorrow to head to my shift at the store.

All I can think about is this warmth deep inside of me, which feels old and new at the same time—the warmth of coming home at the end of a long day.

CHAPTER FIFTEEN

OVER THE NEXT COUPLE OF DAYS, I TRY MY HARDEST
to be Sol. It's easy, somehow—almost like slipping on an
old coat that you didn't remember you had in the back of
your closet.

"I swear to God, I don't know how it happened," Tony
says in the cafeteria on Monday. "But when I got home,
my underwear was full of sand. Like, *full* of sand."

"I don't think I had that problem," I reply, in between
bites of pizza.

"None of us did," Olivia says to me quietly. "Well, no
one except for Tony and Ana María. I'm pretty sure they
were fooling around somewhere when they said they were
going to the bathroom."

I let out a small laugh. It feels nice to understand what
everyone is talking about when they tell stories about the

weekend. It's nice to be a part of the conversation, to lean forward and say, "What?" whenever I don't hear someone else's comments, instead of pretending I did and nodding awkwardly.

Even in the stockroom, I can feel something has shifted. When Bill passes by the big table, nosing around as he always does to make sure everyone is doing their job correctly, he stops the second he sees me inserting a security tag into a silky blouse.

"Nicely done," he says to me. Nick taught me a while ago that, when working with silk or satin, I shouldn't insert the tag directly through the fabric. Instead, I inserted it in the label on the inside of the shirt.

For a moment, I hold my breath, waiting for Bill to say something else, but he simply moves on.

"It's what I've been saying all along," Nick says to me, throwing me a sideways smile. "You're an expert."

The only issue is that schoolwork is starting to pile up, and even though I've tried my best to do homework between my shifts at Wallen's, it's still not enough. I'm sitting in the bio classroom on Thursday when, suddenly, Mr. Vázquez says, "Everyone please hand over your essays!" and my heart stops. I vaguely remember there was an essay I needed to work on for bio, but when I try to think about the details of what it's about or when it was due, my mind comes up blank.

While everyone around me starts shuffling, walking

up to Mr. Vázquez's desk to drop off their essays, my neck starts feeling very hot. And after class, when I have to go up to him and ask if I can get an extension, he gives me a stern look that makes my hands sweat uncontrollably.

"You can have one more day, but that's it," he says.

"Thank you, Mr. Vázquez. Thank you so much."

It is while I'm making my way down to Ari's after school that I realize just what this one-day extension will mean. Because there are other things that have been piling up—a trigonometry quiz that I need to study for, another essay for history, and an entire book I have to read for English lit before the start of next week.

And so, the second I walk into the house, I head straight for Ceci's bedroom and sit at the desk. I push myself to work as much as I can, to do research for my bio assignment, to make a dent on the book for English, and I don't come back out until dinnertime.

"You're pushing yourself too hard, mija," Nancy says to me, shaking her head slightly, while the three of us are sitting around the table.

I don't say anything in response. I can't tell her that it's okay, because it would be a lie. I'm tired, my back hurts, and I can barely see straight, but after dinner, I go right back to my desk.

No matter how quickly the clock seems to be approaching midnight, or how heavy my eyes get, I don't stop working. I finish my research for bio and type out a half-hearted essay. I manage to read a couple of chapters for English, and then I crack open my trig textbook and start solving a few practice problems.

The numbers and formulas on the page are starting to blur, and my mind is starting to feel foggy, when my cell phone buzzes nearby. I swivel around in my chair and rush toward the bedside table to grab it, only to find Diego's name flashing on the screen.

"Hello?"

My heart stops beating as a million thoughts race through my mind. Even though Diego and I have been texting all week, he hasn't called until now. I'd just assumed there wasn't much to say, because even our texts have started to get repetitive—I've been telling him that I'm good, that I'm tired, and he'll give me updates on things that are going on at home, which never seem to be anything different than, *Papi closed the restaurant early again today cause there weren't enough customers.* Or, *Abuela fell asleep on the couch while we were watching a show and missed the entire episode.*

I know that a call at this hour can't mean anything but bad news, and the second I hear my brother's voice coming through the phone, my fears are confirmed. Something terrible must've happened.

"Sol?" he says.

"Yes," I say quickly. "I'm here. Are you okay? Are Papi and Abuela—"

"I'm okay," he says.

"Then what is it? Why are you calling?"

He's silent for a long time, but I can hear him breathing loudly into the phone. Lowering myself slowly to sit on the bed, I put a hand on my chest, trying to bring my heartbeat under control.

"I just miss you," he says in the end.

I nod to myself. Suddenly, I'm the one who's silent.

"I miss you, too," I manage to say after a while.

"Papi's mad again."

"Why?"

"The electricity bill came," Diego whispers. "And he's blaming me and Abuela cause it's really expensive. He says we shouldn't watch so much TV anymore."

"Maybe you and Abuela can play more board games instead," I say. As much as I wish Papi wouldn't take it out on Diego and my grandmother, I can't help but feel the same kind of pressure he must be feeling—pressure to keep the bills reasonable, to save money wherever we can.

"Yeah," Diego replies. "Except they're not as fun with only two players."

It comes unexpectedly—a pang of guilt that hits me right in the chest. Guilt because I haven't been thinking about home as much over the past week, because this weekend was the most fun I've had in years, while Diego and Abuela have had to sit next to each other in the living room, staring down at a board of Chinese checkers because they can't turn the TV on anymore.

Tears come, but I wipe them away quickly. I don't want Diego to realize I'm crying.

"Diego?" I ask softly. "Are you still there?"

I know he is. I can hear him breathing through the phone, but I just want him to say something—anything.

When he finally speaks up, his words send a cold, sharp chill running down my back.

"I'm sad, Sol."

"Why?" I ask, standing up from the bed quickly. "Because I didn't come home last weekend? I can come back this Saturday. I'll—"

"It's not just that," he says. "I just... am."

I think of myself at his age, and the way life was back then. I remember long summer days at the beach and warm winter nights at home. I remember the sparkle in Papi's eyes every time he looked at Mami, and the sound of her laughter, and the colors, and smells, and tastes of her cooking. I also remember the lengths Papi and Mami went to in order to keep us protected from the news, from the violence that erupted throughout the city right around that time. I just wish I had a way to protect Diego from everything that's happening now in the same way that my parents did for me back then.

"I also feel sad sometimes," I tell him. "But this won't last forever. Sadness is like... like waves in the ocean, Diego. It comes and goes. And I will, too—I'll come back, even if I'm not there now."

"Will you be home this weekend, then?" Diego asks after a moment of silence.

"I will," I say, wanting desperately to be there for

my brother. It'll make sense for me to come to Tijuana anyway—after being away last weekend, I need to see Papi so I can hand him my latest paycheck. "You should go to bed soon."

"I know. I just couldn't sleep."

"Try again," I tell him. "It's getting late."

"Will you stay on the line with me? Until I fall asleep?"

"Yeah," I reply. Throwing a quick glance at the desk, where my trig textbook is still lying open, I realize I probably should be turning off the lights soon and getting some sleep myself. "I can do that. Are you in bed now?"

"Yeah."

"Try to relax, then. Close your eyes and breathe slowly. I'll be here."

"And you won't hang up?"

"Not until I hear snoring," I say.

He lets out a small laugh, which brings lightness to my chest.

"Buenas noches, Diego."

"Buenas noches, Sol."

I reach for the switch and turn off the lights in Ceci's bedroom. At first, I can't hear anything coming through the phone, but after a while I'm pretty sure I can hear slow inhales and exhales coming from Diego's end. Even though I'm pretty sure he's asleep by now, and even though my eyes are threatening to shut any second, I stay on the line, trying my best to be there for him.

CHAPTER SIXTEEN

ON FRIDAY, EVERYTHING CHANGES, BUT NOT ALL AT once.

It starts with a whisper. *"Did you hear about Bruno's hearing?"*

As much as I wish I could stop and hear more, I can't just barge into a stranger's conversation. For the rest of the morning, though, I keep my ears alert, trying to pick up on any more news about Bruno, but none comes until later, when I'm sitting in the cafeteria.

"The hearing's happening the third week of November," Ana María announces to the table.

"It sounds so *serious*," Olivia says.

"Well, it sort of is."

"But, like, is it gonna be a trial-style thing where they decide if he's guilty or innocent, or . . . ?"

Simon narrows his eyes. "I don't think so?"

"What's the whole point, then?"

"The board's just gonna decide if they should kick him out or not."

"But he already got suspended," Ari says.

Ana María turns toward her. "So?"

"So shouldn't that be enough punishment?"

"I heard some kids are putting together a petition," Tony says. "They're trying to get a bunch of people to sign it so we can help Bruno not get kicked out."

Before I can ask about this petition—who's putting it together, and how I can sign it—my phone buzzes in my pocket.

It's a text from Diego: **Hey.**

I hold my phone firmly, waiting for something else to come, but it doesn't. Still, that single word is enough to make my heart start racing. Diego never texts me when he's at school. If he's reaching out to me now, it must mean something's going on—especially after the conversation we had last night.

Are you okay? I text him back, my fingers moving quickly over the keyboard. **Is something wrong?**

He doesn't write back. I stare at my phone screen for several minutes, but no new notifications come.

"What's wrong?" Ari asks me. She must've noticed how I've stopped eating.

"I have to make a call," I say, pushing my chair back.

She says something else, but I don't hear what it is. I rush toward the cafeteria doors, among my recent calls.

Someone answers as soon as I step out into the hallway, but it isn't Papi.

"¿Bueno?"

"Abuela?"

"Sol?"

"Why do you have Papi's phone?"

"He left it on the kitchen table. He's—"

"Is that Sol?" I hear Papi's voice coming from the background.

"Why is he home?" I ask. "Why isn't he at the restaurant?"

She goes quiet, and that's when I know it—she's keeping something from me.

"Abuela, why is he home?" I ask, my voice rising.

"He—he's actually on his way out now," she answers.

"Can I talk to him?"

"He says he has to run."

"He should," I say, suddenly aware that there are people walking down the hallway all around me. I turn toward the lockers, trying to keep my voice low and steady so no one will be able to hear what I'm saying. "Lunchtime on Fridays is always busy. He should've opened the restaurant at least an hour ago."

"He knows what he's doing," Abuela says. "You should go back to class."

"It's lunch period."

"Then go back to eating lunch."

I remain silent for a moment, letting my anger out through my breath. "Well, ha-have you heard from Diego? He texted me, but now he's not replying."

"He's at school," Abuela replies. "I'm sure he's fine. Now go. Carry on with your day, and we'll see you here tomorrow, okay, mija?"

She doesn't stay on the line long enough for me to say anything else, which, again, makes me worry that something is deeply wrong, and she's just not telling me what it is.

"Sol?"

"Huh?"

"Are you okay? You seem ... distracted."

I look up from my plate. Ari and Nancy are both staring at me with deep frowns on their faces. It must've been at least ten minutes since I tuned out their voices, but up until now, they'd just carried on with their conversation without me.

"Uh, yeah," I say. "I'm just tired."

Nancy nods, smiling sympathetically. "Of course you are."

"Just one more shift, and then it'll be the weekend," Ari says.

I try my best to smile back at them, and then I put a bite of food in my mouth to have an excuse not to say anything. I wish I had a bit more energy in me, that I could tell them about what's really bothering me, because I know

Ari and Nancy would be able to comfort me. They'd make me feel a little bit better, and lift my spirits at least long enough for me to get through my late-night shift at the store, but I can't bring myself to speak up.

I haven't been able to reach my brother all day. He's still not answering his phone, and my texts have stopped going through, which tells me that he's either run out of battery or has turned off his phone.

I dialed my house number once before I remembered that it no longer exists—not since Papi canceled the landline. That gave me no option but to call my dad's cell again as soon as Ari and I got back home, which was as good as nothing.

"I'm busy, Sol," he said to me when he picked up.

"I—I know, but I'm trying to get in touch with Diego and Abuela, and I—"

"Why don't you call Diego, then?"

"His phone is not working for some reason."

Papi let out a loud groan into the phone. "I'll tell him to call you when I get home."

"But I'm working until midnight tonight."

He offered no words of reassurance. I wanted to tell him I'm worried about Diego, that I have a feeling something is wrong with him, and that we should be finding out if he's even made it home from school, but Papi didn't give me time to say any of that.

"I have to get back to work," he said.

I hoped that at least he was telling the truth—that he

was in the middle of cooking, or serving tables at the restaurant, so I chose not to argue, but now I wish I had.

I wish I knew exactly what is going on at home. I can't wait to be back in Tijuana tomorrow morning, because no matter how much Abuela may insist that I don't need to worry, I have a feeling that I'm needed there, now more than ever.

All through my shift, there seems to be a dark gray cloud hanging over me.

"Is everything okay?" Nick asks when he sees me.

"Yeah," I answer, reaching for a hanger.

Lina tilts her head to one side, staring at me. "You need some rest, honey."

"I'm fine," I answer, forcing a smile. "Just, uh... just trying to get through the week, right?"

Kelly, who's standing at the far end of the table, yells out: "Amen!"

That's all it takes for everyone to drop the subject, and I try to do my work as best as I can, even though I can't resist the urge to check my phone every once in a while. In the end, though, no news comes from Papi or Diego, no matter how many times I check.

When morning comes, I leave a note on the kitchen table, as I've done every other Saturday before heading out.

Thank you again for everything. Have a good weekend, and

I'll see you on Monday! I write, and then I sneak out of the house as quietly as possible.

The ride across the border is different from other weekends. The eagerness I always feel to get to Tijuana, to see my family, to be in my own home, is completely gone. I can't even feel the same relief from a few weeks ago, when I brought Papi my first paycheck. I've received another one—for even more money than the last—but I just can't bring myself to be excited, or happy, or triumphant. There is a deep sense of dread in my stomach, because I have no idea what will be waiting for me when I get to the other side of the border.

I find Papi parked in the same old spot, right behind the taxis. For once, he's not sleeping, but he is staring blankly ahead, his seat belt buckled and his lips pressed tightly together, so deep in thought that he doesn't even notice me until I knock hard on the car window.

"So?" I ask him once I've hopped into the car and slammed the passenger door shut.

"Buenos días," he replies. He doesn't look directly at me, doesn't show any signs that he heard my question. He starts the engine and backs out of his parking space.

"Is everything okay?" I ask.

"Why wouldn't it be?" he replies, reaching for the dashboard. Soft music starts playing from the speakers.

"Diego. I haven't been able to talk to him. Is he—"

Papi lets out a long breath through his nose. "He got in trouble at school again."

"What happened? Did he get into another fight? Is there—?"

"He had his phone taken away," Papi replies bitterly. "He was texting in class."

"Oh." I lean back against the headrest. That must be why he wasn't able to reply even after all the times I tried messaging and calling. But my brother knows better than to be careless with his phone. He's all too aware that he's not supposed to use it at school, so if he was trying to reach me, he must've had something important to say.

When we get home, Papi parks in front of the house, turns off the engine, and removes the key from the ignition, but he doesn't reach for the door handle, and neither do I. We sit quietly in silence, while I try to make sense of all the questions that are spinning around in my head.

But then, instead of asking a question, I choose to say the one thing I'm certain of—the one thing Papi won't be able to deny.

"Something's changed," I say. "Something happened this week, didn't it? Something you haven't told me."

Papi turns toward me. For the first time today, he stares right into my eyes, and in his face, I see a million things that scare me. I see deep wrinkles, which seem harsher than they used to be. I see exhaustion in the dark circles under his eyes and in the length of his beard, which he hasn't trimmed in several days. There's also indecision on his lips, which quiver with words he's unable to say.

"Is it Abuela?" I ask.

Papi shakes his head quickly.

"Or Luis—has he found a job yet? Is he—"

Again, he shakes his head.

He shifts his gaze away from me, looking ahead through the windshield. "The restaurant," he answers in a hoarse whisper.

My first instinct is to turn toward him, but the seat belt jolts me back into place. I don't even reach for the button to unbuckle it. I take in a deep breath, my heart racing as I ask: "What about it?"

Papi turns his head slowly to look at me again, and in his eyes, I find the answer.

"No," I say. "No, Papi, we can't give up on it."

"We need to, mija. We don't have a choice."

"But—but I have another paycheck," I say, fishing it out of my pocket. "Here. We—we can head straight to the bank and—"

"It's not enough," he says. "Our debts have gotten too big. It's one thing to pay the monthly bills and put food on the table, mija, but the debt collectors are gonna come knocking on our door sooner rather than later, and when they do, they're not gonna care about anything except getting their money back."

"Then I'll get more money. I'll find another job, or figure out a way to take even more hours at the store. If you just give me a bit more time, I—I'll figure something out."

I wish I could reach for him. I want to shake him up,

yell at him, so he will come to his senses. We can't give up—not now. There are many more paychecks to come, many more ways to save the restaurant that we just haven't thought of yet. But if we close it down now, then it'll all be for nothing.

"We can't keep throwing money at a lost cause, Sol. Not when there's so many other things we could do with the paychecks you're bringing in. We could stock our own fridge, and cover the bills, and start paying back the debt."

"But once we've rescued the restaurant, it'll help us pay for all those things," I say. "We just need to hold on a bit longer. We—"

Papi shakes his head. "It's too late, mija."

I swallow hard. "You can't make this decision without me. This is my restaurant, too. It belongs to all of us. I mean, we need to ask Luis what he thinks, and—and Diego, also. We need to—"

"The decision has been made for a long time," Papi replies. "Don't you see, Sol?"

There are tears forming in the corners of his eyes. I know he's trying his best. I know he doesn't want to give up on the restaurant any more than I do, but I can't help but feel betrayed by him. I feel so stupid all of a sudden—stupid for thinking that the money I was bringing home would help us save the business, when Papi must've suspected the truth all along: That the restaurant was beyond saving. That he had more important plans for the money.

I don't know what else to say. I don't know what to do

with all the emptiness in my heart, in my stomach, in my hands.

After a while, Papi mumbles something about how Abuela is waiting for us to have breakfast and slowly steps out of the car. I watch as he walks through the front door, and he leaves it open for me before disappearing into the cool dimness of the house.

I know I need to get out. I need to unbuckle my seat belt and go join Papi, Diego, Luis, and Abuela for breakfast, but I can't move. I can't breathe. I can't go sit at the kitchen table as if it were just another Saturday. I need to run, or scream, or do something—anything—that will help us keep Mami's restaurant alive.

In the end, I don't do any of those things. I just remain here for the longest time, taking small breaths through my mouth and staring blankly at the half-open door of the house.

PART TWO

CHAPTER SEVENTEEN

THERE ARE SOME THINGS IN LIFE YOU JUST GROW UP knowing—like your name, or your birthday, or where you're from. Things you never question, because they're so obvious, so... set in stone.

My name is María de la Soledad Martínez. I was born on December 18 in Chula Vista, California. I grew up in Tijuana, and my family owns a restaurant in the heart of the city.

Now that one of those things is no longer true, I feel as though a part of me is missing—as though I'm no longer the girl I've always been, and there's no way to bring her back. I don't think I'll ever be complete again.

My family used to *own a restaurant in the heart of the city.* That sounds so wrong. It doesn't feel real. Some mornings when I wake up, I almost believe that it isn't. For a few seconds, the thought of it feels so absurd—nothing but a bad dream. But then I remember, and my insides crack open all over again, just as they did when Papi told me the restaurant was closing.

The front door creaks open with a loud screech when I push it. I'm not sure if the creaking is new—just one of the signs of abandon that have crept up since we stopped serving customers—or if it had been there for a while.

We didn't even make a big announcement, didn't have an official final night. Papi just slapped a notice on the front door from one day to the next: *Permanently Closed*. We received an endless amount of calls from people we know—people who walked past the restaurant and saw the sign, or who heard from someone or other that we had closed down. They all asked us why, they all said they wished it didn't have to come to this. They all sounded sad that the restaurant had shut down—even those who hadn't bothered to show up when we were struggling to remain open.

My footsteps echo against the walls as I walk in. The place looks nothing like it used to. All the tables and chairs are gone. The space seems so small suddenly, the walls so tall. It's as if they're closing in on me. Still, I can feel something in the air—something that makes me feel like Mami is nearby. I can feel her presence. Staring at the back of the restaurant, where the entrance to the kitchen is, I almost expect her to walk out any second, laughing the way she used to—in a way that filled the entire room—which I'm sure would make the emptiness vanish.

I don't want this feeling to ever go away. I don't want this closeness I feel to her to ever disappear. It makes me so angry to think that we're giving up the only piece of her we had left, that we were unable to do this one thing for her—to keep her restaurant alive.

I blink hard, and hot tears slip from my eyes, falling on the dirty floor.

"I'm sorry," I whisper into the emptiness, and I swear, for a moment I feel as though she's right in front of me. "I'm sorry, Mami."

When there's no answer, I let out a long sigh. I feel cold all of a sudden, as though the temperature has dropped by several degrees.

My legs start feeling weak, so I lower myself to the ground and sit down with my legs crossed right in the middle of the dusty floor. I allow my eyes to close, and I can just see it—I see a full restaurant, the way it used to be on Saturday nights. There are people talking, and eating, and drinking all around me. Mami is standing behind the counter, working at the till, and Luis and I are running among the tables, taking orders. The place smells like food, it sounds like happiness, and it feels like home.

When I open my eyes, the restaurant seems emptier than it did before. Even the presence of Mami has disappeared, and no matter how long I sit here, or how hard I try, I can't find a way to make it come back.

"Where were you?" Abuela asks me as soon as I walk into the house.

"Out," I say.

She purses her lips, not saying anything. From the way she's staring at me, I can tell she knows exactly where I've been, but she doesn't ask any more questions.

I'm grateful that she doesn't, because I know all too well that I wasn't supposed to be at the restaurant today. Papi has already turned in his keys to the landlord, and ads have gone up in search of new tenants. No one knows I kept my key. We must've made so many copies over the years that my dad didn't even remember to ask for mine.

"Is Papi home yet?" I ask. He's been out every day, doing random jobs. He put up ads on lampposts around the city last weekend, and people here and there have been calling him when they need a mechanic to come take a look at their car. He may not be bringing in much money, but these days, every penny counts, and something is better than nothing.

Abuela shakes her head.

"I was about to make some tea," she says. "I'll make you a cup."

I don't have the energy to say no, so I sit down at the table while she gets to work behind me.

"Here you go," she says as she sets a mug in front of me. Abuela swears by chamomile tea. She says it's a cure for almost anything—colds, stomachaches, poor sleep, and even broken hearts. A couple of years ago, when Luis was dealing with bad acne, Abuela managed to convince him that a cup of chamomile tea a day would clear his skin. He did as she said, and drank tea religiously, but it never seemed to work. When his skin finally started to get better, we all knew he'd just outgrown a bad phase, even though Abuela still claimed it had been the tea.

I reach for the cup, feeling the heat radiating from it before my fingers even make contact with the ceramic. I decide to let it cool for a little while, but Abuela takes a long sip from her own mug as if the temperature was just right.

"Diego was asking for you earlier," she tells me.

"Where is he now?"

"In his bedroom."

I nod slowly to myself. My brother has been locked up in his room, claiming to be doing homework, but I'm able to see right through the wall he's trying to put up. I just wish I could find the strength to ask him the questions I want to ask—whether he's mad at me for not saving Mami's restaurant, whether he's struggling at school, whether there is anything I can do to make his life just a little easier.

"How about Luis?" I ask in a small voice. "Has he headed out to work?"

Abuela nods. Luis is the only person in our family who seems to be doing better now. I can't blame him—not really. He started a new job a few days ago, at one of the casinos on Revolución. Now that the restaurant has closed, he is freer than he was before—free to focus on a job that he chose for himself, free to start saving money for his college applications, free from the pressure and the stress of having to save a business that he already knew was beyond saving. He'll be bringing home a few hundred pesos every week, which, again, is not much, but it's something.

Abuela and I fall silent, and I keep myself busy by staring down at my cup, watching the way the steam swirls and vanishes as it rises from the hot tea.

"You're young, Sol," she says softly, and I look up to meet her gaze.

Sometimes, it's easy to forget that she is Papi's mother. He inherited Abuelo's sharp, straight nose and his square jaw, whereas Abuela has always had softer features. Even though her hair is white and her face is lined with years and years of smiles, and frowns, and narrowed eyes, she still has some of the beauty I've seen in old photos. There's something about her perfectly round jaw and her dark brown eyes that has remained the same.

I watch her intently, waiting to hear what she has to say—hoping that she will find a way to ease all the sadness, and the longing, and the regret I've been feeling since I first stepped into the restaurant a few hours ago.

She presses her lips into the faintest of smiles. "You are *so* young, mija."

"So what if I am?" I ask.

"I still remember what it was like—being young. You may think I don't, but I do," she says, letting out a small laugh. "And I remember how change always seemed so final, so... cruel. But in time, you'll realize what I've come to learn after all these years."

"What is that, Abuela?"

"That change gives as much as it takes, and it can open doors you never even knew existed. And that is a wonderful thing. A *wonderful thing*, mija. Because without change, we can't grow. Without change, we can't gain perspective. And without change, it's impossible to see that the bad times only give place to the good, and that nothing worth having in life is permanent."

But I wish it was, I almost say. I hate this—I hate not having Mami, I hate that the restaurant is gone forever. I manage to hold it all in, because I know what Abuela would say in response. She'd only take this as proof that what she's telling me is true, and that I still have lessons to learn.

Soon enough, none of that matters, because something more important grabs my attention: the lime tree outside our window—the one Mami planted all those years ago. My heart seems to stop beating when I realize its branches are almost bare, and what few leaves it still has look frail and dark brown.

While Abuela and I continue drinking our tea in silence, I can't take my eyes off the tree. I wish we could blame its dead leaves on the fall, which has brought with it a wave of cool air, but this has never happened before. The tree has never shriveled up this way, regardless of the season.

I can't help but wonder what Mami would've done if she'd been here to see the tree in this state. I have a feeling she would've watered it, and fertilized it, and done everything she could to save it. She loved to hold on to memories, and tradition—she loved keeping things the way they were. Then again, maybe she would've been quicker than me to listen to Abuela's advice. Maybe she would've made her peace with the fact that the tree's given us plenty of limes over the years, and found it easier to accept that the time has come to plant a new one.

CHAPTER EIGHTEEN

I DON'T THINK I'VE EVER FELT AS LONELY WALKING through the hallways of Orangeville High as I do now.

The voices around me are nothing but noise—noise that I try to tune out as I make my way from one class to the next as quickly as possible. I don't make eye contact with anyone. I just keep my gaze firmly on the hallway ahead of me, even as I feel the lockers and the walls closing in.

In the cafeteria, I go back to being silent most of the time. They all try—especially Ari, Olivia, and Camila. They ask about my weekends at home, and about work at the store, but even though I answer all of their questions, I can't find a way to act bright, or happy, or to lower my walls.

Dinners with Ari and Nancy have also been quieter

than usual. After I told them the restaurant was closing down, something seemed to change between us. Maybe it's just the fact that my stay at their house has become more permanent. Because now that we know the restaurant will never become our main source of income again, this is just the way life is now. Papi will keep bringing in money from odd jobs, Luis will keep working at the casino, and I'll keep working at Wallen's.

My name is María de la Soledad Martínez. I was born on December 18 in Chula Vista, California. I grew up in Tijuana, and I left home at sixteen years old, to move in permanently with my childhood friend and her mom.

Maybe Abuela wasn't entirely wrong when she said change can bring unexpected things. Because, since the restaurant closed, I've found it a lot easier to accept that I don't have to be anyone other than Soledad. After trying and failing to be Sol for years, I've finally made my peace with the idea that I don't have to run away from my loneliness or my sadness. Lately, I've been trying to embrace them, to welcome the idea that this is who I've been meant to be all along. I am Soledad Martínez—always have been, and always will be.

"Uh... Soledad?"

I keep walking. I'm already running late for next period, and the chances that someone would be talking to me in the hallway are just too low. There must be a different girl named Soledad they're calling after.

"Wait, Soledad!"

I turn around to find a short guy with shiny black hair walking toward me. I don't think I've ever seen him before, but from the way he's smiling, he seems to know me.

"Hey," he says, hugging a green clipboard against his chest. "Bruno told me about you."

I shake my head slightly. "What?"

"I—I mean, he told me to reach out to you," he says. "I'm Irwin. I'm putting together the petition so the school board will let Bruno stay."

"Oh." I haven't given this much thought lately. The whispers have persisted—whispers about Bruno, and the school board hearing, and the petition that's going around, but I haven't paid much attention to any of it. I haven't paid attention to anything, really—not my classes, not my exams, not my homework assignments. All that matters is working at the store—so much that my dreams are filled with nothing but hangers, and racks, and warehouses so dark and big that I get lost within their depths.

Irwin raises his eyebrows at me. "So... will you sign it?"

"Yeah," I say, nodding. "Yeah, of course. Do you have a pen?"

The list isn't too long—there's probably fifteen or twenty names above the line where I sign mine, which makes me wonder if he's just using a fresh sheet, or if these are the only people who have been willing to stand up for Bruno so far. Either way, I don't have the strength to ask.

"Good luck," I say as I hand him back the pen and clipboard. "And thanks for doing this."

I manage to give him a small smile, and then I turn away. Before I can take even a step forward, however, he stops me.

"Uh, Bruno said something else," Irwin says, which makes me turn back toward him, curious. "He—he said you two used to commute together sometimes."

Slowly, I nod. The early mornings when I would run into Bruno on the bridge already feel like forever ago. It's as if all that used to happen in a different world, a different lifetime, even though it's only been a couple of months since I stopped doing the commute daily.

"Well... I just thought, if we're able to get people to speak up for Bruno during the hearing... you might be a good person for it."

"Me?"

"Well, you were there that day in the cafeteria, right? You saw everything that went down between Bruno and Jack, so maybe you could tell your version of what happened. And—and you also know Bruno. You'd be able to tell the people from the school board about him."

"I don't—"

"I mean, you have a similar background. You're both from Tijuana."

"So?"

"So they might listen to you. They might see all the ways that you and Bruno are similar, and how hard you both work. You might be able to sway their opinion."

"No," I say in a whisper. "No, I can't."

"But Bruno needs—"

I shake my head. "You can have my signature for the petition, but that's it."

The thought of talking in front of all those people from the school board makes me nauseous, and not only because I've always been terrified of speaking in front of crowds. There's also something about what Irwin is saying that sounds so wrong—the idea that I might be able to help the board see the ways in which Bruno and I are similar. Maybe Irwin means no harm. Maybe he's desperate for solutions and trying whatever he can think of, but I can't do what he's asking me to do—I could never stand in front of the board and try to convince them that Bruno has to stay in school because he and I are quiet, or because we're good students, or because we don't usually get in trouble. If they can't see for themselves that Bruno belongs in this school because he was born in this country, and because he needs an education, and because he deserves to have dreams for the future, then nothing I could say will sway them.

"You don't have to decide now," Irwin says quickly. "You can let me know once you've thought about it. We could really use your help, Soledad."

The bell rings in that moment, and I'm grateful it does. With one last half-smile at Irwin, I turn around and run down the hallway toward trig.

Even after I've sat at a desk and the teacher has closed the classroom door, my heartbeat doesn't slow down. At first, I think it's because I ran here, but after a while I realize there's something else in the back of my mind—another reason I can't do what Irwin has asked me to do.

My heart gives a violent lurch when I think about sitting in front of a bunch of people and telling them about how I used to cross the border every day. No one's ever questioned my place in this school—not the teachers, not the principal's office, not the school board. But if the people from the board started asking me questions about why I used Ari's address for registration and why I haven't always lived in her house, I don't know what I would do. I don't think I'd be able to forgive myself for willingly walking into that situation, for putting my own spot in this school at risk.

But then I start thinking about the few names on the petition, and the look on Irwin's face when I turned him down, and the hoarseness in Bruno's voice the last time I talked to him. I wish I was brave enough to speak up for him. I wish I could find a way to help—that I could do more.

※

I wake up before dawn on a Thursday morning in October. The early morning shifts haven't killed me yet, but they very well might. I'm not sure how much longer I'll be able to keep doing this—how many more weeks I'll be able to get up and go to work after getting barely any sleep.

It's not just about me, either. I'm worried about Nancy. The more tired she looks every morning, and the quieter the car gets during the drive, the more I tell myself that I might not be able to accept her offer to drive me up to San Diego on Tuesdays and Thursdays much longer.

I get dressed in the darkness of Ceci's bedroom. Turning on the lights would be too harsh on my eyes, so I move between the shadows, guided only by the soft glow of the moon coming into the room through the thin curtains.

My eyes keep shutting, and my body is so heavy I'm having a hard time fitting my legs through the holes of my jeans. Somewhere outside the door, I hear low voices, which tells me Nancy has already turned on the early morning news while she waits for me.

When I step out of my bedroom, however, I find Nancy sitting on the couch, her eyes tightly shut and her mouth hanging open. She's wearing her pajamas, and there are infomercials playing on the television. She must've fallen asleep out here last night.

"Nancy?" I whisper.

She doesn't move.

"Nancy," I say again. I really don't want to wake her—especially not when she's been working long shifts at the salon and she's probably had a terrible night's sleep sitting here—but the time on the microwave is getting dangerously close to four thirty, and the only way I'll get to work on time is if she drives me.

I put a hand on her shoulder and shake her gently. Nancy jolts awake, staring at me with wide eyes and a frightened look on her face.

"Who is it?" she says. I'm not sure if she's talking about something she saw in a dream or if she's wondering who I am, but I take a few steps backward so she can see me clearly.

"It's just me," I say.

Nancy's eyes slowly focus on me. "Oh, mija, what are you doing awake?"

"It's Thursday," I answer, feeling a heavy weight landing on my stomach as I watch Nancy's face. Her eyes move quickly as she comes to the realization of what this means.

"Ay, Dios mío," she says, propping herself up from the couch. "I'll get dressed. Don't worry, mija, we'll get you to work on time."

She rushes down the hallway and into her bedroom, and I'm left there standing in the middle of the living room, feeling like the biggest burden.

The drive to the store is silent. I mostly just stare out the window, but whenever I turn to look at Nancy, she's got the same blank expression on her face. Her hands are loosely wrapped around the steering wheel, her shoulders slumped. She also blinks a lot, which is what worries me the most. I know exactly how she's feeling—the fogginess, the lingering shock of realizing you've overslept. I'm no stranger to any of that. I just hope she'll be able to get some more sleep as soon as she gets back home.

"Have a good day," she says to me as I open the passenger door of the car.

"Thank you, Nancy. For everything. I—"

"Don't worry, mija," she says. "You should get going, it's almost five."

I run into the store, up to the staff room, and clock in at six minutes past five. I try my best to hurry downstairs, but I know it won't make much of a difference at this point. I'm officially late.

When I walk into the warehouse, the first person I notice is Nick. He always is, really. This morning he's wearing the same red plaid shirt as on the day we first met. His scruff is getting a bit long, which means he'll probably show up tomorrow with a freshly shaved face, and his brow is furrowed as he looks down at his hands, deeply focused on work.

I go to the corner, pick up a crate, and head over to the table to join him.

"Hey," he says to me.

"Hey."

"Sleep well?"

I nod, glancing briefly into his eyes as I pop the crate open. "How about you?"

He nods back, the corners of his lips twisting into a subtle smile.

Things have been different between us over the past couple of weeks, and I wish more than anything that we could go back to normal. I just don't know how.

During the first few days after Papi told me the restaurant was closing, everyone was worried about me. Nick, Lina, Kelly, Marcos—they all noticed that something had changed deep within me, even though I couldn't find the strength to tell them about what was going on at home. They asked if I was okay, if there was something wrong, but I kept insisting I was fine.

Soon enough, people stopped asking. Everyone seems to have gotten used to my silence—even Nick, because he no longer tries to make conversation, no longer cracks jokes. He just works peacefully by my side, not even talking to the rest of the table, trying his best to keep me company even though I haven't been the easiest person to be around lately.

I wish I could find a way to make him see how grateful I am for the fact that he hasn't given up on me, how much I appreciate him being here next to me, day after day. I also wish I could get him to ask me all those questions one more time—if I'm okay, if there's anything wrong. I may not have been ready to answer them truthfully before, but I'm ready now—ready to tell him about the restaurant, about what's going on with my family. I just don't know how to bring it up, so I keep hoping he will—that he'll speak up and help me break down this barrier I've put up, because I have no idea how to lower it on my own.

"Soledad?" Bill's voice comes from behind me suddenly.

I turn around quickly, feeling anxiety rising in my chest, because I know exactly what this is about. Bill must've noticed I showed up late, and he's about to give me a hard time for it.

But then, when I approach him, he doesn't seem at all

upset. He lifts up a piece of paper, which looks a lot like the sheet where everyone's schedules are written out for the week, and says, "You haven't taken any weekend shifts lately."

"Uh, I..."

"I thought you *wanted* weekend shifts."

"I—I do."

If I'm being honest, all I want is to be home on weekends. I want to be with Diego and Abuela, to sneak out and go to Mami's old restaurant, even if it's empty, and even if it's only for a while. But now that Bill is asking, I really have no excuse. I should be taking every single opportunity I get for longer shifts.

"Well, that's good," Bill says. "Because I need people for this Saturday and Sunday."

Once we've settled on my hours, I head back to the table, telling myself I'll at least be able to hang out with Ari and all of them after work this weekend. The thing is, the thought of joining their weekend plans doesn't bring me the same type of joy as it did before.

"What was that about?" Nick asks me as I reach into the crate I was working on and pull out a few pieces of clothing.

"Just scheduling weekend shifts."

From the corner of my eye, I notice the way Nick's eyebrows shoot up quickly. "You'll be around this weekend?"

"Yeah," I reply, letting out a long sigh. "I guess I will be."

There's a brief moment of silence between us, during

which we both reach for hangers at the center of the table. But then, with a sigh of his own, Nick turns to me and says, "Is everything okay, Sol? I—I know you've told me a million times that you're fine, but… I don't know. Something feels off."

I swallow hard. This is it—the question I'd been hoping he would ask, but all of a sudden there's a knot in my throat that reminds me of why I'd had such a hard time answering honestly before, why I'd been trying to avoid telling him the truth.

"It's just…" I blink, trying to keep myself from crying. "There's been a lot going on lately."

Nick doesn't say anything. He just stares at me expectantly, and that's when I tell him everything—about Papi closing down the restaurant, about how it feels as though we have lost Mami all over again, about how all the progress we made in the year since she died has vanished all of a sudden, and now it's as if we're back at square one.

I try my best to keep my voice steady, to take deep breaths, to slow down anytime I feel like I'm getting too close to tears. The last thing I would want is to start crying inside the stockroom, even though Nick has a way of making me feel as though it would be okay even if I did—as though I could cry, or scream, or flip over the table we're working at, and it would all be fine. As though there's nothing I could possibly do that could make him judge me.

"But you're not," he says to me.

"What?"

"You're not back at square one. I—I mean, it sounds like you're a lot stronger than you give yourself credit for."

I can almost hear Abuela in his voice. Or is it Ari I'm thinking of? Either way, I can picture one of them telling me not to be so hard on myself, to look around and notice all the things I'm too stubborn to see at times.

"Thank you," I say, not looking directly at him. "But you don't have to—"

"I know I don't *have* to say it," he interrupts me. "But it's true."

"I'm sorry I didn't tell you about all of this sooner. I know I've been acting like—"

"You don't need to be sorry," he says quickly. "I'm just happy you trust me enough to tell me now."

My entire body fills up with warmth as I realize that I do trust him, and that maybe I don't deserve all his patience, or his understanding, or his willingness to be right here next to me for the past two weeks.

"So... what would you say about hanging out on Saturday?" he asks me. "You know, after our shifts."

In the back of my mind, I think of all the reasons I should say no—because I should spend that time doing homework instead, or because I should ask Ari what she's up to before I agree to other plans, or because no matter how much I want to say yes, I'm not sure I'm ready to think of Nick as anything other than a friend.

But then, when I turn toward him and stare into his

puppy eyes, my heart melts. There's no way I could say no, even if I tried. And so, nodding slowly, I say, "Yeah. We could figure something out."

Neither of us says much for the remainder of our shifts. All I know is that the second I walk out of the store an hour later, there's a weird sensation in the deepest part of my stomach—one that feels a lot like longing. As I start making my way up Fourth Avenue toward the MTS station, I get the sudden urge to turn back the way I came. I want to return to Wallen's, and go down to the warehouse, and spend a bit more time with Nick, even if it only means standing there in silence while we work on the clothes.

I've never experienced this feeling before, but I've heard about it—mostly from characters in telenovelas. I've heard them describe how there are some people that you could never get enough of—how, sometimes, you can start missing someone the second after you say goodbye to them.

I don't know if this is the same thing, or if it'll even last. But, as I step onto the trolley, all I can think about is Nick, and his brown eyes, and the fact that we're hanging out this weekend.

"This is a blue line trolley," a voice overhead announces. "All passengers must have a..."

The trolley starts moving, and I stumble my way toward a seat, my legs feeling weak. I have no way to explain what is going on inside my chest right now. Because, among the deep sadness, and anxiety, and guilt that's swirling around in there, I also feel something exploding—a warm glow that breaks through the hopelessness, breathing new life into my lungs.

At least for right now, there's nothing and no one in the world that could dampen the pure joy that the thought of Nick brings me. And as the trolley rolls onward and the streets rush past the windows, the glow inside of me only keeps growing stronger and stronger.

CHAPTER NINETEEN

When I tell Nancy and Ari that I'm spending Saturday evening with a boy, they both stare at me with shocked looks on their faces.

"Well... how did you meet him?" Nancy asks me. There's something in her voice that warms my heart— a gentle curiosity that she's hoping will come across as casual, even when I know she's trying to find out every detail about where I'm going and who I'll be with.

"At work," I say, looking down at my plate.

Ari chokes on her glass of water. "Is it Nick?" she asks. "Did he ask you out?"

I lift the fork up to my mouth, but before taking a bite of spaghetti, I turn toward Ari and nod.

"*What?*" she shrieks. "Well, is it a date?"

"I'm not sure. I mean, we're friends, but I don't know if we're—"

"That's good," Nancy says quickly. "Starting off as friends is always a good idea. There's no need to rush into anything else, you know?"

I laugh a little, thinking about Mami. She would've said the exact same thing, which makes me grateful to at least have Nancy, and to know that she's looking out for me.

"What are you two doing on Saturday?" Ari asks.

"I don't know yet," I answer. "He said he'd pick me up at six."

Ari's eyes widen. "He's gonna pick you up *here*?"

"I'll make sure to be home all night on Saturday," Nancy says. "That way you'll be able to call me, and I can go pick you up if you need me to."

"Thank you, Nancy."

While Ari asks me questions about how Nick asked me out, and whether I have any suspicions about what he might have planned for our date, I can't stop smiling. Because even though Papi, Abuela, Luis, and Diego aren't here, there's something about tonight that makes me feel as though I'm eating dinner next to my family.

Even though we're not related by blood, and even though a lot has changed since I first moved in with them, Ari and Nancy feel like home, and I couldn't be any more grateful for that.

Nick rings the doorbell at exactly six p.m. on Saturday, just as he said he would.

"Sol!" Nancy's voice echoes throughout the house. "Sol, he's here!"

"I'm coming!"

Ari asked me if I wanted to borrow makeup or any clothes, but I said no. I figured that if a t-shirt and a pair of jeans are good enough for work, they should be good enough for a date. I did, however, wash my hair and spent a solid half-hour doing my braid, trying to make it look as perfect as possible.

"Be safe, mija," Nancy says to me as I step out of my bedroom. "And remember, you can—"

"—call you anytime," I say. "Don't worry, I won't forget."

Ari comes to wrap her arms around me. "Have fun," she whispers into my ear. "And promise to tell me everything later."

"I will," I say. "I promise."

I hug her back, and then I turn toward the front door. When I open it, I find Nick standing on the front steps with his hands in his pockets.

"Hey," he says to me, smiling. He's wearing a white t-shirt and his old, dirty Timberlands. He looks different somehow, but it takes me a second to realize why: He's pushed his hair back with gel.

"Hi," I answer, my voice a little too high.

"Hey!" he says again, looking over my shoulder.

Turning around, I see that Nancy and Ari are still lingering by the living room, watching me and Nick with big smiles on their faces.

"Oh, hello," Nancy replies, waving at him. "Nice to meet you!"

Before she can say anything else, Ari whisks her away into one of the bedrooms, and I turn back around to face Nick, feeling myself blushing.

"Sorry about that."

"No, no," he says, flashing a smile at me. "You ready to go?"

I nod once, stepping forward to walk out of the house.

"My truck is parked just around the block," he says.

"Where exactly are we going?"

Nick lifts his eyebrows. "You'll see."

He leads the way down the sidewalk and around the corner. I'm not sure what I pictured when he said he drove a truck, but I don't think it was this. Parked beside the curb is an old pickup, which must've once been painted red but has now become a rusty shade of brown. It has bumps and scratches here and there, and it looks like it could use a good wash. Somehow, though, it feels so perfect. Now that I've seen it, I don't think there's any other car in the world I could picture Nick driving.

I jump into the passenger seat and buckle my seat belt. A second later, he hops in and starts the engine.

As he pulls away from the curb, I sneak a sideways glance at him. None of this feels real. It's as if I'm in a dream and I might wake up any second, but when Nick cracks the windows open and a soft breeze starts blowing in my face, I'm reminded that it isn't. I'm really here, and so is he, and we are really driving through Ari's neighborhood on our way to an unknown destination.

"Are we going into the city?" I ask as we drive past a sign on the side of the road that says we're heading north.

"Nope," Nick answers, throwing me a quick smile.

Before I can ask where he's taking us, we get onto the highway and the wind starts blowing at full speed. Nick turns up the music, and I turn toward the open window, watching shops, and trees, and dry patches of land flashing past us.

After about twenty minutes, Nick slows down. He drives off the road to take us down a dirt path, past a few sad-looking trees, and he stops in the middle of a clearing.

"This is it," he says, turning off the engine. He must be able to see the confusion on my face, because he lets out a small laugh. "We're having a picnic... sort of. Come on, I'll show you."

He opens his door, and I do the same. I jump out, landing on dry grass, and walk toward the back of the truck. Nick opens the tailgate to reveal a bunch of things on the truck bed: A cooler, a blanket, a couple of lanterns, and a big bag of chips.

I'm not sure what to say. He seems to have put a lot of thought into this, so I feel like I should thank him, or ask if I should've brought anything. Instead, I blurt out: "So... we just sit on the grass?"

Again, he laughs. "No, not on the grass."

He hops onto the truck bed and reaches for the blanket. In one sweeping movement, he stretches it open and lays it out so we can sit on top of it.

"Come on up." He offers me his hand. I take it, feeling electricity running through my veins when his skin makes contact with mine.

"You can sit," he says to me after I've been standing next to him awkwardly for a couple of seconds.

I do as he says, leaning my back against the side of the truck, and I watch as he leans over to open the cooler and pulls out two bottles of beer. He cracks them open, hands me one, and comes to sit next to me.

"Cheers," he says, clinking his beer against mine.

"Cheers." I take a small sip out of my beer, while Nick takes a long one. The sunlight is quickly disappearing. The sky is shifting from light blue to gray, and all around us, the night seems to be coming alive with the chirping of a thousand insects, which blends in with the sound of cars speeding down the highway. Through the trees, I can make out their headlights flashing by like hundreds of fireflies vanishing into the distance.

"It's getting dark," I say softly.

"That's the whole point."

I turn toward him, searching for answers in his face.

"The stars look different from here," he tells me,

resting his head against the side of the truck as he looks up at the sky. "We're far enough from the lights of the city, and it's supposed to be a clear night."

"So . . . we're stargazing?"

"We are," he says, smiling. "You're gonna be the director of NASA one day, remember?"

I almost choke on my beer, laughing. "Maybe not the director of NASA," I say. "But . . . I do wanna be someone."

"Who do you wanna be?" he asks.

"I mean, I keep telling people that I'm not sure, but . . . maybe I am. I've had engineering in the back of my mind for the longest time, and I just . . . I like the idea of knowing how to fix things, and build things, and . . . and change things, you know?"

"That makes sense," Nick says. "But I didn't ask *what* you wanna be. I asked *who* you wanna be."

I take a swig of my beer, thinking. I used to be so certain I wanted to be Sol—and maybe I still do. Maybe I'll never fully give up on that idea, never be able to grow comfortable with the thought of being Soledad for the rest of my life, no matter what I've been trying to convince myself of lately.

"I'm not sure," I answer finally. "Someone different."

"I think you're already pretty great."

A chill comes running down my back as I look into his deep brown eyes. I don't think anyone has ever said this to me before. I've never really been satisfied with just being me. When it comes to my family, I'm always telling myself that I need to be less afraid, less overwhelmed by the pressure of having to succeed for them. Around Ari and her friends, I feel the need to be less quiet, less awkward, less shy. And during my toughest moments, I tell myself that I need to be less sad, less anxious, less like Soledad. But maybe that's part of the problem. Maybe I've been trying so hard to become less and less that now there's hardly any of the real me left.

"It's true," he says. "And you should know it—even if I wasn't here to tell you this."

I nod slowly, noticing how it's getting harder to make out his features. The light around us is shifting, bathing everything in a soft, muted glow.

"How about you?" I ask.

"Huh?"

"Who do you wanna be?"

Nick is silent for a long time. An insect screeches loudly somewhere nearby, but to me, the only sound that matters is that of Nick's slow breathing.

"I used to think I wanted to be famous," he says. "You know—be one of those singers who *makes it*. But after the last year, with my mom being sick, and having to push back my college plans, all I want is just... to have a boring life. I wanna be one of those people you see in movies who live in nice houses in the suburbs, and drive Toyotas, and go on vacation once a year to... like, Orlando, or something."

I narrow my eyes at him slightly. "Why do you want that?"

221

"Because those boring people seem to at least have all the most important things. I mean... they're not scrambling for money, they're not worried about what other people think about them, they're not trying to make impossible dreams come true. They have a job, a family, a friend group... and that's all they need, really. And wouldn't that be nice? To just have everything you need? To not spend your time wishing for things you can't have?"

I think back to a time when that was my life—when I had everything I needed. When Mami was still here, and Papi hadn't yet become as harsh as he is now, and everything was the way it was supposed to be. Nick may have a good point, but if I know him—and I think I'm starting to—a boring life won't be enough for him. Not when he has dreams as big as the ones he told me about before.

"It could be nice," I answer. "But... maybe you don't have to become that person."

He shrugs.

"I mean it. Maybe... your mom is gonna get the transplant. And maybe you'll be able to go to college, and you'll meet people who will believe in you, and who will help you get to where you want to go. And then, in a few years, you'll be looking back thinking about how you almost gave up on your dreams before you even gave yourself a chance to go after them."

He stares at me for a long time. I'm not sure what's going through his head—if he thinks I'm crazy, or if he's trying to convince himself that what I'm saying is true. Or maybe he's realizing the same thing as I am: that he and I are much more similar than either of us knew—that we're both harsh on ourselves sometimes, that we both want big things, and that we're both terrified of what will happen if those things don't become a reality.

Even though I keep waiting for him to speak up, he doesn't, and before I know it, I've stopped waiting. I blink slowly in the soft light, taking small sips of beer and paying attention to the rhythmic sound of Nick's breathing.

"Look," he says suddenly, pointing upward. The sunlight is all but gone by now, so that the first stars are starting to appear, shining bright against the deep gray sky.

"How did you find this place?" I ask him softly.

"I was driving down the road one day, and I just… decided to stop."

"Do you come here a lot?"

"Only sometimes. When I need to think about stuff," he says. "After everything you told me the other day, I thought this would be a good spot to bring you. I figured you might like to have some peace and quiet—to be in a place where you can listen to your own thoughts again, you know?"

My heart flutters. Maybe it's just the beer, but everything feels a lot simpler all of a sudden. With the stars shining above, the sounds of the night buzzing nearby, and the heat of Nick's body right next to me, I feel like I have everything I could ever need.

"Thank you," I say to him.

He meets my eyes, and just like that, I know something

is about to happen. He leans toward me, and I lean toward him. Slowly, he kisses me, and the trees, and the chirping of insects, and the lights of cars driving up and down the highway disappear. All that matters in this moment is the feeling of Nick's strong arms holding me and the tickle of his beard on my skin. And as I open my mouth slightly, allowing his lips to melt into mine, I can't help but feel as though kissing him is the easiest thing in the world. It's as if I'd memorized the shape of his mouth in another life, and now I'm just remembering, remembering, remembering.

When we finally lean away from each other, everything around me seems to come back to life gradually. Blinking a few times, I realize the night seems a lot brighter than it did before. The moon is nowhere to be found, but the stars glowing above are enough to light up everything around us.

Nick smiles at me, and I smile back, but we don't say anything. For a brief moment, it's as if neither of us knows what to do, but then Nick takes a swig of his beer, and I do the same, only to find that my bottle is empty.

"I'll get us fresh drinks," he says.

He gets up to grab another two drinks from the cooler—sodas this time—and he returns to sit next to me a second later. Even though the air is starting to get chilly, his body is still warm against mine. And as we sit in peaceful silence, I quickly stop thinking about the cold, or the insects, or the cars flashing past on the highway. All I could possibly care about is the glow of the stars and the feeling of our lips touching.

CHAPTER TWENTY

THE FOLLOWING WEEK GOES BY IN A BLUR OF EATING dinner with Ari and Nancy, showing up at school, and spending my early mornings and late nights in the warehouse next to Nick.

Whenever we're working around the big table, Lina, Kelly, and Marcos seem to make an effort to set up at the opposite end of wherever Nick and I are. I can't help but suspect that they've noticed something has changed between me and him, but none of them says anything. They just focus on giving us space, and a part of me is grateful. Because during the hours I spend by his side in the stockroom, it's easy for me to imagine us back at that clearing in the woods. It's easy to block out everything except the feeling of him beside me and the sound of his deep voice.

"Can we hang out again this weekend?" he asks me

during our shift on Thursday, staring at me with hopeful eyes.

"I have to go home," I answer, my heart hurting a little. "But I'll be around next weekend. I promise."

At school, it becomes impossible to deny that the attempts I've been making at keeping up with my workload are not nearly good enough. I receive a history test back with a big, red D on the corner, and I walk into English to find that I was meant to have read several chapters of the new book we've been assigned, so I have no choice but to spend the entire period with my head down in a corner of the classroom, hoping that I won't get called on for answers.

In between all the madness of the week, Diego calls me a few times. He doesn't sound the same as he used to. He sounds more serious, more mature, but I can tell he's trying his hardest—trying to reach out to me, trying to go back to being his old self, trying to heal from the wounds that losing Mami's restaurant has reopened for all of us.

When I walk into the house on Saturday morning, he's already awake and sitting at the kitchen table while Abuela makes breakfast.

"Hey," I say, walking up to him. "How was your week?"

"It was okay," he replies.

Before he can say anything else, Abuela turns to me and says, "Dios mío, it feels like forever since you were last here."

"It's only been two weeks."

"It feels like much longer, mija."

While I help her finish making breakfast, I notice that once again, we're having nothing but scrambled eggs and coffee. There is no bacon, no chorizo, no pan dulce. Closing the restaurant was supposed to be for the best. It was supposed to help us put food on our own table, instead of spending the money on paying rent for the restaurant and buying ingredients from suppliers, but I haven't yet seen any of the improvements Papi promised.

Once we're done eating, I set up at the dining room table to do homework. What I truly want is to leave the house quietly, sneak into the restaurant using my key, and just be there for a while. After the stressful week I had at school, though, I know I can't afford to waste any time. I have to focus on homework.

I keep hoping that Diego will come and join me at the table, but he doesn't. He simply lies on the living room couch, staring up at the ceiling. Papi hasn't stopped insisting that we need to keep the electricity bill down, so my brother doesn't even turn on the TV. Instead, he keeps busy by throwing a small ball up and catching it, again and again.

"Do you have any homework?" I ask him after a while.

"I finished it all."

"Really?"

He meets my eyes for the briefest second, nodding, but I'm not sure I believe him.

"Well, do you want me to look it over? Make sure it's all good?"

"No," he answers. "Should be okay."

I don't want to push him too hard, so I drop the subject. In the end, he puts the ball down on top of the center table in the living room and heads off into his bedroom.

A part of me wants to go after him, and keep him company, and find a way to get him to talk to me, but I don't leave my seat at the dinner table. I stay focused on my schoolwork, hoping that by the end of the weekend, I'll at least have made a dent on everything I need to get done.

I'm neck-deep into a reading for English, highlighting passages furiously and making notes, when I hear a door open down the hallway, and I look up, thinking Diego has finally emerged from his room. But instead, Luis walks out, staring at me with wide eyes.

"What are you doing?" he asks me. There's something awkward about his voice, about his posture, as though he's not quite sure how to approach me.

"Homework," I say. "You?"

It's a stupid question, really. I know he's only just woken up, but I still wait to hear his response.

"I was, uh... gonna head out to work soon," he says. "But... I've been wanting to talk to you."

My eyebrows shoot up. I can't think of anything Luis could possibly want to say to me. I can't even remember the last time we chatted, or the last time the two of us were alone together in the same room.

"O-okay," I say, pushing my books aside. "We can talk."

He pulls a chair back and sits down in front of me.

Perhaps it's been too long since I've seen him from up close, because he looks different. His scruff is getting thicker, the lines around his eyes and forehead deeper. Long gone is the moody nineteen-year-old who would wear the same leather jacket every day and sneak out to meet some girl he was dating. Sitting in front of me is a full-grown man.

"I need a new job," he says, staring straight into my eyes.

"I thought you liked working at the casino."

"It's not bad," he says. "But the money's not enough. Fifty dollars a week isn't gonna help us get out of this mess."

I look down at the table. Papi has been trying to avoid talking about his debts, so I haven't asked him how big they are, but I do know most of the money we're bringing in is going toward paying them off. It's the reason we still can't turn on the TV for longer than an hour in the evening, the reason the fridge is still empty and our plates still not full enough.

"What are you thinking of doing?" I ask my brother.

"Well, that's the thing," he answers. "I thought you could help me. Maybe I could find a job in the US."

"Luis, I don't—"

"If I worked the same amount of hours right across the border, I'd be making over two thousand dollars a month, Sol," he says, leaning closer to me. "*Two thousand* dollars. That would be more than enough for all of us—enough for you to stop working, enough to pay off Papi's debts, enough to save money for my college tuition."

"But I can't help you get a work permit. I don't know how I could—"

"Then think of something," he says to me. "Maybe—maybe you could help me find a job at the store where you work, and they wouldn't need to find out I'm not a citizen."

"They will ask," I answer. "They'll ask for your social security number, and then what will you say?"

Luis leans back in his chair, staring at me with narrowed eyes. Suddenly, everything about his attitude changes. He becomes serious, cold, as if he's put up a wall from one second to the next.

"You just don't wanna help me, do you?"

"Of course I want to help you! But I can't do what you're asking me to do."

"What are we meant to do, then? Are we supposed to keep living like this?"

"I know we need more money," I say. "I just... I don't have the answers you want. I don't know how to get the money any more than you do."

The truth is, maybe there is a way. I could work enough hours at the store to make the two thousand dollars a month Luis is talking about, which would save our family once and for all. I just don't see how I'd be able to work at Wallen's full time and keep up with school. When I think about dropping out of Orangeville, about not graduating next to Ari next year, about throwing away my college dreams, my throat starts getting tighter and tighter, until I can barely breathe.

"I get it," Luis says after a moment of silence. "You're not around most of the time, so you don't care. As long as you get your fancy high school degree, and your college acceptance letter, and all the food you could possibly need at your friend's house, it doesn't make a difference to you how the rest of us have to live."

"You know that's not true," I say sharply, looking into his eyes. "You know I care."

"You don't really act like it sometimes."

"That's not fair." I don't mean to raise my voice, but all of a sudden I'm yelling, and I can't stop myself. "I know we need more money. I *know* it. But I'm already giving everything I can, and I can't just help you find a job across the border. It's not that easy."

Luis's jaw tightens, his cheeks become redder. I'm almost certain that he's about to start yelling back, but when he speaks, his voice is no louder than a whisper.

"It was easy enough for you."

His words cut through me like a knife, because maybe there's a part of him that's right. It's getting harder and harder to make sense of the reasons why I'm an American citizen when he isn't, why I have a future to look forward to when he doesn't, why I'm able to get food, and electricity, and everything I need at Ari's when the rest of them have been struggling.

I wish I could speak up, but I can't think of anything to say, can't even remember how to use my voice. All I can do is sit still and watch as Luis pushes his chair back and storms out of the house without so much as throwing me another glance.

~~\|/~~

My brother's words stick with me for the rest of the weekend. I can't seem to find a way to run away from them, even though I don't even see him again during my remaining time in Tijuana. By the time Papi, Abuela, Diego, and I sit down to have dinner on Saturday night, he's still at work, and the next morning, he sneaks out of the house without anyone noticing.

"We'll find a way, mija," Papi says when I tell him about the things Luis said to me.

"But he's right, Papi. We need more money. At some point, we're gonna need to—"

"You don't have to worry. Your brother might not be able to see it, but *I* can—I can see how hard you've been working."

I don't ask the question I'm most afraid to bring up. I don't ask what he thinks about the idea of me starting to work full time, because maybe I don't want to hear his answer.

Later in the evening, however, while I'm sitting in the living room next to Abuela and Diego playing Chinese checkers, a part of me wonders if Luis has a point. I'm the only person in our family who can work in the US—the only one who can get us out of this mess once and for all. So if I was truly as selfless as I claim to be, wouldn't I put my family before everything else? Wouldn't I be willing to postpone my education and my dreams so I could make sure they'll be okay? Wouldn't I make the decision that needs to be made all by myself, drop out of Orangeville, and ask Bill for full-time hours?

"Sol, te toca."

"Sorry?"

"It's your turn, mija."

I look down at the board, trying to understand what's going on. It's as if someone else has been playing instead of me, and I'm just stepping into her shoes halfway through the game, because I can't even recall any of the moves I've made so far.

"I—I'm playing red, right?"

"No, yours are the purple ones," Diego whispers beside me.

I make a move, and Abuela goes after me. "You kids have your turns," she says, standing up from the couch. "I'll run to the bathroom."

Diego moves one of his checkers. I do the same, and suddenly there's nothing for us to do except wait for Abuela to come back.

"Are you sure you don't need help with your home-work?" I ask Diego. "We have a couple of hours before dinner if you want me to—"

"No," he says, shaking his head once. "It's fine."

"How are your grades? Have you gotten a report lately?"

Diego looks away from me, but I notice the way his

face turns red. And then, without saying anything at all, he lets me in on all the things he's been trying to hide.

"It's okay," I say, because I can tell that his lips are trembling, and I don't want him to start crying. "Diego, it's okay. We can find a way to bring your grades back up. You don't have to—"

"It's not just my grades," he says, and a single tear comes rolling down his face. "It's those kids."

"The ones who were saying things about you? The ones who've been—"

Diego nods, looking down at his lap.

"What have they done?" I ask.

I move closer to my brother, taking the spot on the couch where Abuela was sitting a minute ago, and grab one of his hands.

"Diego," I say. "Tell me."

"There's a boy. Andrés."

"Andrés," I repeat, telling myself that it's important for me to remember this name for later. "Is he one of the kids who has been giving you a hard time?"

"No," Diego answers, shaking his head. "No, it's the opposite. He—he's my friend."

Even though my heart is beating hard, and even though my brother is still crying, something warm fills my chest in that moment. Diego and I are similar in that way— we've always found it difficult to make friends, except that there's one big difference between me and him. I've always had Ari, while Diego hasn't had anyone. He's made friends here and there over the years, but there's never been any-one who has stuck by his side, no one who has stayed with him the way Ari has stayed with me.

"That's good," I say. "It *is* good, isn't it?"

"Yeah," Diego replies, still not looking directly at me.

"How did you become friends?"

"He also likes drawing. That's how I started talking to him—cause I was working on my sketchbook during recess one day, and he asked to see the picture."

"What's the problem, then? Why are those other kids bothering you?"

"They're saying things about us," Diego says. "About me and Andrés. The same kinds of things they used to say about me before—that we're girly, that we're different." He lets out a long sigh. "That we're...boyfriends."

My mind races as I try to understand what he's saying—or, rather, what he hasn't quite dared to say out loud. A part of me wants to lean over and wrap my arms around him. I want to remind him of how much I love him, how he is perfect exactly the way he is, but I resist the urge. Maybe he doesn't need any of that. Maybe what he needs is for me to not make a big deal out of any of this, for me to just be here for him and help him feel less alone.

"Well," I say slowly, "you're probably too young to have a boyfriend."

It happens unexpectedly. Diego lets out a chuckle. For a moment, I'm not sure if he's sobbing instead of laughing, but then I notice the trace of a smile on his face.

"Yeah," he says, nodding to himself.

"But, if a boyfriend is what you want—you know, one day, when you're older—then... you shouldn't care what those other kids say about you."

"It's hard not to care."

"I know. But it's just as hard to pretend to be someone you're not. So, if you have a new friend, just... don't let anyone stop you from enjoying that. Focus on being there for Andrés, and hopefully he'll be there for you, too, and maybe that'll make it easier to tune out those stupid kids."

I'm not sure if I'm saying the right things. I'm not sure if this is what he needs to hear, or if I'm giving him the right advice, but I just want him to know that I am on his side. I want him to be certain that I love him, and that I'll always be here for him, no matter what.

We hear a door opening down the hallway. I know Abuela is about to come back any second, so I pull Diego closer to me and wrap him in a hug.

"I love you," I say. "*So* much. You know that, don't you?"

"I know," he whispers into my ear.

"What's going on here?" Abuela asks when she sees us.

"Nothing," I answer. "I'm just... thinking about how I'm heading back to California tomorrow."

"Well, mija, you know we always miss you when you're gone," Abuela says as I move aside so she can sit back down between Diego and me. "I hope neither of you cheated while I was in the bathroom. Is it my turn?"

She stares down at the board, and while she stretches out a hand to move one of the red marbles, I sneak a glance at Diego. When he meets my eyes, I smile at him, and the corner of a smile twists in a way that tells me he's trying his best to smile back.

CHAPTER TWENTY-ONE

ARI AND I HEAD UP TO SAN DIEGO FOR OUR AFTER-noon shifts at Wallen's right after school on Monday. The sky has been undecided between blue and gray all day, and now it looks like neither. There's a thin layer of fog floating overhead, which is making the sunlight soft and opaque.

"Ceci's coming home this weekend," Ari says once we're on the I-5 North.

"Oh, nice. When's she getting here?"

"Saturday. But don't worry—you can sleep in my room while she's here."

I make a mental note to clean up the room a bit this week—maybe move my clothes to the far corner of the closet, and make sure the desk is clear. I wouldn't want Ceci to come home and feel as though a stranger has taken over her bedroom.

"Are you excited to see her?"

"Yeah," Ari says. Her window's rolled down, so her hair is flying around her head. "It's the first time she's coming home since she left for college."

"Well, I'll try not to get in the way of your family time too much. I'm working Saturday and Sunday, and I'll be out with Nick at some point."

Ari lets out a laugh. "Get in the way of our family time?" she says. "Sol, you *are* family. I'm sure Ceci will be happy to see you."

I let out a small laugh as well. Perhaps I've held on too much to the image I used to have of Ceci when we were kids—of the girl who was so possessive of her things, who would never play with us. Perhaps I'll need to get to know her all over again—the girl who has agreed to let me sleep in her bedroom, and who used to bake with Ari all the time, and who managed to get into San Francisco State on a scholarship.

"My mom wants all of us to go into San Diego for dinner on Saturday. Maybe somewhere in Little Italy," Ari says. "You should come—I mean, if it doesn't get in the way of your plans with Nick."

"We don't really have plans yet. We just said we'd do something this weekend."

Ari turns toward me, her eyes filled with curiosity. "How are things going with him?"

"Great," I say. "I… I mean, I think so, anyway." Even now, thinking of Nick makes my heart skip a beat. The truth is, as long as I get to hang out with him again this weekend, I know I'll be able to get through whatever happens over the next few days—I'll be able to push through work, and school, and the thought of what might be going on at home.

"Do you remember those bets we used to make when we were younger? About who would be the first of us to have a boyfriend?"

"Yeah," I say, shaking my head a little. "I always said it was gonna be you, and you always said it was gonna be me."

"Exactly." Ari smiles, her gaze fixed on the road. "Guess I won."

"He's not my *boyfriend*," I say. "But, you know, he's... nice."

Ari rolls her eyes at me. "It sounds like he's more than just *nice*."

"How about you?" I ask, trying to deflect the attention away from me. "Is there anyone at Wallen's that you like?"

"Not really, no."

"At school, then?" I ask. Other than the childish bets we used to make, Ari has never talked much about romance, never given much thought to the idea of being in a relationship.

She shakes her head. "I'd rather focus on friends. There'll be plenty of time for everything else once we get to college."

"Yeah. I guess that's true."

"Not to say you shouldn't see where things go with Nick," she adds, taking her eyes off the road for a second to look at me. "You've seemed a lot happier since you went on that date with him."

In the back of my mind, I can't help but wonder if Ari has a point—if it would be smarter to wait until we're in college to worry about romance, if I'd be better off focusing on school, and work, and my family. But then, when I step into the stockroom a while later to find Nick's big, brown puppy eyes staring right at me, I can't bring myself to ignore the tingling in my hands, the beating of my heart against my chest. I can't find a way to imagine what it would be like to work here without him around, or what the last few days would've been like if I hadn't been able to hold on to the idea of our second date.

I'm so busy staring back into his eyes that it takes me a moment to realize that the place is emptier than I've ever seen it. While the door slowly swings shut behind me, I take a look around the stockroom, trying to think of any possible reason why more than half the staff could be missing. Before I can get my thoughts in order, though, Bill approaches me and lets out a loud exhale through his mouth.

"Oh," he says. "It's good you're here. Go on, get to work. There's plenty to do today."

I don't linger. I sneak away quickly to go pick up a crate from the pile, and then I set up at the big table next to Nick.

"What's going on?" I ask him. There's only two other people working around the table, whom I've only ever seen a few times before. Everyone else who should be here today—including Lina, and Kelly, and Marcos—is absent.

He crinkles his nose slightly. "There's a cold going around. I think it started with Marcos, cause on Friday he said his kids were staying home from school, and then he called in sick over the weekend."

My throat starts to feel really dry, and I'm not sure if it's because I haven't drunk any water since lunch, because my anxiety is acting up, or because I might actually be coming down with something.

"So everyone who's not here is home sick?"

Nick nods, raising his eyebrows. Right at that second, Bill lets out a loud sneeze, which makes the few of us working around the table turn sharply toward him.

"Don't even mention it," Nick whispers in my ear. "He's been blowing his nose nonstop, but he keeps saying he's not sick."

"Soledad!" Bill calls from across the warehouse. For a moment, I'm scared he overheard what Nick just whispered to me, but then he says, "Focus, please. We're still getting through the morning shipment, and we have to empty every single crate before the end of the night."

I nod once and get to work right away. Bill has a good point. The pile of crates does look bigger than ever, and getting through it is taking much longer than usual—not just because there are only four of us working around the table, but because Bill and the other two employees keep getting pulled away.

Their walkie-talkies beep endlessly, mostly with requests from salespeople upstairs—can you check if we have this t-shirt in a size medium? There's a customer looking for this dress in blue, could you take a look around to see if we have it? Could you bring out the replenishment racks for the men's department?

There are usually enough people in the stockroom that these requests are easy to manage, but today, Bill and the other two employees all look overwhelmed as they go in and out the door, carrying single pieces of clothing, armfuls of hangers, or clothing racks filled with stuff, while Nick and I keep working on the crates.

At some point, it's only me and him in the stockroom. Even though it feels weird—the emptiness, the silence— I'd be lying if I said I don't like it better this way. Just me and Nick, working side by side.

"No way," he says a couple of hours into our shift, his mouth falling open. "Did that really happen?"

"I swear it did," I answer. "Poor Luis had to go around with no eyebrows for six months."

I've been telling him old stories from the restaurant, like the time Luis stood too close to the flames when he was eleven, and his eyebrows singed off.

"He was so scared to go to school the day after it happened," I say. I may be laughing now, but I remember how shaken all of us were back then. "My mom offered to paint his eyebrows on with makeup, but he refused."

"Well, did he—"

We're interrupted by the sound of a walkie-talkie pinging.

"Bill, could we get the modern replenishment for men? It's taking a while."

We look around. The warehouse is still completely empty except for the two of us; Bill must've forgotten his walkie-talkie on top of the table before heading back upstairs. Nick reaches out to pick it up while I slip a sparkly dress onto a hanger.

"Hey, this is Nick from the warehouse," he says into it. "I'll bring the modern racks up."

Putting the walkie-talkie back down, he looks up at me and smiles.

"I'll be back in a minute. You okay to stay here on your own?"

"Of course." I'm almost done with the crate I've been working on, and the pile is starting to look a lot more manageable.

"Cool," he says, wheeling a couple of racks along as he makes his way toward the door. "I'll be back soon."

With Nick gone, the warehouse seems bigger and colder than it ever has, but I try not to think about it too much. I push myself to work as fast as possible, telling myself that my shift will be over before I know it, and I shouldn't leave Nick and the rest of the team with a ton of crates to finish on their own.

I insert a security tag into an expensive dress, and then I pick up all the hangers to go sort them in the women's evening wear rack.

I've barely had a chance to go drop the empty crate

among the pile and pick up a new one when I hear beeping on the keypad outside, and the door swings open.

"Hey," Nick says. "Did you miss me?"

I'm about to blurt out I couldn't have missed him—that he was only gone a few minutes, but I stop myself in time, and try to think of something nicer to say.

"You know I did."

He comes up to the table, smiling as far as his lips will go. Before taking his spot beside me, he sneaks up from behind to give me a quick kiss on the cheek, and all of a sudden the stockroom seems a lot brighter and warmer than it did a minute ago.

For the rest of the week, it feels as though the only thing people at school can talk about is Bruno and the hearing. The petition has gotten more signatures, but there are now whispers about a different type of petition—one that has been circulating among the parents, which says that Bruno is a threat to our school, and he should not be allowed to stay.

"I heard they already have over a hundred signatures," Ana María announces to the table during lunch on Wednesday.

"Who started it?" Ari asks, brandishing the apple that she's holding in her hand.

"Who do you think?" Simon whispers from the other side of the table.

Jack Akers's parents. I should've known. Even though I've tried to ignore him as much as I can, I've seen him walking around school lately, complaining about how much pain he's still in, and how difficult his recovery has been. More than once, though, when he thinks no one is paying attention, I've seen him laughing, or talking loudly, or chewing gum without a care in the world.

"Is there anything we can do?" Olivia asks suddenly. "You know, to help Bruno?"

"Just sign the petition that Irwin's been passing around, I guess," Simon replies. "Have you all signed it?"

While everyone around the table nods, a pang of guilt hits my stomach.

"Irwin asked me to, uh... to speak on the day of the hearing."

Ari turns sharply toward me. "What do you mean?"

"He said I might be able to sway the school board's opinion—that I should go talk about Bruno, and convince them to let him stay at Orangeville."

"Well, that's good," Olivia says. "I mean, if it'll help Bruno..."

"I just... I don't think I can do it."

I look down, not wanting to meet their eyes, not wanting to see the disappointment on their faces. I already have a lot going on, and the last thing I need is to add more weight to my shoulders.

"What do you mean, you can't do it?" Ana María asks

me. There's no judgment in her voice, but I still can't bring myself to look at her as I answer.

"I just... can't." I try to remember the reasons I had for saying no to Irwin—the fear of speaking in front of the school board, the possibility that they might ask questions about where I'm from and why I haven't always lived in California. But, all of a sudden, it's a lot harder to make sense of them—it's harder to convince myself that I shouldn't at least try to speak up.

"It's okay," Ari says, touching my arm. "You don't have to do anything you don't want to."

From the corner of my eye, I notice that Olivia and Simon are nodding. After a long moment of silence, Tony clears his throat and starts talking about his driver's license test, which he's taking tomorrow, but I find it hard to focus on what he's saying.

All I can think about is Bruno, and the fact that the hearing is only a couple of weeks away. And as Ana María's words spin around in my mind, I start to feel anxiety rising in my chest. *What do you mean, you can't do it?*

The truth is, once the day of the hearing comes around and Bruno's future is decided, all I'll be left with will be the thought that I had something to offer—something that may have helped him—and I was either unable or unwilling to hand it over.

The end of the week comes as a relief. It's not only the fact that this is a pay week, which means I'll be getting a check tonight, but I also can't wait to see Nick. I can't wait to spend a few hours next to him and come up with a plan for our second date this weekend.

Before heading out for my shift, I eat dinner early next to Ari and Nancy, as we do every Friday.

"Sol, could you use your employee discount to buy some towels at the store tonight?" Nancy asks halfway through the meal. "I'll give you the money, and all."

Ari looks up from her food. "We already have lots of towels."

"I know, but I want Ceci to have a fresh set for this weekend."

"Sure," I say, smiling at Nancy. "I'll get them."

I take the trolley up to San Diego right after we finish eating and head straight for the bath section as soon as I walk into the store. Nancy didn't specify which color she wanted, so I pick a set of light blue towels that's on discount. After paying for them, I head up to the fourth floor so I can stuff them in a locker and clock in before the start of my shift.

The stockroom has gone back to normal by now. Everyone who was sick earlier in the week has slowly but surely returned to work, and the place feels as lively as always tonight.

"Sol!" Lina says when I join the table. She may have been gone for barely a few days, but now she's standing between Kelly and Marcos, smiling brightly at me as if we hadn't seen each other in years.

"How are you feeling?" I ask.

"Good, good. Just happy to be back."

"What was the stockroom like without us?" Kelly asks.

I turn to meet Nick's eyes, only to find a suppressed smile on his face. As great as it is to have everyone back, it's hard to deny that the last few days were some of the best ones I've had since I started working here. With a near-empty stockroom and no one to distract us, Nick and I were able to forget about everyone and everything, and just focus on each other.

"It was miserable," he answers, which earns him sympathetic glances from Lina and Kelly.

"Well, we missed you guys as well!" Lina says, tilting her head to one side.

While she talks about all the shows she caught up on during her sick days, I keep waiting for the right time to turn toward Nick and ask about our plans for the weekend. But before I've had a chance to say anything, I hear my name being called from across the warehouse.

"María de la Soledad?"

I look up to find Helen, the woman from Human Resources, standing at the doorway. I only ever see her when she hands me my paychecks, except for the few times I've run into her on the elevator and we've been forced to make awkward small talk. I have no idea why she would come all the way down here looking for me.

"Yeah?"

"Can you come with me for a second?" she asks.

My first instinct is to think about my paycheck. Maybe she has questions about the hours I logged over the last couple of weeks. Or perhaps—I think hopefully—she's about to offer me a different job. With the holidays getting closer, maybe sales positions have opened up, and I might be able to get a job similar to Ari's, with convenient after-school shifts.

Whatever her reason for wanting to talk to me, Helen doesn't reveal even the slightest trace of emotion as I follow her out of the stockroom.

"Uh . . . any fun plans for the weekend?" I ask her while we ride the elevator up to the fourth floor, trying to break the dead silence between us.

"Not really," she says, pursing her lips. She doesn't offer anything else, doesn't ask me about my own weekend, and so I choose to drop it and wait out the elevator ride in silence.

Helen leads me through the same hallways we went down when I came in for my interview, and she stops in front of the open door of one of the small offices.

"After you," she says with a small nod.

I walk into the office, but I've only taken a couple of steps before I stop in my tracks. There is someone already in the room. Bill is standing in a corner with his arms crossed over his chest, looking more serious than I have ever seen him.

Any hope I had that this could be something good slips away immediately. My arms and legs feel numb as I sit down on one of the chairs in front of the desk and wait for Helen to take a seat across from me.

"María, I asked you here to talk about a delicate matter," she says.

My mind starts racing. I resist the urge to turn toward Bill. I wish I could look into his eyes, read his expression, and get a sense of what is about to happen, but I force myself to stay still.

Helen remains silent for only an instant, but it seems to go on forever, as I try to think of any reasons why I might be in trouble. Could they have discovered a lie I told during my interview? I can barely remember the questions Helen asked me, but maybe I wasn't a hundred percent truthful. Or maybe this is about the other day, when Nancy overslept and I made it to my shift a few minutes late—maybe they're about to give me a warning about clocking in on time from now on.

"When you first joined the team at Wallen's, you received training on the store's theft policy. Is that correct?"

Theft? I ask myself, even as I nod, vaguely remembering the pamphlets Helen gave me and a brief talk Nick and I had about the consequences of stealing from the store.

"Then you must be aware that we have a no-tolerance attitude toward stealing."

I have no idea where or how I find the strength in me to speak up, because my heart seems to be stuck in my throat. "But—but I haven't stolen anything," I say.

Helen turns to look over her shoulder, and Bill uncrosses his arms, taking a step forward.

"Soledad, do you remember working on a crate of dresses earlier this week?" he asks.

"I—I work on a lot of crates every day."

"The one I'm talking about came in on Monday. It was a new product shipment from Erdem." He pauses briefly to observe my reaction, but I remain motionless in my seat. "In fact... we have footage of you working on it."

I *think* I remember. This must've been one of the crates left over from the morning shipment—the ones I was rushing to finish because half the warehouse was out sick and Nick and I still needed to get through a lot of work before the end of my shift.

Helen leans forward over the desk. "The footage shows you working inside the stockroom, all by yourself."

"I was only alone for a few minutes," I say firmly.

"The thing, María, is that the dress we're talking about is worth over sixteen hundred dollars. It's listed on the shipment slips, but when a customer came by asking for it, it was nowhere to be found. We had no option but to look back and see what had happened."

Helen falls silent. I feel as though I'm under a spotlight, as though she and Bill are both looking at me carefully, searching for any signs that might give me away. I try my best to keep my face straight, even as my hands start sweating uncontrollably.

"I am not accusing you of stealing," Helen says. "I want to make that very clear. But we *are* investigating what happened, and part of that involves asking: Did you take that dress home with you on Monday evening?"

I'm speechless. The room around me seems too bright all of a sudden, because I can't even believe we're here, having this conversation. I can't believe this is happening, or that it will ultimately come down to my word against theirs, because there's no one else who can back me up.

I'm not sure how long it takes me to speak up, but finally, I clear my throat. "I didn't take anything."

Helen and Bill stare into each other's eyes. I can already tell they don't believe me, but there's no way to make them see the truth. I've never stolen anything in my life. I would never risk my job here, but there's not much I can do if they've already made up their minds.

Helen lets out a long sigh that fills the entire room. "I'm afraid we're going to have to put you under administrative leave—at least until we get a bit more clarity on this situation."

"Wh-what does that mean?" I ask.

"It means that, while we figure out what happened here, it would be best if you didn't come in for your scheduled shifts."

"So... am I fired?" I ask, my voice shaking.

"No," Helen says firmly. "You're still an employee at the store. That has not changed... *yet*."

"Will I still get paid?"

Helen purses her lips. "Unfortunately, no."

My stomach twists. I stop breathing. The room around me starts getting brighter again, and I start to feel like I'm spinning. It's lucky I'm sitting down, because I'm certain I would've crumbled on the spot if I had been standing.

"I have a few papers I need you to sign," Helen says. "Please wait here until I go get them, and I'll explain the next steps to you."

She gets up to leave, and I'm left alone in the room with Bill. I can't speak up, can't even turn toward him. I'm not sure if he's trying to meet my gaze, if there is something he wants to say to me, but I don't even care right now—not while the world around me is still spinning so fast that I feel like I'm going to pass out.

CHAPTER TWENTY-TWO

THERE ARE A FEW THINGS ABOUT TONIGHT THAT I don't remember.

I don't remember stepping out of the office. I think I cried at some point, but I can't be certain. Helen must've guided me out of there and walked me toward the exit of the store, because I don't think I would've been able to do those things on my own.

I don't remember what either of us said when we parted ways, or if we said anything at all. I barely even remember walking up to the MTS station, but I do know the air inside the trolley felt grim and silent, as if someone had died.

Even now, I'm not sure how I managed to get myself all the way down to Palomar Street and to Ari's house. All I know is that the sound of the front door banging shut behind me makes me jump, bringing me back into my body, into the real world.

"Who's there?" Nancy calls from within her bedroom.

A light comes on, and a second later she appears, wearing her pajamas.

"Oh, mija, I wasn't expecting you until much later," she says. "Did your shift end early?"

I remain still by the door, unable to move, unable to say anything. All I can think about is having to break the news to Papi that I've been put on leave—that I may not be able to bring paychecks home for a while. Even worse is the thought of having to explain *why* this is all happening. Tears form in my eyes when I think about the look on Abuela's face when she hears I've been accused of stealing, the disappointment there'll be in Diego's gaze.

"Sol," Nancy says. "Mija, what's wrong?"

In a quick movement, she comes to stand next to me and guides me toward the kitchen table. I sit down on a chair, and she sits down right next to me, holding on tight to both of my hands.

"Where's Ari?" is the first thing I ask.

"She's still out," Nancy says. In the back of my mind, I remember the plans Ari and all of them mentioned earlier today—they were going to see a movie, and then they were going to head to Camila's house.

"Tell me everything," Nancy says. When I meet her eyes, I see Ari in them. I see friendship, and kindness, and eagerness to help.

And so I tell her. I tell her about my shift at the store on Monday, and how I had to rush through some of the crates. I tell her that the security cameras show me working by myself inside the stockroom, and the fact that a dress has gone missing—a dress that costs more than three of my paychecks combined.

"They... they asked me if I took it," I say, trying my hardest to keep my voice steady even though my chest is heaving. "They think I stole it."

"Then they must not know you," Nancy says softly. "But I do—I know you, mija, and I know you would've never done that."

I nod to myself, trying to slow down my breathing. This still doesn't feel real. I can't help but wonder if it's nothing but a strange nightmare I dreamed up, because I'm only just beginning to understand everything that this means—that there'll be no more shifts at Wallen's with Nick, no more commuting to and from San Diego, no more money to bring to my family.

"Did they fire you?" Nancy asks me after a moment of silence.

"No," I say. "Not yet. But... I just know they're not gonna let me come back. I'm gonna have to find a new job, and... and my family—they're gonna have to—"

"Slow down," Nancy says. "Do you have any idea what really happened? Can you think of where that dress might've ended up?"

"No," I say. "Nothing like this has ever happened—even

when I put the clothes on the wrong racks by accident, they always ended up where they needed to be. I've never gotten in trouble."

I think about Nick. I think about the fact that he must've been waiting for me to come back down to the stockroom, but I never did. A sharp pain comes to my stomach when I think that he'll have to hear from Bill later on that I've been accused of stealing, and that I won't be coming to work anymore.

"I need to go home." The realization hits me harshly, suddenly. It's almost as if a bucket of cold water has been dropped on top of me, because no matter how much I've wanted to fool myself into believing that this is my home, that I'm a sister to Ari, and a daughter to Nancy, none of those things is true.

I'm only here because of my job at Wallen's, because I need somewhere to sleep so I can make it into my early and late shifts. But now, without my job at the store, I don't think there's any room for me in this house. There's no place for me in this family, no reason for me to be here any longer.

"You can leave in the morning," Nancy says. "Why don't you try to get some sleep?"

With a sideways glance at the time on the microwave, I see it's not even nine yet. I might be able to get back to Tijuana before the streets start to feel unsafe.

"No, I—I should really try to get back."

Nancy frowns for a long moment, but she doesn't try to stop me. Slowly, I get to my feet and stumble my way into Ceci's bedroom so I can start packing.

I yank open the closet door to grab the duffel bag I brought with me all those weeks ago. I throw it over the bed and start taking clothes off their hangers, telling myself I should take everything. I don't think I'll have any reason to come back next week.

While I pack, tears fall from my eyes, but I force myself to sob quietly. I don't want Nancy to hear me crying.

Once I'm done, I wipe my tears and walk out of the room carrying my duffel bag over one shoulder and my school backpack over the other. Nancy is still sitting in the kitchen, her back straight and her eyes wide, exactly as she was when I left her.

I stand awkwardly in front of her for a second, not knowing what to say.

"Thank you, Nancy—for everything. I—"

"You don't have to thank me," Nancy replies, getting up from her chair. "You're always welcome here. And you'll be back soon. I know you will be."

I press my lips together, trying to stop myself from crying. Perhaps she's right—I'll have to come back sooner rather than later. I'll need to find a new job, and keep making money to help my family, but I have no idea when that will be—or what life will look like by the time that happens.

In a sudden movement, Nancy takes a step closer to me. "I'll drive you, mija."

"I can take the trolley. It's fine."

"No," she says. "Come on."

Without another word, Nancy turns toward the door, and I follow her. I don't have the energy to argue right now, or to refuse her help, so I hop in the car with her and sit quietly in the passenger seat while we make our way through the near-empty streets of her neighborhood.

The traffic on the highway going to San Ysidro can be pretty bad on Fridays, but today it moves at a decent pace. It takes us less than thirty minutes to get there, and Nancy brings me as far as she can—all the way to a sign that says TO MEXICO, which has an arrow that points toward the entrance of the tunnel.

"Thank you again, Nancy."

"You're welcome, mija," she says to me. "Say hi to your family for me."

"I will."

I reach for the door handle. I'm about to pull it when I remember something.

"The towels," I say, and all of a sudden, I can't hold it in. The tears I've been trying to hide from Nancy come pouring from my eyes, and there's nothing I can do to stop them.

"I forgot the towels," I sob. "I—I bought them, but I put them inside a locker in the staff room, and ... and I didn't remember to grab them before leaving the store."

"That doesn't matter," Nancy says, reaching for one of my hands and squeezing it. "Ari will get them on Monday. Don't worry about that, mija."

"But—but Ceci," I say. "She won't have fresh towels, like you wanted her to."

"It doesn't matter."

She pulls me in for a hug, and I allow myself to fall into her arms.

"It's okay, mija," she whispers as she touches the back of my hair with one hand. "It'll all be okay."

I have no idea how long we remain there, parked along the sidewalk right in front of the entrance of the tunnel to Mexico. I just keep crying into Nancy's shoulders, and she keeps her arms wrapped around me, waiting patiently for my eyes to run dry.

The sky is an inky shade of black tonight. As I walk toward the entrance of the tunnel, there is no sign of the moon. I'm pretty sure it was shining when we left the house earlier, but its soft glow has now all but disappeared.

I don't think I've ever crossed the border on my own this late. Mami and Papi would've never allowed it. The tunnel feels empty and bleak, and when I reach the border agent's desk, I'm one of the few people waiting in line.

"¿Todo bien?" the officer says to me.

He's asking if I'm okay. There must be something about the late hour, or about my red, swollen eyes, that's making him curious. He stares at me fixedly, reading my expression as if I were a book.

"Sí," I answer. "Todo bien."

I let out a long sigh when I step out into the night air and start making my way down the ramp. There are bright lights illuminating my path, but as soon as I get off the ramp, I feel as though I've been submerged in darkness. I look around the esplanade, feeling cold and lonely all of a sudden. Without the street vendors and the taxi drivers, this place looks a lot different, and it doesn't help that the moon has still not reappeared from behind the cloudy skies.

I take a few steps forward, my heart beating fast as I step deeper and deeper into the shadows, but then I hear the sound of a car engine starting, and two headlights come to life, breaking through the darkness.

For a moment, I'm scared to come closer. The model of the car and the identity of the driver are hidden behind the stark brightness of the headlights, but then, when the passenger door swings open, my heartbeat slows down a bit.

"Get in, mija."

I half-run toward the car and quickly shut the door behind me.

"Hola, Papi."

He locks the doors quickly and then turns to stare at me, making me feel as though I'm about to be interrogated.

"What's going on?" he asks.

"I, uh..." I answer in a small voice. I clear my throat and try again. "I'll explain when we get home."

He nods once before putting the car into gear, and I relax my shoulders. I wasn't brave enough to tell him about everything that happened over the phone, so I just asked him to pick me up at the border. I'll have to tell him the truth soon, and I am terrified of what will happen when I do, but for right now, I'm at least grateful that he isn't asking any more questions.

I rest my head against my seat, feeling a battle inside me that is unlike anything I've ever felt before—sadness because I wish I could've stayed with Nancy a little while longer, but peace because Papi is beside me. Terror at the thought of telling him that I've been put on leave, but hope at the thought of giving him my latest paycheck, which Helen handed to me before I left the store. Helplessness because my time in California was cut short so suddenly, but deep relief because I'm finally home.

We find Abuela waiting in the living room. She's wearing her nightgown, and her face looks glossy, which tells me she has already applied her night creams. There is a rosary in her hands and a lit candle with a picture of a saint on the center table. She must've been praying.

"Sol," she says, getting up as soon as she sees me. "What happened?"

I struggle to speak up. I try hard to find the words to explain to her what's going on, but in the end I let out my breath in a long exhale and step forward to hug her.

"Mija," she says, wrapping her arms around me, and that's when I realize this is exactly what I needed—a hug from Abuela. For a second, it all goes away—the sadness, the anger, the disappointment. I just wish she didn't have to let go of me. I wish she could make all of this go away for good.

"What happened?" she asks again, leaving her hands on my shoulders as she stares into my eyes.

The door clicks shut somewhere behind us. Papi has walked into the house, and I am very aware that he can hear what I am about to say.

"I... I think I'm gonna get fired."

"*What?*"

I lower myself onto the couch. Abuela does the same, but Papi remains standing, his hands firmly on his waist.

"Sol, what are you talking about?" he demands.

Abuela gestures at him to sit down, and so he does. With the two of them staring at me, I feel more ashamed than I've ever felt in my life.

I explain everything to them—how there's an expensive dress missing, how Helen thinks I may have taken it. I tell them that they won't be paying me until they figure out what happened, and that they might not allow me to come back to work at all.

"Ay, Dios mío," Abuela sighs as soon as I'm done talking.

Papi leans forward, his elbows resting on his knees, and his hands over his mouth.

"Is it true?" he asks me. "Did you steal that dress?"

"*Armando!*" Abuela hisses at him, but the damage is done.

A sharp pain hits me in the chest—pain because it has really come to this. Because our situation has become so desperate that Papi has to wonder if I'd be capable of this, because he's acting as if he doesn't even know me. And maybe it's true that he doesn't. Maybe after all these weeks of being apart, he's no longer sure who I am, and maybe I'm no longer sure who he is, either. The man he used to be when I was younger would've never assumed the worst of me, would've never asked me this question.

"No," I say, my voice barely there. I'm all too aware that Diego is sleeping just down the hallway, so I try my best to speak softly. "But it doesn't really matter to them. They gave me my check for the last two weeks, and they said they'll call when they have news."

"So—so they did give you the money they owed you," Papi says, looking more awake all of a sudden.

I nod, fishing the check out of my pocket. I offer it to him, but he doesn't take it, so I just lay it neatly over the coffee table.

"What do we do now?" I ask.

Both of them look away from me. I should know already that they don't have the answer to that. Because without the money from my job at the store, we're left without options. There's nothing to do, no other way to pay the bills. We may have this last check, and Papi might manage to make it last a while, but once this money is gone, all we'll have left is the money he's making from whatever jobs he's able to find, and what Luis brings in from the casino.

In the end, I'm the one who speaks up. "I'll find another job."

Papi and Abuela don't move. I'm not sure they even heard me. I never imagined this was possible—that both of them could ever be left speechless, but that's exactly what happens. The light of the candle flickers, making their expressions look bright one second and shadowy the next. The seconds pass, and still, neither of them can find the right words to say.

"I'll start looking tomorrow. Something will come up." Even as I say it, I think about how long it took me to find a job the first time around. This time, I don't imagine it'll be any easier—especially if I can't get a good reference from the managers at Wallen's. Even if it only takes a few weeks to find something new, by the time anything turns up, it might be too late. We'll be forced to spend the next several weeks with no gasoline for the car, no way to pay back Papi's debts. At least Luis's paycheck will prevent us from starving, I tell myself—it'll allow us to keep putting food in the pantry, even if it's just rice and tortillas.

I have no idea how long we sit here. I wish I could say something else—that I could promise them I'll find a way, and that it'll all be okay in the end. Even more so, I wish they could make the same promises to me. I wish they would wrap their arms around me and tell me they're proud of me, that they know I'm trying my best, and that we will all fig- ure out a way to dig ourselves out of this mess together. I wish they would remember that I'm not the only one who's responsible for feeding the family, and that I'm not the adult here, but it's probably too late for that.

CHAPTER TWENTY-THREE

At night, I see Mami in my dreams. She doesn't really say or do anything. She's just *there*. The first time I dream of her, on Friday, she looks as she did in her final months—her hair gone, her face sunken, her eyes filled with pain. But there's still something about her presence that brings warmth to my heart, that makes me feel less alone, so that when I open my eyes in the morning, all I want is to go right back to sleep, just so I can be with her for a little while longer.

On Saturday night, she reappears, only this time she looks different. She's the person she used to be when I was little—the woman with long, wavy brown hair, and full lips, and a sparkle in her eyes. She's wearing one of her Sunday dresses—a flowery piece that she used to wear to Mass—and she's smiling at me.

"Where were you?" I ask her. "We've been looking for you."

She stares at me, her expression unchanging.

"Mami, where were you?" I ask again, and she frowns slightly. That's when I realize she can't hear me. She must be able to see my lips moving, must be able to tell that I'm trying to ask her a question, but she can't make out what I'm saying, no matter how many times I repeat the question.

I reach for her, but there's a barrier between us—a glass wall, which I press my hands against, wanting desperately to take her hand.

"Mami!" I yell, realizing she's trapped on the other side of the glass. Or maybe I'm the one who's trapped. Either way, we need to find a way to break it. "Mami, don't worry. I'll get us out of here."

I turn around, hoping to find a hammer, or a rock, or anything to shatter the glass with, but there's only emptiness behind me—stark, white emptiness, which stretches for as far as my eyes can see.

I wake up feeling strangely cold. I pull the blankets closer to me, staring up at the ceiling in my bedroom, trying hard to hold on to the image of Mami in her Sunday dress, but the emptiness wins. I feel it creeping in, settling inside my chest, sneaking into every single one of my fingers and toes.

"You look pale," Abuela says to me during breakfast. There are no eggs this morning, no coffee. Instead, there's some dry cereal and an apple for each of us, which we eat eagerly. "You should spend some time outside, get some sun."

I look up from my bowl of cereal to find Luis staring right at me. His hair is as messy as it always looks in the morning, but his eyes are alert, staring at me unblinkingly. I can tell exactly what he's thinking—that there's no time to waste. I need to start looking for new jobs right away, start coming up with ways to make up for the income we've just lost.

As much as I wish I could do all that, I can't seem to find the energy for it. My entire body feels weak and heavy, and so, after breakfast, I decide to listen to Abuela's advice and set up a chair out in the backyard, hoping that the fresh air will help breathe some life into me.

I sit facing the sun, folding my hands on top of my lap and trying my best to feel the warmth of the sunlight, but I just can't find a way to relax.

The only thing I see when I close my eyes is Mami's face. And this time, I can hear her voice clearly, telling me to get up, and go out, and do something. She's telling me not to give up, not to lose hope—to figure out a way to fix our family.

I just can't do any of the things she's telling me to do. I can't do anything except sit here, frozen in my chair, while a deep, dark feeling of restlessness swirls around inside my chest.

I spend the rest of the day in front of our family computer—a clunky old thing that makes whirring sounds for no reason and always finds a way to freeze at the wrong moment.

I'm scrolling through job search websites, applying to every single opening I can find between San Ysidro and San Diego, when my phone starts buzzing, and I lift it up to see Nick's name on the screen.

My first instinct is to just let it ring. Texts have come nonstop—texts from him and Ari, wanting to know what happened and how I'm doing, asking if there's anything they can do. I just haven't found the will to respond to them. I haven't found a way to put my feelings into words, or to explain that there's no point in dwelling on what happened at Wallen's—not when there are much more urgent things that I need to worry about.

Before I can make up my mind about answering, the phone stops ringing, and so I turn my attention back to the computer screen. When it starts ringing again a few seconds later, though, I can't bring myself to ignore it.

"Hello?" I answer.

"Sol?"

"Nick?" Just saying his name makes my heart hurt, because this wasn't the way our weekend was supposed to go. We weren't supposed to be in different cities, in different countries. We were supposed to be at the beach, or going to the movies, or maybe even back at that spot in the woods, surrounded by soft starlight.

"I've been so worried about you," he says. "From the

moment I realized you weren't coming back down after talking to Helen. And then I asked Bill what happened, and he told me about the dress."

"Yeah," I say, my voice barely there.

"Sol, I talked to them—to Helen and Bill. I told them there was no way you could've—"

"Nick, I—"

"—and everyone else is saying it, too. Lina, Kelly, Marcos, and even other people in the warehouse—they're all on your side, and we're trying to—"

"I should focus on the future," I say, and he goes quiet immediately. "I need to start thinking about finding a new job."

"I get that," he replies. "But Sol… we could still make this right. We need to find a way to get you to come back."

I remain quiet, because I'm not sure what to feel. A part of me is grateful that Nick is trying his best, grateful that the people in the stockroom are speaking up for me, but I'm also tired of thinking about it—about the unfairness, about the look on Helen's face when she said she was gonna put me on leave. I'm tired of being mad at her and Bill for the way they treated me, even after all the hard work I put in from the day I first started.

I swallow through a knot in my throat. "I really wanted us to go on that second date this weekend."

"We will," he says. "We'll go on a second date, and a third, and a fourth, if you want to. Just focus on what matters right now—and I will, too. I'll keep trying to fig-ure out what happened to that dress."

"Thank you, Nick. You're so—"

"I'm here for you," he says. "Don't forget that, okay?"

"I won't," I reply, trying my hardest to hold on to him—to the thought of seeing him again, to our long con-versations at work, to the memory of our first kiss. And despite the fact that I already feel as though it all hap-pened in another lifetime—as though he and I now live in different worlds—there's still something about the sound of his breathing coming through the phone that brings a ray of light to my chest, even when the rest of the world feels darker than ever.

I wake up to the sound of my alarm on Monday morning after another full night of dreaming about Mami. Instead of rolling over to get a few more minutes of sleep the way I usually would, I throw the covers off and get up imme-diately, eager to escape from the uneasiness of my dreams.

Breakfast with Papi feels weird. I take slow spoonfuls of cereal, washing them down with chamomile tea, while Papi sits very still in his chair, looking out the window at the lime tree in our backyard.

As soon as I get to school, I start looking for Ari. I'd never really thought about how difficult she can be to find in a crowd, but I suppose it's true that she's shorter than most people, so she's not precisely hard to miss. There's also her blunt, shoulder-length haircut, which seems to be more common than I had ever realized. Every time I spot a girl with dark hair that looks like hers, my heart leaps for an instant, until I realize it is someone else and not Ari.

She sees me before I see her. I barely have a second to register that she's standing in front of me when she closes the distance between us and wraps her arms around me.

"I'm sorry I wasn't there for you on Friday," she whispers into my ear. "You should've called me. I would've come straight home if you'd told me about what happened."

"Your mom was there. That was more than enough," I whisper back. "And I'm sorry, too. I'm sorry I didn't reply to your messages. I've been so—"

"It's okay. I get it," she says. Somehow, it's as if she's able to understand everything that happened this weekend—the conversation I had with Papi and Abuela when I got home on Friday, and my dreams about Mami, and the fact that dinners with my family were much more silent than usual.

"How was Ceci's visit?" I ask as we start moving down the hallway.

"It was pretty good. She showed up with blond hair, and my mom was pissed. She kept saying that Ceci should've come to her before dyeing it, but I tried to stay out of it."

"And dinner in Little Italy?" I ask.

"Best pizza I've had in my life. But I kept thinking about how you were supposed to be there, and how the four of us should've had a fun weekend."

It hurts my heart to see the sadness in Ari's eyes, to

hear the honesty in her voice. I want to find the words to tell her how badly I wish I could've been there, how much I thought about her over the last couple of days, how grateful I was to know that she was there for me, even if I couldn't find the strength to write back to her messages.

"I'm gonna miss having you around at home," she says before I can say any of that. "The more I think about what happened at the store, and that dress, and all... I mean, it's so ridiculous. We should fight it. We should go speak with Helen, and tell her that—"

"Nick's already done that. I don't think it'll work."

"But they can't do this to you. They can't—"

"Ari, it's okay."

"But it's not," she says. "I just... I wish things would stay the same. My mom and I like it when you're there with us."

Something inside me melts. My heart feels less heavy, my shoulders a lot looser. Without warning, I pull her in for a hug and sink my face into her shoulder. Her arms remain stiff by her sides for a second, but then she hugs me back with all her strength, and nothing seems to matter—not that we're standing right in the middle of the hallway, not the fact that we're blocking the entrance to the cafeteria.

"I'll come back," I say. "As soon as I find another job, I'll come back."

I pull away from her and stare into her eyes. There's doubt written all over her face, as though she's not quite certain I'm telling the truth, but she must not realize what

I know—that I *need* to find another job. That staying in Tijuana is not an option.

"Come on," she says suddenly. "Let's go get lunch."

"I should really go to the library. Talk to you later, though?"

"Of course," she answers. "Talk later."

She turns around to go into the cafeteria, but I can't resist the urge to call after her.

"Ari?" I say, and she turns back around to face me. "Thank you for being there for me."

"Always."

She smiles at me, and I smile back. We stare into each other's eyes for a second, until we realize we can't stand here any longer. She makes her way into the cafeteria, and I start walking down the hallway toward the library.

While I sit down in front of a computer, I don't think about all the homework I need to catch up on, or about the stress of continuing my job search. All I can really think about is what Ari said: *My mom and I like it when you're there with us.*

Perhaps it's been true all along—maybe we really are a family, in our own little way. Because things may change—I may live at Ari's house one day and go back home the next. And she and I may grow older, or make new friends, or grow apart, but we'll always find a way back to each other. Just as sisters do.

CHAPTER TWENTY-FOUR

For the next few days, I spend lunch period in the school library. It's nothing but a small room with a few shelves lined against the walls and four old computers set up side by side along a big desk, but at least it's quiet, which is all I've been wishing for lately. Today, the only other people in here are two freshman girls, both of whom are busy looking at their phones even though they have books spread open on the table in front of them.

I sit down in front of one of the computers, take out my lunch—a plastic bag with some cereal that I packed last night—and I start eating slowly, trying not to be too loud even though there's hardly any risk of anyone complaining.

While I start going through job listings, my mind is

filled with images from dinner last night—Diego complaining about eating rice again, Papi snapping at him, saying that rice is all there is, and Abuela trying her best to keep the peace by saying she'd make quesadillas the following evening to switch things up a bit.

There was also Luis's chair, which I couldn't stop looking at, even though it was empty—empty because he was still out at the casino, because he was out there trying to make money, because he's the only one in the family who's working right now.

Every time I send a new job application, a wave of emotions takes over my chest. Hope, as I tell myself that maybe this could be the one—that I could get an offer to work as a waitress at Chili's, or a sales associate at the H&M in the Las Americas Outlets, or as a stockroom associate at Walmart. But then, a second later, I start to feel afraid, because of the decisions I'll have to make once a job offer does come.

It's becoming more and more obvious to me that Luis was right. We can't keep living like this. And the only way to get out of this situation will be to ask for full-time hours once I get a job offer, even if it means dropping out of Orangeville, and postponing college, and thinking of new dreams for myself that don't involve becoming an engineer.

My phone pings suddenly. A part of me is hoping to find a message from a recruiter—maybe a request for an interview, or something. I would even be grateful for a rejection, because the lack of news has been getting on my nerves, but instead, there's a message from Nick.

I miss you.

My heart swells, beating fast against my chest. Typing as fast as I can, I write back: **Miss you, too.**

Any luck with the job search?

Not yet, I write back. **But I'll let you know as soon as something happens.**

By the time I head to trigonometry at the end of lunch hour, I've submitted over a dozen job applications, which at least makes me feel like I've accomplished something.

I try my best to pay attention in class, but it's becoming harder and harder. I've never found it this difficult to keep myself motivated, not even in the months after Mami died, not even during my first weeks of work at Wallen's, when I was so exhausted I could barely stay awake. Back then, I at least had something to work toward—the idea of getting my high school degree and getting into college. Now, there's none of that. Nothing but a clock that seems to be ticking in the back of my mind, reminding me that the time is fast approaching when I'll need to drop out of school.

The instant the bell rings at the end of class, I reach for my bag to start packing up my books. I'm following a group of kids toward the classroom door, when Miss Acevedo clears her throat.

"Sol?" she says. "Could you stick around for a few minutes?"

I freeze on the spot, my mind racing. I wait by her desk until the classroom starts to empty, and then she turns toward me with a deep frown on her face.

"Sol, here's the thing," she says, removing her glasses. "You scored a forty-seven on last week's quiz."

"Oh."

"I've noticed you've been distracted lately," she says. "How is everything at home?"

"Everything's, uh… okay," I answer under my breath.

Miss Acevedo purses her lips, nodding slowly. "I just want to make sure we get you the help you need. Your grades have been dropping steadily since the start of the school year, so… maybe there's something we could do to change that."

I know she means well, but this isn't what I need right now. I don't need the added weight of Miss Acevedo's expectations on my shoulders. All I want is to be done with this conversation and go on with my day.

"Would after-school tutoring work?" she asks me.

"I don't think I'd have the time for it."

"You *need* to make time," she says. "You've always been such a good student, Sol. I wouldn't want to have to fail you at the end of the school year."

There's something about that word: *fail*. Something that makes my head spin, my hands feel numb. It's suddenly hard to understand why I'm here, or how I ended up in this situation, when I've always worked so hard, when I've always put school before everything else.

"Okay," I say. "I… I'm sure we'll figure something out. For tutoring, and all."

My ears start buzzing, so I don't even hear Miss Acevedo's response. Whatever she's saying right now doesn't matter, because it's all hitting me suddenly—the fact that it'll all be for nothing. After two years of crossing the border, of turning in assignments on time, of studying and keeping my grades up, I'm about to lose everything.

Over the past couple of days, I've been trying to prepare myself for the idea of dropping out of Orangeville and starting to work full time. I thought I knew what it all meant, but the truth is this isn't what I want—not even close.

I want to do better at school. I want to keep my grades up, and get a good GPA, and do well on the SATs, and get into San Diego State. I want to become an engineer, so that when younger girls hear about me—a girl from Tijuana who became someone—they'll find it a little easier to believe that they can achieve their own dreams.

I walk out of the classroom. The hallway is loud and busy as people make their way from one class to the next, but I move slowly, staying close to the walls in case I need to hold on to them for support. My chest starts to feel tight, and I find myself trying to remember what I'm supposed to be doing. Is it lunchtime yet? What's next period? Do I have another class to get to?

The noise of the hallway gradually becomes more muted, my mind clearer. That's when I realize I need to head to bio. But while I sit in class, I can't find a way to focus, no matter how badly I wish I could. I keep thinking about Mami, and how she never got to finish high school herself. Mami, and how she always put her hopes and dreams on me and my brothers, because we were meant to do all the things she was unable to do. Mami, and all the ways I'm letting her down by giving up on the future she wanted me to have.

※

"You should go to sleep early," Abuela says to me while we do the dishes after dinner that night.

"Why?"

She throws me a knowing glance from above her glasses. "Do you really need a reason?"

Dinner was different tonight. Luis has been making friends with the kitchen staff at the casino, so he was able to bring back chicken fingers and fries that he got for free. None of it was very fresh, so we had to heat it up in the oven, but there was enough food for all of us, which made the air around the dinner table feel almost joyful while we ate.

Now that it's just me and Abuela standing in the kitchen, however, there's something solemn in the air between us. It's almost as if she can feel my exhaustion, feel the weight I've been carrying on my shoulders all week.

"You need to put yourself first, mija," she says. "You deserve to take some time to rest."

I look down at the dish I've been rinsing. It's completely clean already, but I can't seem to find a way to lift it up and put it on the rack.

"One of my teachers said something to me after class today," I say after a moment.

"Something nice, I hope."

I shake my head. "She said I need to try harder to keep my grades up."

Abuela stares at me fixedly for a moment, while we both breathe in the stillness of the kitchen around us.

"I just don't think I can do it anymore."

"You have to, mija."

"I *want* to, but... what's the point, really?"

"The point is that you're strong," Abuela replies. "And you've managed to do it this whole time. For over two years, you've managed to wake up early, and get yourself to school, and keep your grades intact. I know things have been hard lately, mija, but you have the strength to do all of it. I know you do."

"That's the thing, Abuela," I say, reaching for the knob to turn off the water. "I'm not sure those things matter anymore."

"What do you mean?"

"Luis said it to me the other day—we need more money, as soon as possible. And if I started working full time, I could make around two thousand dollars a month. That would be like forty thousand pesos. We could pay back Papi's debts, and the bills, and put real food in the fridge for a change. It could—"

Abuela puts the sponge down. There are still several

dirty dishes waiting by the sink, but she wipes her hands on a towel and turns around to open one of the cupboards.

"What are you doing?" I ask.

"I'm making us a cup of tea."

"Why?"

"Because you look like you need one."

I'm not sure exactly what she means, but I don't argue. When I offer to help with the tea, she refuses, telling me to go sit at the kitchen table instead. And so I do—I sit in my usual chair, watching as Abuela moves around the kitchen, fills a pot with water, and sets it over the stove.

"Here you go," she says as she places two cups on the table and lowers herself to sit down next to me.

"I don't get it," I say, not reaching for my cup. "Shouldn't we finish the dishes first?"

"Don't worry about that," Abuela says. "You already have too much on your mind, and it's not doing you any good."

"It's not like I can do anything about it," I say. "I mean . . . it's always gonna be up to me, isn't it? I've known it all along—that I'm gonna have to take care of you and Papi when you're older, and that I'm gonna have to help pay for Diego's college when the time comes. But . . . it was also up to me to save the restaurant, and I couldn't do it. And now it's up to me to find a way to make enough money so we can get our old lives back, and if I can't, then . . . where does that leave us?"

"Mi amor," Abuela says. I know she's trying to think of

something to say that will make me feel better, but that's not what I need right now. What I need is to talk about the truth.

"No matter how many posters he puts up around the city, Papi isn't getting any closer to making enough money," I say. "And neither is Luis. So, unless a miracle happens, I'll always have to be the one to save our family."

Abuela reaches for her tea, takes a long sip, and sets her cup down. I'm waiting for her say something, but she doesn't, so after a while, I stop waiting. I allow a peaceful silence to settle between us, and once I'm certain my tea won't be hot enough to burn my mouth, I reach for it and take a sip.

"You're not completely wrong," Abuela says as I lower my cup. "You will be the one to save this family. But not in the ways that you think."

I watch her intently, waiting for her to explain what she means.

"You'll be the first person in our family to go to college, Sol," Abuela says. "Think of your parents, of me and your Abuelo, of all the people who came before us. None of us has done the things that you will do. Vas a ser enorme, mija. And you will prove to us—to your brothers, especially—that this family can do extraordinary things."

Before any of this happened—before the restaurant started struggling and our family fell apart—I was so certain of all this. I always believed that I was going to go far—just as Ellen Ochoa had done, and maybe even further than her. But now, as I sit here with my entire body heavy from exhaustion and my mind foggy with stress, I can't bring myself to dream the way I once did. I can't imagine the future I once felt was within my reach.

"It's too late," I say. "College, and everything you just said... it's impossible now."

"The thing is, Sol," Abuela says, "you're already doing impossible things. And look at you—you're still here, still fighting, and you won't stop."

"I want to," I say. "I want to keep fighting, but I don't know if I can."

"You will," Abuela replies, and there's no doubt in her voice. "I know you will, because things have not been easy, mija, but you haven't given up. And if you feel over-whelmed, and tired, and like you can't keep going much longer, that's because you've already *done* so much. If doing the impossible was easy, anyone would do it, but you're not anyone. You are María de la Soledad Martínez, and you will continue to do impossible things.

"I know that you're scared of the future now. But wasn't it scary to start going to school on the other side of the border? Or looking for a job? Or moving away from home?"

"But—"

"The money you've brought back over the last cou-ple of months has made a big difference to all of us," she says. "There's no way to deny that, mija. But maybe we've lost sight of things a bit. It shouldn't be up to you to fix things—or not *only* up to you to, I should say. We all need to do our part, and for you, that means focusing on school, and college applications, and yes—maybe a part-time job."

"But Papi said it wasn't enough. When he decided to close down the restaurant, he said that—"

"Then he will find a way to do his own part better," she says. "And so will Luis. But none of this means you should be giving up on your dreams, Sol. In fact… I don't think it's ever been more important for you to hold on to them."

For all this talk about strength, and going far, and holding on to my dreams, I feel incredibly weak all of a sudden. I can't even seem to be able to finish my tea, or get myself out of this chair.

And so I let Abuela help me. I let her pull me up from the chair, and guide me down the hallway, and lower me onto my bed. She helps me out of my clothes and into my pajamas. She undoes my braid and runs a brush through my hair, humming while she does.

Deep down, I wish I could return to a time when I could just let someone else carry all this weight for me. I wish I could be a child again, and not have to worry about anything. But while I sit here with Abuela brushing my hair, I hear her voice inside my mind, repeating the same words over and over again: *You're already doing impossible things… and you will continue to do impossible things.*

CHAPTER TWENTY-FIVE

THE AIR IS CHILLY AS I WALK ACROSS THE ESPLANADE on Monday morning—or chilly for Tijuana standards, at least. There are people wearing coats and scarves all around me, which makes me wonder if I should've brought a thicker sweater.

I'm watching the rising sun through the metal grating walls of the tunnel, hugging myself to keep warm as I move slowly with the line, when I realize that Bruno is just a few people ahead of me.

I leave my spot and walk up to him. The instant I touch his shoulder, he turns around, looking alarmed.

"Oh, Sol," he says. "Where did you come from?"

"I was just back there," I say. "How's it going?"

I should know better than to ask that question by now. Bruno lets out a long sigh, not looking directly at me.

"I'm just... you know."

I nod quickly. "I know."

We fall silent. It's hard to believe now that we used to stand here in line every day chatting about anything and everything that crossed our minds. I wish we could go back to that—back to the mornings when our biggest concern was making it to school on time, when we didn't have to worry about disciplinary hearings, or searching for jobs, or paychecks. I wish we could go back to being two kids from Tijuana who crossed the border every day to go to school, and nothing more.

"I signed the petition," I say, breaking the heavy silence that has fallen between us.

Bruno glances into my eyes briefly. "Thanks."

"Is it true that there's a different petition going around with the parents?"

He meets my eyes again, pressing his lips together. And then, he nods.

"They're gonna win," he says. "I already know."

"Maybe they won't. Maybe we can still find a way to—"

"Jack's parents have the school board in their pocket. They've been putting so much pressure, and... there's nothing I can do about it. I kinda just want it to be over already so I can move on with my life."

"What will you do?" I ask as the line moves and we take a few steps forward. "If they..."

"I'll probably have to skip the rest of the school year."

His words hit me straight in the heart, because this is

exactly what I was considering up until a couple of days ago. I can feel the same type of dread he's feeling right now—the regret, the fear that all these years of working hard for his education will have been for nothing.

He shrugs. "No other school is gonna take me right now—especially not with... you know, my *track record*."

Anger rises in my chest—anger at Jack, who will carry on after this as if nothing happened. Anger at his parents, who are taking this much further than they should. Anger at the principal, who's put Jack's version of the story above Bruno's, and at everyone who has signed that stupid petition to kick Bruno out of school.

"I'll probably find a job—same as you, so I can help my parents out for a bit," Bruno says. "And then I'll sign up for school in Tijuana—someplace where they have no way to find out about what happened at Orangeville."

The anger keeps getting hotter and hotter—especially when I realize I'm angry at myself, too. I'm angry at the fact that I turned down Irwin when he asked me if I could speak up for Bruno at the hearing.

I want to apologize to him. I want to tell Bruno all the reasons why I simply can't put myself in the spotlight, but I can't bring myself to say any of that.

"Bruno, I—"

"I wanna hear about you," he says. "Tell me what's new."

I can see the exhaustion on his face, the dark circles under his eyes. I can't imagine anyone has wanted to talk to him about much other than the disciplinary hearing lately, and he must be desperate to talk about something else.

"I'm looking for a new job," I reply. I tell him about the type of job that I'm searching for—something entry-level, near the border, with good hours, which sounds more and more impossible to find with every word I say.

While we move slowly with the line, though, I start to realize it—how it's not too late yet for me to help him, for me to speak up about what really happened on the day he got into a fight with Jack.

"I'm sorry, Bruno," I say suddenly, once we're getting close to the room with shiny floors where border agents are waiting to check our passports.

He turns toward me, frowning. "What are you—"

"When your friend Irwin asked me if I was willing to speak in front of the school board, I told him that I couldn't, but I was just scared. I'll do it, though. I'll be there, if you still want me to."

His expression shifts. His frown disappears, his eyes widen, and the corner of his mouth twists into something that could almost pass for a smile.

"Do you mean that?"

"I do. The hearing's this Friday, isn't it?"

"Yeah," he answers. "But, Sol, I'm not sure if the board will let you be in the room, or if they'll even be willing to listen to—"

"We need to try. Maybe... maybe there's someone we

can talk to. We can ask if they'll let me be there, and I'll tell them all the truth about what happened that day in the cafeteria."

Bruno lets out a long sigh, turning to face the front of the line. I can tell that he's trying not to get his hopes up, but that he also can't help but think about what a difference this could make. If the school board was just willing to listen to our side of the story, then maybe not everything will be lost. Maybe there'll still be a way for him to remain at Orangeville.

For the last few minutes of waiting in line, neither of us says much. But right before we step up to talk to the border agents and we're forced to go our separate ways, he turns to me and nods once.

"Thank you, Sol. For being willing to help."

I can't find any words to say back to him, because the truth is that I should've done this much sooner. I should've been brave enough to agree when Irwin first asked me. I should've been there for Bruno from the start.

⁂

Over the next couple of days, all I can hear inside my mind while I walk through the hallways at school is Ari's voice saying, *No one's looking at you, Sol!*

No matter where I go, or which way I turn, I can't help but feel as though there's a pair of eyes staring right back at me. At first, I'm convinced that it's all in my mind, that I'm having flashbacks of what it used to feel like to walk into the cafeteria. But then, by the time Wednesday rolls around, it becomes harder to fool myself into believing that this isn't real.

No one's looking at you, Sol! I try to tell myself as I make my way to the cafeteria. Except that they are—everyone *is* staring.

In the gazes that surround me, there's curiosity, and wonder, and anticipation. People seem to be waiting for me to *say* or *do* something, but I don't. I just keep putting one foot in front of the other, carrying my heavy backpack over my shoulders.

"Everyone's talking about you, Sol," Ari says to me once I'm sitting beside her.

Olivia nods. "Everyone."

"Why?" I ask. "I haven't done anything."

"Rumor has it that you're gonna speak at Bruno's hearing on Friday," Camila says. "People are dying to hear your side of the story."

"Oh."

"Is it true?" Ari asks me. "Are you really gonna speak in front of the school board?"

"I don't know yet," I answer. "I—I mean, I said to Bruno I would, but I haven't talked to him since Monday. I'm not sure if the school board's gonna be willing to hear what I have to say."

"Well... you can ask Bruno himself," Olivia says.

I turn around in my chair to find Bruno and Irwin walking toward our table, looking slightly nervous.

"It worked, Sol," Bruno says. "The board said that you can come speak on Friday."

For a moment, my ears buzz with the sound of different voices. Everyone around the table starts talking at the same time while I take small breaths through my mouth, only vaguely aware of the fact that Ari is touching my shoulder.

"Sol, are you okay?"

"Yeah," I answer. "That—that's good."

"This is changing things already," Bruno says. "Everyone knows you saw what actually happened, so now that you've agreed to speak up, some people are starting to question whether Jack's gonna win. They're starting to question his version of the story."

Irwin nods beside him. "A lot more people have signed up for Friday since yesterday."

"What do you mean?" I ask.

"We're getting a group of us together to go to the school district's offices," Irwin answers. "I—I mean, we're not allowed inside the room while the board is discussing, but we wanna organize a silent protest outside the building. We're meeting right after school, and we're gonna make signs, and everything."

"Do you think that'll help?" Olivia asks.

It's Bruno who nods. "The more people who show up, the better," he says. "We gotta prove that there's more people on our side than on Jack's—especially with all the pressure his parents have been putting on the board."

"We'll be there," Ari says beside me. "All of us."

While the rest of the table nods, I turn toward Bruno, feeling tightness in my throat as I remember the hearing's only two days away.

"Bruno, what should I say?" I ask him. "When I'm in front of the board, what do you think I should—"

"Just tell them the truth," he replies. "That'll be enough."

"Okay," I say, nodding. "I can do that."

Bruno smiles, and suddenly, he looks a lot more like the kid who used to join me on the bridge before any of this even started—like the kid who used to love talking about music, and his sister, and his dog. For the first time in a long time, I see him—the real him, and not the kid everyone's been whispering about lately.

Throughout the rest of the day, I try my best to keep to the sidelines, even though the spotlight seems to be following me everywhere I go. Every time I look up, I find someone new staring at me.

After years of being invisible, of moving through school as quietly as a shadow, I'm not sure what to make of this. I'm not sure what to do with all this attention, or how to feel. In the back of my mind, I wonder if this is what a part of me has wanted all along—being seen, being heard—and whether I'd rather go back to being Soledad, at least for a little while.

Whenever I walk into a classroom, I try my best to

find a seat toward the back so people will find it a bit more difficult to stare at me. And while I push myself to pay attention, and take notes, and catch up with everything I didn't bother to learn over the past couple of weeks, there's something about what Abuela said to me the other night that fills my entire body with hope. Because, as impossible as this all seems—getting through the rest of the week with the eyes of the entire school on me, and sitting in front of the school board on Friday, and finding a way to help Bruno—perhaps it's true that I'll be able to find the strength within me to do it.

When the bell finally rings at the end of the day, I rush straight toward the school doors, eager to get home and be with my family. I've barely made it halfway down the front steps, however, when I look down at my phone screen and see something that makes me stop in my tracks—a missed call from a San Diego area code.

My first instinct is to think about all the job applications I've sent out over the past week. Maybe someone is finally reaching out to schedule an interview, or to offer me a position. But then, when I think of Helen and Bill and how they must also have San Diego area codes, my entire body seems to turn to stone.

I am still frozen on the steps, debating what to do, when my phone starts buzzing with a call from the exact same number.

With shaking hands, I press the answer button and lift the phone up to my ear.

"H-hello?"

"María de la Soledad?"

"Yes," I answer, my mind racing. "Yes, it's me."

"This is Helen, from Wallen's Department Store," she says. "I'm wondering if you'd be able to stop by this afternoon."

I mumble a response. Between the adrenaline rushing through my veins and the fear of what this might mean, I can't even think clearly, but I'm able to register all the most important details—four o'clock today. Helen wants to talk. She has important news.

The second I hang up, I start to follow the crowd that's rushing toward the MTS station. And when I get there, instead of heading toward the San Ysidro platform, I go to the San Diego one and hop on the northbound trolley, my heart beating fast as my hopes, and my dreams, and my entire future seem to flash past the windows.

Helen didn't tell me where to meet her—or, if she did, I can't remember—so I go stand near the entrance to the staff room.

I've only been waiting here for a couple of minutes before the door opens and Helen steps out. "María," she says. "Thanks for coming."

She holds the door open for me, and I follow her toward the office. I wish she would've just told me what's going on when we spoke on the phone, or that I could at least read her expression and get a sense of what's coming, because the anxiety of not knowing is killing me.

It feels as though I'm holding my breath up until we're sitting across from each other at her desk, and she says, "We've finalized the internal investigation."

I lean forward in my chair, wanting to say something, but my words get caught in my throat.

"We have come to the conclusion that the dress must've been left inside one of the shipment crates. Either that, or the supplier never sent it."

"Wh-what does this mean?" I ask in a small voice.

"It means that we were wrong to assume you were to blame," Helen says. Somewhere underneath her collected front, I can tell that she is embarrassed, but she's trying her hardest not to let it show. "We owe you an apology, María de la Soledad. And you can return to work, if you wish."

Yes, I almost say. *Of course I'd like to come back.* But there's something stopping me—something that keeps me frozen in my seat. After what she and Bill put me through, after the way they so easily accused me of something I didn't do, a part of me wants more. I want more than a job at a place that will turn its back on me from one moment to the next, more than what Helen is offering me right now.

But then I think of all the job applications I've sent and haven't heard back from, and the grim silence that has filled the house during dinner since I stopped working, and I come back to the same answer I was going to give her. At least for now, this is my best and only option.

"I do," I reply, nodding slowly. "I want to return."

"Great," Helen says. "I'll add you to the schedule for next Monday, if that sounds good to you."

"Yeah." I'll have to talk to Ari and Nancy, ask if they'd be okay with me coming back to their house next week, but I can't see why they wouldn't agree. "That should work."

Helen makes a note on a piece of paper, and then, with a small smile on her face, she tells me she's looking forward to having me rejoin the team.

As soon as I walk out of the store and into the soft November sun, my resentment toward Helen starts to fade away, and instead I think about all the people I need to tell about this news. I'll need to tell Papi, and Abuela, and Ari, but my first instinct isn't to call any of them. I pick up my phone and, as my chest swells with hope and pure relief, I look for Nick's number among my contacts.

"Sol," he says when he answers. "How are you?"

"I'm..." I let out a long sigh. "I'm great, actually. I—I have news."

"Did you find a job?" he asks, sounding a lot more alert.

"No," I answer. "But I just talked to Helen."

Even through the phone, I can tell that Nick has stopped breathing. "What did she say?"

"She apologized for what happened with the dress...

and then she asked if I want to come back to work next week."

"And what did you say?"

"I said yes. I—I'm coming back on Monday, and I just—"

"That's great!" Nick replies, and something explodes inside of me—the ray of light that only he is capable of bringing into my chest. "Sol, I'm excited to see you."

"I'm excited to see you, too."

I hold the phone tight against my ear, thinking about what this means—that I'll be able to go back to seeing him every day, that I'll get to have dinner with Nancy and Ari in the evenings, that I'll be able to hand Papi a check every two weeks once again.

"Maybe... I don't know. We could have that second date this weekend?" he asks me.

"I—I'll be in Tijuana. But we can hang out next week. We could even—"

"We'll figure something out," he says to me. "Just... focus on coming back."

We stay on the line for a little while, until he tells me that he needs to go. As I walk up the street toward the trolley, I tell myself that all I have to do now is get through Bruno's hearing on Friday, and then I'll be able to breathe normally again.

CHAPTER TWENTY-SIX

On Thursday night, Luis brings back leftovers from the casino again—more chicken fingers and cold fries—so we all eat quickly, eagerly, as we do whenever our plates are full enough that we don't have to play around with our food to make it last as long as possible.

When I got home yesterday and told them all that I'd gotten my job at Wallen's back, we had a near-celebration. Papi gave me a big hug, sighing into my shoulder in a way that made his lungs deflate and his entire body feel heavy as I held him. Abuela made quesadillas for dinner with a block of cheese she'd been saving, and Diego and I turned the TV on for a while before it was time for him to go to bed.

"I'm glad it all worked out in the end," Luis said to me.

"Thanks," I replied. There was something in his voice

that made it sound as though he was struggling to get the words out, as though there were other things he wanted to say. But I could tell that, deep down, he was feeling relieved, because it'll no longer be up to just him to bring money in.

Tonight, some of that victory still lingers in the air, but there's something else, too—a silence that seems to have fallen all around us after I mentioned that I'll be speaking at Bruno's hearing tomorrow.

"¿Estás segura de que esto es lo correcto, Sol?" Papi asks me suddenly.

I look up from my plate and meet his eyes. He's asking if I'm sure—if speaking in front of the board is the right thing to do.

"Sí," I reply. "Estoy segura."

"But what if..." His voice trails off, but I know exactly what he's not saying. I know he and Abuela have been thinking about this all through dinner—about the fact that the people from the board might ask about my proof of residency documents, about the possibility that I might only get myself in trouble by walking into this situation.

"I need to do this, Papi," I say. "Because if it was my future being decided instead of Bruno's, I'd want someone to speak up for me. I'd want to know that I'm not alone."

Papi nods slowly to himself. He doesn't look convinced, but he doesn't argue.

I keep eating, dipping my fries in ketchup. The truth is, I'm not convinced either, but it's too late to back out now. The only thing left to do is hope that I'll be able to make a difference tomorrow, and that it won't all be for nothing.

⁌

From the moment I get to school the next day, Bruno's name is all I can hear.

"—two o'clock, but I heard everyone is—"

"Bruno le dijo que—"

"—pero don't worry, las pancartas van a estar listas—"

"I know! Yo tampoco creo que Bruno—"

Bruno himself is nowhere to be seen. I wonder how he's feeling, which side of him is winning—the helpless side I saw on the bridge earlier in the week, or the hopeful one I saw a glimpse of two days ago, the one who thinks he might just have a chance.

As I make my way through the hallways, the stares follow me more than ever before. I suppose it doesn't help that I'm wearing a flowery dress, which seems to be attracting much more attention than my usual jeans and t-shirt would. I wanted to look as formal as possible for the hearing, and after trying on a couple of Abuela's ugly blazers, I realized that one of my mom's old Sunday dresses would be my best bet.

The instant I walk into the cafeteria at lunchtime, I stop in my tracks. I have never seen it so packed. Half of all the kids in here must be skipping class, because every single table is full, even though not everyone seems to be eating. There are people moving all over the place, speaking loudly, passing markers around, and drawing on big, bright posters.

BRUNO BELONGS HERE, says one of the signs that's lying on a table close to me.

"Hey," says Camila when she sees me. "Here's a marker, and there are posters over there."

The energy at school continues to rise all throughout the day, and the light in the hallways seems to continuously change—at times it's dark and grim, as though someone has dimmed the lamps, and at times so bright that it's blinding. And as the buzzing of voices becomes louder and louder, I realize it's not only the people who support Bruno who are speaking up.

"The hearing's probably gonna last less than ten minutes," I hear a kid say spitefully as I pack up my things after history class. "The board's already made up their minds."

By the time the final period bell comes, a dead silence falls all around school. After a full day of loud voices and even louder opinions, it's as if everyone has finally accepted the fact that there is nothing left to do but wait.

Instead of going to my final class of the day, I head toward the school doors, where Bruno is waiting for me so we can head over to the school board building.

"Are you ready?" he asks me. He's wearing a suit, his hair is gelled to one side, and he looks every bit as nervous as I feel.

"Yeah," I answer, even though I don't feel ready at all. "Are you?"

He shrugs in response, which tells me everything I need to know.

My shoes echo loudly against the hardwood floors when I walk into the conference room where the hearing is happening. I've been standing right outside the doors for over an hour, so my legs are starting to feel a bit numb, but I manage to put one foot in front of the other and sit down at a long table, right across from the members of the school board.

There are five of them—three women and two men. When I looked them up online earlier this week, they were all smiling in the photos that were posted on the school district website. Today, they all look serious, with their hands folded neatly over the table and their lips pressed into straight lines.

"Tell us," says one of them—a woman with long, curly hair that I recognize as Sally Rivera, the president of the board. "How well do you know Bruno Rodríguez?"

There's a bottle of water on the table right in front of me, but I don't reach for it, despite how dry my throat feels. Instead, I swallow hard and say, "Pretty well, I guess."

"Would you describe him as your good friend?"

"Sure. I—I mean, I've known him for two years."

"Do you spend much time with him at school?"

"Not at school, no. He's a senior and I'm a junior, so

we're not in any of the same classes, but we sometimes hang out outside of school."

"My understanding is that you two sometimes commute together, is that right?"

I open my mouth to answer, but no words come out. Suddenly, I feel that urge again—the urge to reach for the bottle of water, to drink a few sips. I wish I could lift an arm, pick it up, and unscrew the cap, but my hands remain frozen in my lap as the five board members stare fixedly at me.

"We're not here to talk about where you live or don't live," Mrs. Rivera says, staring into my eyes. "We're only here to talk about Bruno, okay?"

I let my breath out in a long, trembling sigh. "Okay," I answer. I clear my throat, and try to answer the question again. "Yeah—we commute to school together sometimes."

"And in the time that you've spent with Bruno, have you ever perceived him to be aggressive? Or a threat to you or other people in any way?"

"No," I answer, shaking my head firmly. "Never."

One of the board members—a man wearing glasses who's sitting in the far corner—is typing furiously into a laptop, surely writing down every word we're saying. The *tap, tap, tap* of his keyboard is ringing in my ears, but I try my best to keep my attention focused on Mrs. Rivera.

"Can you tell us about what happened that day in the

cafeteria? The day Bruno got into a fight with another student?" she asks.

"Bruno and Jack started arguing," I say. "Jack said that—"

"I'm sorry to interrupt," says a woman with blond hair who's sitting right next to Mrs. Rivera. Jessica Martin, I'm pretty sure her name is. "But could you start from the very beginning? What were you doing before the conflict started?"

I nod, clearing my throat again. And then I tell them everything—how I was standing in line for food, and Bruno came up behind me. How he and I were talking, not paying much attention to what was going on around us, and how Jack complained that the line wasn't moving.

"He pushed his way past me, and he almost knocked over my tray. That was when Bruno spoke up. He—he said to Jack that he couldn't just do that, that he couldn't skip past us. Only he said it in Spanish, and that's when Jack... started saying things."

Mrs. Rivera frowns slightly, so that her eyebrows come closer together. "What exactly did he say?"

"That Bruno shouldn't be speaking Spanish. That we weren't in Mexico. It wasn't anything I haven't heard before, but... it seemed to get to Bruno."

"How did the situation escalate? When did it become physical?"

I blink slowly, trying my best to remember. "I—I think Bruno stepped forward, toward Jack. And then..."

I don't want to say the wrong thing. I don't want to fill in the gaps where my memory fails me, but I can't seem to remember exactly what happened in that moment.

It comes to me in slow motion—the image of Bruno, Jack, and me standing by the cashier line. I can almost feel the weight of a food tray in my hands, can feel the tension rising, can see the hurt look on Bruno's face.

"Jack pushed Bruno," I say. "Bruno pushed him back, and that's when it happened—when they started fighting."

Mrs. Rivera nods slowly, and she's not the only one. Miss Martin raises her eyebrows, nodding as well, and the man who's typing away shakes his head slightly.

"I can't make this into anything other than what it was," I say. "The two of them *did* get into a fight, and Bruno *did* punch Jack. But… but it was Jack who threw the first punch."

I watch Mrs. Rivera's reaction closely. I can tell this is not the first time she's heard this, but she still narrows her eyes at me.

"Are you completely sure of that?" she asks.

"A hundred percent," I say. "They were struggling on the ground, and Jack hit Bruno on the side of the head. That was when people started pulling out their cell phones and recording, but… the videos only show half of it. It was Jack who started the whole thing. He's the one who seemed to have a problem with us just because we were speaking in Spanish—he's the one who tried to get under Bruno's skin."

There's a moment of silence—a moment during which the tapping of the keyboard is all I can hear.

"And now, it's Jack who's determined to prove to Bruno that he doesn't belong here—that he doesn't deserve to finish high school, and do something with his future."

"María de la Soledad, perhaps we should—"

"I just... I don't think many people understand what it means for some of us to be able to come to school at Orangeville. I mean... we all go to the same classes, and turn in the same assignments, and eat in the same cafeteria next to each other every day. We're all technically running in the same race, but some of us started ten feet behind. And... sometimes it's hard to understand how we're meant to get to the finish line. How we're supposed to do impossible things if obstacles keep being thrown at us even when we try to catch up with everyone else."

I'm not sure where these words are coming from, but I do know one thing. All the fears I thought I would feel in this exact moment are completely gone. After being so uncertain, so anxious about talking in front of the school board, it has turned out to be shockingly easy to show up today, to use my voice, to step into the shoes of Sol.

It's all much simpler than I used to think—finding the strength that is buried deep within me, and doing things that once seemed impossible, and becoming the person I've always been meant to be. And now that I've realized this, I don't think I'll be able to go back to being Soledad. Not entirely, at least.

I wait with my hands firmly set over my lap, holding my breath as Mrs. Rivera blinks slowly. I wonder what's going through her mind—if I've managed to convince her that Bruno deserves a chance, if this will make any difference in the board's decision whether to expel him.

I'm almost sure that we're not done yet, that they're all gonna launch into a million other questions about Bruno, and Jack, and that day in the cafeteria. But then, as quickly and suddenly as she asked her first question, Mrs. Rivera gives me a vague smile.

"Thank you, María de la Soledad," she says. "That'll be all."

☀

The crowd waiting outside the building is much smaller than I thought it would be. For all the talk about Bruno earlier today, and all the people helping out with the signs in the cafeteria, the protest looks a lot smaller out here. Twenty or thirty people, maybe, most of whom are starting to look exhausted from standing here for too long.

"Well?" Irwin asks me as I walk down the front steps of the building. "How did it go?"

The entire crowd shuffles as some people lean forward, trying to listen in on what I'm about to say.

"I'm not sure," I answer.

Irwin's expression falls. I wish I could tell him that it went well. I wish I could give him something more than this, but I don't have the ability to comfort him right now—not when my heart is beating fast against my chest, reminding me that the board's decision will come sooner rather than later, and we're all gonna have to deal with it once it does.

I turn toward the crowd instead, scanning one face after another. I recognize most of these people from Orangeville, but there are a few that I'm sure go to a different school. And then, when I find Ari's gaze staring back at me, my heart stops beating altogether.

Irwin asks me something else, but I don't even hear what it is. I step forward to make my way through the crowd, and when I reach the spot where Ari is standing, I fall straight into her arms.

"Sol," she says. "Is everything okay?"

"I don't know, Ari," I say into her ear. "I just hope I did everything I could've done to help him."

"You did," Ari says. "I know you did."

When I pull away from her, I realize that everyone else is standing right beside us—Camila, Olivia, Ana María, Tony, Simon. They're all carrying signs, but no one is lifting them up anymore. Camila's is starting to look a bit worn around the edges, and Tony has rolled up his and is carrying it under his arm.

"How long have you all been out here?" I ask.

"Since the last bell of the day rang, so... definitely more than an hour," Olivia answers. "A big group of us walked over from school."

"Is Bruno still in there?" Simon asks me, nodding toward the building.

"Yeah. I saw him just now, when I walked out of the conference room."

"And the people from the board? What were they like?"

"They were... serious," I answer. "I couldn't really tell whose side they were on."

"Do you think they'll make a decision today?"

"I don't know. I hope they will," I say, thinking about Bruno. Thinking about how agonizing the wait must be for him, how badly he must be wishing for closure on this whole thing, regardless of what the board decides in the end.

I'm not sure how long we stand here, staring at the front doors of the building. Whispers travel from one side of the crowd to the other, and a few people come and go, yet the doors remain still.

"That doesn't look too good," Camila says suddenly, pointing toward the sky. There are dark clouds forming in the distance, and they seem to be rolling in our direction.

"What should we do?" Ana María asks from behind me. "Is there any point in waiting out here?"

"I don't know," Tony whispers back. "The school board might not even—"

He chokes on his own words, because right at that moment, the doors of the building open.

Everyone seems to go silent at the same time. We stop

whispering, stop moving, stop breathing. It's as if even the wind has stopped blowing and the seconds have stopped passing as we all turn to face the front.

Bruno walks out of the building and blinks repeatedly, as though he's been blinded by the light. For a moment, he looks shocked, as he stares out at all the people who are gathered here for him, but then he turns toward Irwin.

"Well?" Irwin asks.

Bruno nods, the corner of his mouth twisting into a smile, and the entire crowd bursts into cheers.

I try to make eye contact with him, wanting to get confirmation that his nod really did mean what I think it did—that he's gonna be able to stay, that the school board voted in his favor—but I can't even find his face in the crowd as everyone hugs, and smiles, and lets out sighs of relief.

The dark clouds close in on us and big drops of rain start falling from the sky, but no one seems to care. All that really, truly matters is the energy in this little corner of the parking lot, the sound of the loud voices all around me, the pure relief swelling inside my chest.

CHAPTER TWENTY-SEVEN

THE DARK CLOUDS LINGER FOR A WHILE. THE RAIN IS at times stronger, at times lighter, but even while I stare out the window of the trolley on my way home, there are raindrops sliding down the glass, making everything outside look hazy and blurry.

When I walk into my house, it's completely silent. There's no buzzing of the refrigerator, no sound of voices, no sign of anyone here.

"Hello?" I call out, but there's no reply.

With every step I take deeper into the house, my heart seems to fall lower and lower. During the whole ride to the border, I kept thinking about getting home and telling my family about what happened at the hearing. I've been wanting to share the good news with them, but now all I can think about is the eerie silence that surrounds me.

I pull out my phone, thinking about calling my dad, when all of a sudden I start to make out a noise—the hush of whispered voices.

I tiptoe my way toward it, and it leads me all the way to Luis and Diego's bedroom. As I lean closer to the door, the voices become clearer.

"—wait until she gets here."

"Maybe we should go now."

"We might not even need to go. I think he's just sleeping."

I push the door open to find an odd scene in front of me. Diego is lying on his bed, looking fast asleep. There's a big bruise on his face, a bump on his forehead, and his hands are gently folded on top of his stomach, while Papi, Luis, and Abuela stand over his bed.

My dad is the first to notice me standing at the doorway.

"Sol," he says. "We were wondering when you'd be home."

"What happened?" I ask, my heart rate speeding up.

"He got into trouble again at school," Luis says. "Some kid pushed him, and he fell and hit his head."

"Is he okay? How did—"

"We think he's okay," Papi answers.

"He didn't give us many details," Abuela whispers from the corner where she's standing. "But your dad and I talked to one of the teachers when we went to pick him up, and she said Diego's been struggling with bullies lately."

"Well, what do we do?" I ask, taking a step closer to Diego's bed. "Does he need to see a doctor? Do we need to—"

"That's what we were talking about just now," Papi answers. "He kept insisting he was fine. We helped him get into bed, and now he's been sleeping for a while."

"I read online that it's not a good thing, though," Luis adds quickly. "It says you shouldn't sleep after a head injury."

Abuela nods. "Maybe we should try to wake him up."

"We shouldn't bother him," Papi whispers. "Let's let him sleep, and we'll see what he says when he wakes up."

I fall silent, my mind racing. I'm not sure who to side with, or what the right thing is to do. Maybe Abuela is right—we should try to wake him, and make sure he's feeling okay. Then again, if Papi is right, and he's only tired, then we should let him rest. He's had a hard enough day.

One moment of silence turns into another, and all of a sudden none of us knows what to say. And while we stand here around Diego's tiny bed, dozens of memories start to creep into my mind. There's something about this whole thing that reminds me of when Mami first got sick.

Looking around at Papi's, Luis's, and Abuela's faces, I see so many of the same things as I did back then. There's despair in Papi's eyes as he stares down at Diego without blinking. Abuela's pressing her hands against her lips, and I can almost hear the prayer she's saying to herself, even though no words are coming out of her mouth at all. Luis is frowning, frowning, frowning, standing frozen with his arms crossed and his shoulders arched back. And me... well, I'm not sure. I remember feeling numb back then. I remember standing motionless in front of Mami, unable to believe that she was really sick, unable to wrap my head around the possibility that she might leave us.

But now, it's not numbness I feel. It is desperation, restlessness. I'm finding it hard to stand still. Because, while Papi, Luis, and Abuela retreat into themselves, feeling just as hopeless as they did back when Mami was sick, I know this isn't the same. We're not the same people, and this is not the same situation. There must be something to do.

"Can we call Roberto?" I ask Papi. He's the doctor who treated Mami. He had to deliver so much bad news to us over time that he became something other than a doctor to us—he became a part of our family, someone who knew everything that went on in our house, who understood every single challenge we were going through. I'm sure that if we called him now, he'd be willing to help us. He'd be willing to answer our questions, and maybe even come take a look at my brother.

"I haven't spoken to him in over a year," Papi replies.

"Call him," I say. "Please."

"I'm just not sure if he'll—"

"Who are you going to call?" a voice comes all of a sudden—a voice I wasn't expecting.

Turning toward the bed quickly, I see Diego has opened his eyes. He's leaning his head against the pillow, staring at all of us with a slight frown on his face.

"Diego!" Abuela says, rushing to his side.

"Are you okay?" I ask, at the same time that Luis demands, "How are you feeling?"

"Annoyed," Diego replies, and I can't help myself—I let out a small laugh. "Why'd you wake me up?"

"We were worried about you," Abuela says. "We weren't sure if you needed to see a doctor."

"Is that why you've all been watching me while I nap?"

I meet Luis's eyes. Somehow, I can tell he's also trying hard not to laugh.

"How are you, Diego?" I ask. "Luis told me you hit your head, and we just thought—"

"I'm okay, I think," he says.

Almost at the same time, the rest of us let out a sigh. We meet each other's eyes, breathing a lot easier now that Diego is sitting up on the bed and talking.

After a moment, though, I find something else in the silence. It's a lot like the restlessness I was feeling a minute ago, except I can now see it on everyone else's faces: Papi's, Abuela's, Luis's. I can tell they're all trying hard to figure out what to say, what to do, even though no one seems to be able to move.

I'm the first to find my voice. "What happened?" I ask. "Diego, how did you—"

"It was the same kids as before." He swallows hard. "I was just sitting with my friend Andrés. We—we were eating, and drawing in our sketchbooks, and they came up to us."

"What did you do?"

"Nothing, at first. They started saying mean things, and we tried to ignore them, until…"

Luis leans closer to him. "Until what?"

"Until I started talking back, and that's when it happened."

"That's when they pushed you?" Abuela asks.

Diego starts nodding but stops quickly, wincing in pain.

"He can't go back to that school," Papi says, shaking his head firmly.

"What should he do, then?" I ask him. "Where else is he gonna go?"

We all fall silent again, realizing that Diego has no choice. We have no way to pay for private school, but we can't let the bullies win. He can't stop going to school just because of them.

"We'll go talk to the principal," Abuela says. "Your father and I."

"And I'll walk you to and from school every day," Luis says to Diego. "Make sure those kids know you have an older brother who'll stand up for you."

I take a step closer to the bed, sitting down next to Diego.

"And I'll be there for you," I say to him, staring deep into his eyes. "It doesn't matter if I'm at Ari's—you can always call me. Day or night."

Even though he hardly looks like himself with the big bruise beneath his eye, I can tell he's listening intently—and that he's trying his hardest to believe me.

"We won't let those kids win," I whisper. "We're all here for you."

Without warning, tears come pouring from his eyes. He doesn't sob, doesn't make a sound. He sits very still, crying quietly, and that's when my own eyes start burning with fresh tears.

I pull him into a hug, and he falls into my arms easily. And while he cries into my shirt, I sneak a glance up at Papi, Abuela, and Luis. They've all stepped closer to the bed, and I can feel them all beside me. Luis puts a hand on Diego's back, while Papi squeezes my shoulder, and Abuela tries to wrap her arms around all of us.

And for the first time in I don't know how long, I don't feel alone when I'm next to them. I can hear their heavy breathing, can almost feel their hearts beating at the same time as mine. Somehow, I can feel Mami near—the way I used to when I walked into the restaurant, the way I some-times do when I close my eyes and try to remember the sound of her voice.

Maybe this is who we would be if she had never left

us. Maybe, if the cancer had never come, or if the doctor had delivered better news when she got her diagnosis, or if she'd managed to beat it, we would've remained united, and strong, and less afraid, just as we used to be.

But now, I think that we might just manage to become those people again. We might figure out how to escape from all the pain, and the fear, and the grief that has held us back from the moment we first heard Mami was sick. We might be able to help Diego get through the school year, and find a way to pay back Papi's debts, and help Luis send out his college applications, and put food on the table—as long as we stick together.

"It's all gonna be okay," Abuela whispers suddenly. I know she's talking to Diego, but her words still bring me comfort, still bring warmth to my chest, as if she'd spoken them directly to me.

I have no idea how long we remain here, huddled together around Diego. The rain keeps tapping softly against the window, and the sunlight starts fading, but we don't move.

I don't know what we're gonna eat for dinner, or when we're gonna turn the lights on, or what I'm gonna do about all the homework I have to do. The only thing I'm certain of is that, in this moment, I have everything I need right here next to me.

CHAPTER TWENTY-EIGHT

I'VE BEEN LOOKING AFTER THE LIME TREE IN OUR backyard lately, following my mother's old advice—spray it with three parts water, one part liquid soap.

"It's deadly to the pests, but harmless to the plant," she used to say.

I've been doing this as often as I can, feeling my heart growing every weekend when I see it looking a little healthier. The leaves are turning greener, the fruit is blooming. It's almost illogical—how other trees seem to be dying down now that winter is almost here, but this little lime tree in our backyard is flourishing.

I just wish I could be around more, so I could water it every day. When I leave home on Monday mornings, I always remind Papi to look after it. At first, I wasn't sure if he would bother listening to me, but he has, and it hasn't only been him. Abuela, Diego, and even Luis—they've all been taking turns going out to the backyard once a day while I'm gone, spraying the leaves with soap and making sure it's watered.

"It's looking better," Papi says to me while we make dinner on a Sunday in December. "The tree."

I nod at him. I know the long days of going around the city, answering calls to fix issues with people's cars, have been taking their toll on him, but he's been a bit more energetic lately, a little less angry.

We carry our plates to the dinner table. Once we're all sitting around it, Papi clears his throat.

"I talked to Rafael this morning," he says as he breaks off a piece of bolillo and dips it into his soup.

We all look up at him. He hasn't mentioned his old boss from the car shop in a long time, so I can't help but hold my breath, hoping he's about to deliver good news.

"Has he asked you to come back to work?" Abuela asks.

"Not exactly. He's retiring at the end of this year, and he wants to sell the car shop."

My stomach drops. Since I returned to work at Wallen's, we may have been able to keep up with the bills and start eating something other than rice and tortillas, but we're a long way from gathering enough money to be able to start a new business.

"What did you tell him?" Luis asks, frowning slightly.

"That's the thing," Papi answers. "He agreed to let me take over the shop and split the profits with him until I'm able to buy him out."

Something happens around the table right at that moment. We all seem to relax our shoulders at the same time, because this sounds a lot like the moment we've all been waiting for—the sign that things will finally start getting back on track for all of us. A second later, however, a deep sadness falls over the dining room, and I know exactly what everyone is thinking about—Mami's restaurant. Because the thought of starting a new business that doesn't include her—or her ideas, or her food—feels almost like a betrayal. The place we loved—the one we tried and failed to save—is gone, and nothing else could ever replace that.

"Your mom and her restaurant may be gone," Papi says slowly, as if he knew exactly what I'm thinking. "But we're still here. And we need to find a way to make a living."

"Does this mean Sol is gonna be able to come back home soon?" Diego asks. He's been a little less quiet during dinner over the past few weekends, a little more curious about what the rest of us talk about.

I hold my breath, waiting to hear what Papi says, because maybe that is exactly what this means. Perhaps, if Papi starts making enough money at the car shop, I could finally come back home.

Before my dad can find the right words to say, Luis speaks up.

"If I get the job at Costco, it might," he says. I've been helping him look for new jobs and prepare for interviews over the past couple of weeks. We've been trying to find a better job for him—one with better hours and better pay, and he had an interview at the Costco in Zona Río on Friday. It would mean a decent check coming every two weeks—not to mention an employee discount on food, and house supplies, and everything we might need.

"It's too soon to say," Papi adds. "But, if that's what Sol wants... yes, she could come back home at some point soon."

If that's what Sol wants. His words keep ringing in my ears long after we've finished eating dinner. It's funny, how I've been wishing for this ever since I moved in with Ari, but now I'm not so sure—I'm not sure I'm ready to give up dinners at her house, or shifts at the store, or seeing Nick every day. I'm not sure I'd be able to get used to the idea of not having to provide for my family, of not having to be an adult anymore.

The next morning, Papi and I head out of the house in a rush. He drops me off at the border as he always does, and I walk quickly across the esplanade, toward the ramp. The wait on the bridge has felt shorter lately, the sun rising in the distance a little brighter. Maybe it has something to do with Bruno, who I seem to be running into a lot.

Today, I've barely been waiting in line for five minutes before he sneaks up behind me with a smile on his face.

"Morning," he says.

"Morning."

Ever since the whole disciplinary hearing ordeal ended, something has changed between us. We're more than just two kids who sometimes commute together, more than two kids from Tijuana. We've become friends—real friends.

"Good weekend?" Bruno asks me.

I smile and say, "Yeah," and that's all it takes for us to start talking our hearts out—about the places we went to, the food we ate. He tells me about how his little sister is learning to play the drums, which has been giving everyone at his house constant headaches, and I tell him about Diego, and how he's been doing better ever since Papi and Abuela went to talk to his teachers and Luis started walking him to and from school every day.

I've also been telling Bruno about Nick. I've told him about our second date, when we picked up In-N-Out and went back to our spot in the woods, and about our third date, when Nick took me to Coronado Beach and tried to convince me to go into the water even though it was freezing. I've also told Bruno about the way Nick makes me feel, and how every time my skin touches his—even when it's by accident—it's as if he sends a shock wave through my body, making me feel electricity that's unlike anything I've ever felt before.

It's weird sometimes, having Bruno as a friend. I constantly find myself worrying that I've overshared, that I've said too much and he'll think I'm weird, but I've slowly started to learn that there's nothing I could possibly say that could make him judge me. That's the thing about being friends with someone who's also struggled with figuring out where he belongs—there's a silent promise at the heart of our friendship that we can each come exactly as we are.

Bruno waits for me outside of passport control, and we walk together toward the MTS station. We go our separate ways when we get to school, but not without first agreeing that we'll see each other at lunch. He and some of his friends have joined our cafeteria table. Irwin, Johnny, Arturo—they're all nerdy, and they're all just as obsessed with that Santa Monica–based rock band as Bruno is, but they've meshed surprisingly well with the rest of the table.

The day slips by. Keeping up with my schoolwork hasn't gotten any easier, but I've been trying harder to pay attention in class and take notes. It doesn't change the heaps of homework I have to get through every day, but not having to play catch-up with what we're learning in class has at least made things a bit easier.

When the last bell of the day rings, I meet Ari out in the parking lot as usual.

"You ready to go?"

I've also been feeling a bit different around her, even though nothing has really changed. During the time we spend together in the car driving up to San Diego, while I eat meals with her and Nancy, when all three of us cuddle up on the couch to watch TV, there's a lightness between us that I can't really explain. All I know is that it feels a lot like when we were kids—easy, effortless, as natural as meeting up with your neighbor who lives right around the corner, or playing with your best friend at recess.

Today, we drive with the windows rolled down. The December air is crisp, but my skin feels warm every time a ray of sunlight hits me directly.

"Your birthday's coming up," Ari says to me, smiling slightly.

"Yeah." I've never been a huge fan of my birthday. Even when we were little, it was Ari who would have the big birthday parties, with princess dresses and big piñatas, but I always preferred doing something smaller: having a picnic, or going to the beach, or to the movies. This year, I don't think there'll be any of that. All I want is to have a Sunday at home—a Sunday with my family. That's the best birthday I could possibly ask for.

"We should do something fun," Ari says.

"Like what?"

She sneaks a quick glance at me. "We'll figure something out." There's something about the way she's smiling that makes me wonder if she has a surprise planned, but I don't ask.

Lately, Wallen's has been much busier than usual. When we get there, we have to make our way through a mass of customers who are moving around the store anxiously, carrying big bags, checking lists on their phones, and speaking loudly among themselves. Everyone told me that working in retail during the holidays would be crazy, but I don't think I fully understood what they meant until now.

Ari and I make our way up the busy escalator toward the fourth floor, and the minute we approach the staff room door, it swings open and five different people walk out quickly, looking stiff and stressed. It's not just the customers who go crazy around this time of the year, apparently. It's all of us.

Still, coming back to work at the store has been a relief, and not only because of the paychecks. The instant I stepped back into the warehouse on my first shift after the whole ordeal with the dress, I realized how much I'd missed this place.

I'd missed Lina, and Kelly, and Marcos, who were so happy to see me, you'd think I was their long-lost daughter.

Mostly, I'd missed Nick. I don't think he's ever looked cuter than he does today, even though he hasn't changed anything. He's wearing a plaid shirt and his same old jeans, and his blond hair is pushed back. When he sees me staring at him, he smiles, cramped teeth and all, and my chest flutters.

"Hey," I say to him as I join him at the table.

"Hey," he answers. "We were all just talking about you."

"About me? Why?"

He's barely opening his mouth to answer when I hear a woman's voice calling my name.

"Sol?"

I turn around to find Helen standing at the door. She's carrying her clipboard, and there are circles under her eyes that tell me she's also been a bit more stressed than usual lately.

"Yeah?"

"Do you have a couple of minutes to chat?"

My stomach is filled with dread. I can't help but think about the dress, can't help but wonder if she's about to reopen that whole thing. But when I meet Nick's eyes, I have a feeling he already knows what Helen wants to talk to me about, and he's smiling.

"You should go," he says, nodding toward the door.

"Uh... okay." I walk over to Helen, my heart beating fast against my chest. But then, when she smiles, I manage to let my breath out through my nose.

"I wanted to ask if you'd be interested in a sales position," she says as soon as we step out of the stockroom.

"Uh... sales?"

"Yes, sales. We need as many hands as we can get on the floor during the next few weeks. But, if you're happy in the new role, you could switch over from the warehouse team permanently."

My first thought is that I don't want to leave the warehouse—I don't want to leave Nick, or any of our friends. I can't imagine myself coming into work at the store every day and not seeing him, but then I start to think about the possibility of no more early morning or late shifts, no more rides from Nancy at four a.m. or lonely trolley rides at night.

"Would I be able to work after school?" I ask.

"Well, yes. We could find you afternoon shifts."

I almost agree right away. I'd probably be stupid not to accept this, but there's something that holds me back—the thought of what Papi said last night during dinner. Maybe I need a bit more time to find out whether the money he'll be making at the car shop is enough, to figure out what *I* want.

"Can I think about it for a few days?"

"Let me know once you've decided," Helen says. "The sooner, the better."

When I return to the warehouse, Nick is still smiling. He watches me intently as I walk around the big table and join him.

"How did you know?" I ask.

"How did I know what?" He's trying his hardest to seem clueless, but the smile at the corner of his mouth betrays him.

"That she was gonna offer me a sales position," I answer anyway.

"Because she asked a couple of us earlier if we also wanted to switch over to sales."

"And what did you say?"

"Well… Kelly said she might do it. But I'm happy where I am. I think I'm gonna stay."

My heart falls. A part of me had been hoping he'd say he was gonna switch over as well, because that would've made this decision a lot easier.

"You should take it, though," he says. "If that's what you want, I mean."

As I stare into his eyes, a deep sadness settles at the bottom of my stomach. "But I wouldn't work next to you every day anymore," I say. "We'd have different shifts, different hours."

Nick shrugs a little. "We'll find a way to still see each other," he replies. "Even if you told me you were moving halfway around the world, I'd still want to find a way."

I look down, not wanting him to see me blushing, but the truth is that I feel the same. Even if I didn't work in the warehouse anymore, or if I quit my job at Wallen's, or if I moved halfway around the world, I'd still want to make time for Nick, to hang out with him on weekends, to see if we could become anything more than what we are now.

"Tell me," he says as I open up a crate and start working. "Did you catch up on *Pasiones* over the weekend?"

"I did," I say, nodding. I spent Saturday night sitting on the couch with Diego and Abuela, watching *Pasiones de tu Corazón*. We started watching it again recently, which hasn't been easy to do after missing two whole seasons, but we're trying our best to catch up.

"I can't believe Amara's sister got shot," Nick says. He started watching it, too—mostly because I kept telling him about it—and I'm not sure how he's doing it, but he's managed to keep up with the show pretty well even though it's all in Spanish and he doesn't speak a word of it.

"This week's episodes are gonna be crazy," I say. "Or, I mean, craz*ier* than usual."

"Oh, they will be," he replies. "Maybe, you know, we should watch it together sometime?"

I smile at him. "That would be fun."

Suddenly, I can just see it—I can see us watching *Pasiones* side by side, and hanging out in the afternoons, and inviting him to come down to meet my family in Tijuana one day.

One day, I tell myself. Because, for now, I'm grateful to have just this: These few hours of standing beside him, working, laughing. These moments that seem to belong to only the two of us, even when we're in a big old warehouse, surrounded by people, piles of crates, and clothing racks.

"So? Are you gonna take it?" Ari asks me.

I'm sitting around the dinner table with her and Nancy. I've been telling them about what happened at the store earlier, and they've been listening to me intently.

"Yeah," I say. "I think so."

"It'll be great, mija," Nancy says, nodding quickly. "Those crazy work hours will be the death of you if you stay in the warehouse, I'm telling you."

"That's true."

"And we'll be able to drive to and from the store together every day," Ari says.

"Yeah."

"And you're welcome to stay with us either way," Nancy adds, leaning a little closer to me. "Esta es tu casa, mija."

I've been thinking about this a lot—the fact that afternoon shifts might still not allow me to go back home at the end of each day. Because if my shifts end at eight, and it takes me over an hour to get to the border... well, there would be no point heading home at that time, only to be up again by five a.m. the next morning to go to school. I just wish I could figure out a way—that I could go back home for good and still earn enough money to help my family.

"Thank you, Nancy," I answer. Just when I start to feel a bit overwhelmed by the thought of having to make a decision soon, I change the subject. "When's Ceci getting here?"

"On Saturday," Ari says. "But don't worry. The air mattress is supposed to arrive before then."

Ceci will be done with finals soon, so she's coming home for Christmas. Nancy ordered an air mattress online so I can sleep in Ari's room while Ceci is here, and even though a part of me would rather just sleep on the couch, I couldn't complain—not when they're so determined to make it all work so I can live with them even when their house is full.

I wonder what would happen if I no longer lived here, if I went back home for good. I'm scared that we would lose this—that we'd lose this closeness, that Ari would go back to being a friend instead of a sister, and that Nancy would become my friend's mom, instead of someone who is able to bring me warmth, and comfort, and help when I need it most.

But, as the two of them smile back at me, I realize that now that we've become family, there's no going back.

And there is no amount of time or distance that could ever change what they mean to me, or what I mean to them.

"Luis?" Papi says halfway through dinner on Saturday evening. "Do you wanna tell them, or do you want me to?"

Luis looks up from his plate. Judging from the spark in his eyes, I'm able to guess what he's about to say even before he opens his mouth.

"I got the job," he says, a wide smile spreading across his face.

"What?"

"The one at Costco."

The dining room is loud all of a sudden, as the rest of us gasp and laugh.

"I knew you'd get it," Abuela says once the noise dies down, her voice shrill with excitement. "When do you start?"

Luis isn't used to receiving this much attention, but it's easy to see that a part of him likes it. "Next week."

"And the money's even better than we'd thought," Papi says. "Tell them."

Luis looks up from his plate. "It's a pretty decent wage," he says. "So I'll definitely be able to send out college applications for next year."

"And you can come home," Diego says, turning to me. "You *will* come home, won't you?"

I put my fork down. Suddenly, I feel like I'm floating.

I haven't told them about the sales position that Helen offered me earlier this week. It's not like I've wanted to keep it a secret, but I just haven't found the right time to talk about it. I haven't felt ready to have a conversation about coming back home, or about my future.

You will prove to us that this family can do extraordinary things. I hear Abuela's voice inside my mind all of a sudden. Maybe she's right—maybe, despite how hard it was to leave home, and move in with Ari, and start working at the store, we all needed this, and not just because of the money I've brought back every two weeks.

Maybe we all needed to realize that we could do more, that we could become more, and perhaps I'm not the only one who's managed to do something remarkable. Maybe all of us have already done extraordinary things, because even despite Mami's absence, we're all here, sitting around the dinner table, talking about the future. And that is more than I thought was possible after she left us.

I wake up on Sunday to the feeling of warm sunshine hitting my face. It takes me a moment to understand what is happening, where the sunlight is coming from. But when I roll over and blink a few times, I see Abuela staring at me over her shoulder. She's standing by my bedroom window, opening the curtains to let the light in.

"Feliz cumpleaños, mija," she says.

I lift my head up from the pillow. "Gracias, Abuela."

She smiles at me and lowers herself to sit at the foot of the bed with her hands on her lap. "Seventeen years old," she whispers.

The number sounds a bit odd, coming from her lips. Seventeen. It sounds so... young somehow, and I don't feel young. I feel as though I should be much older, as though I have aged several years in the past few months alone.

For a moment, she lingers, not moving, not saying anything. She just stares at me with her eyes slightly narrowed, almost as if she were trying to recognize me. As if there were a stranger lying in my bed—as if I'd woken up as someone entirely new this morning.

"Nancy told me you were offered a sales position at Wallen's," she says.

It takes me a few moments to find my voice. The first questions on my mind are how and when she spoke to Nancy, but then it becomes obvious: the fact that they've been having phone conversations all along, the fact that Abuela has been checking in on me this whole time.

Slowly, I nod. "Yeah."

"And?" Abuela asks me. "Are you going to take it?"

After days and nights of asking myself this exact question, I've pretty much made up my mind. The answer has to be that yes, I'll take it. I'll keep living at Nancy and Ari's, head to work every day after school, and bring paychecks back every couple weeks. The real answer, though, is that I want to be here, at home. I want to spend my afternoons doing homework next to Diego, and my evenings having

336

dinner with my family. I want to be here to help Luis fill out his college applications, and to hear Papi's stories from the car shop when he comes back from work every night.

"You don't have to, you know?" she says softly.

"What?"

"You should come back, mija. You should quit and come back home for good."

"What about the money?" I say.

"If we need extra money, your dad will make sure we find it," Abuela answers. "It's his turn now—his and Luis's. You've done what you had to do, and it's not your job to carry this burden anymore."

"I also have to think about college."

"Well… when the time is right, maybe you can look for a new job closer to home that will allow you to save money for college," Abuela says. "I know how hard the past few months have been for you—dealing with all the pressure, all that weight… and now you deserve to recover, to look after yourself, so you can later focus on the bigger and better things that your future will bring."

I swallow back a knot in my throat. There's lightness in my chest that I haven't felt in months, joy inside my heart when I hear these words, but I know it's probably gonna be harder than Abuela is making it sound. It always is.

"Breakfast is almost ready," she says, getting up from the bed and turning toward the bedroom door. "Meet us out there."

"Thanks."

DANIEL ALEMAN

I get out of bed and make my way to the kitchen, to find that everyone is already waiting for me. There are no balloons, no decorations, not even a special breakfast, but having my whole family here is everything I could possibly want.

"Happy birthday!" Diego says when he sees me.

Papi pulls me into a hug, while Luis smiles at me from the corner of the kitchen.

"We'll have a celebration today," Abuela says.

"We really don't need to—"

"I'm making tamales."

I choke on my own words. I've never been able to say no to tamales, and so once we've cleared the table after breakfast, I help Abuela get started. We set a big pot over the stove to make the dough, we put tomatillos, onions, and chiles into the blender to make the salsa, and we soak the corn husks. And while we work, all I can think about is what she said to me earlier.

I don't know if I can do it—if I can let go of this weight I've been feeling over the past few months, if I can go back to being Papi's daughter, and Diego and Luis's sister, and Abuela's granddaughter. I don't know if I can just pretend I've forgotten about money, and the bills, and the need to bring paychecks back home, and start worrying only about my friends, and making plans with Nick, and—one day, when it's right—a new job that allows me to come home every evening, so I can save for my college applications.

But then, when the tamales are cooking and I step out

338

through the back door into the white sunshine, I feel different, almost as if I were stepping into a dream, where everything feels easier, and happier, and less complicated than I'd made it out to be.

The sky is deep blue and the leaves of Mami's old lime tree are bright green. Diego is walking around barefoot on the grass. Luis is helping Papi set up a table and folding chairs so we can have lunch outside, and Abuela is inside finishing up the tamales.

"So?" she whispers to me a while later, sneaking up behind me. "Will you do it, Sol? Will you stay?"

I look into her eyes, realizing this has been the real answer all along. One day I'll have to leave home for good. I'll have to move to California to go to college and do all the things I said I would. But when I do, it'll be because I want to, and not because I have to. In the meantime, I'll keep crossing bridges every day.

And if ever I feel lonely, I'll try to remember that I have a family on both sides of the border. I'll think of Nancy and Ari. I'll think of warm nights under the starlight next to Nick, and of this exact moment beside Papi, Luis, Diego, and Abuela.

I'll think about the fact that my life is here, but also there, and I'll keep coming and going, just like waves in the ocean.

ACKNOWLEDGMENTS

I'VE WRITTEN MANY BOOKS OVER THE YEARS, BUT THIS was by far the most challenging one. I'm grateful, first and foremost, to my mom, who read draft, after draft, (after draft!) of this novel. Ma, thank you for always being readily available to give me your thoughts about the story or simply for a chat. To my dad, my sister, and my brother: Thank you for being there for me always.

This book is, in many ways, for my late grandmothers. To my Abuela Lety, who had her first encounter with grief at an extremely young age and was never able to escape from it: I understand you better now, and I wish I could've shared this story with you. And to my Abuela Tere, who had no option but to harden as a result of her own grief: You were one of the strongest women I've ever met.

My brilliant editor, Farrin Jacobs, guided me through the intimidating process of writing a sophomore novel. Thank you for your expert insight, your patience, and your faith in this story, Farrin. I am so grateful to Brittany Groves, Erika Turner, and Mishma Nixon for their

ACKNOWLEDGMENTS

invaluable support, to David Curtis for his beautiful cover illustration, and to the rest of the team at Little, Brown Books for Young Readers, including Crystal Castro, Bill Grace, Sasha Illingworth, Savannah Kennelly, Cassie Malmo, Amber Mercado, Annie McDonnell, Esther Reisberg, Christie Michel, Emilie Polster, Marisa Russell, Victoria Stapleton, and Megan Tingley.

Pete Knapp, my literary agent, has already heard this a million times, but I'll say it again: Thank you for believing in me, for your relentless support, and for your flawless advice. To Stuti Telidevara, Andrea Mai, Emily Sweet, Abby Koons, and the entire team at Park & Fine: Thank you for everything you do.

I'm grateful to my film agent, Mary Pender-Coplan, and everyone at UTA—I'm so lucky to have you in my corner!

To Jacky Carrasco, Paulina Reynoso, Frida Quevedo, Char Walther, and Jimena Sierra, who knew me through my most awkward phases and are somehow still my friends: I am so thankful to have you by my side. It wasn't until we were all at the beach together that this story fully clicked for me. Vanessa Castillo, who long ago used her voice when I was unable to use my own: Thank you for being my friend, and for all the lessons you taught me.

Conor McDermott, thank you for your patience and unwavering support while I was working on this book. Matt La Placa, I miss you and can't wait to be reunited. Elizabeth Grant, thank you for being an inspiration to

342

me always. Luis Ernesto Guerra, I am so grateful for your support, both then and now. To Karla Gutiérrez, Sarah Ellwood, Victoria Gies, Lucy Boyko, Sarah Devine: Thank you for being on my team even after all this time.

I am grateful for the friendship and support of so many people, including Ana Sofía Ibarra, Norma Vargas, Emilio Sosa, Jorge Carrillo, Bianca Guilbert, Daniela Morales, Valeria Mayor, Jonathan Benitez, John Nesbitt, Brittney Clendenan, Lauren Lawson, Renee Cervantes, Taylor Steele, Joel Ferrier, Kate Pinchin, Mikyla Kay, Laura Schreiber, Lindsay Holmgren, Leyla Erdan, and Jess Panetta.

Thank you to the authors who have provided encouragement, friendship, or advice, or who have simply inspired me with their talent and passion for storytelling: Adi Alsaid, Cory Anderson, Maria E. Andreu, Maya Ameyaw, Paul Coccia, Lane Clarke, Elora Cook, Zoraida Córdova, Kess Costales, Alda P. Dobbs, Payal Doshi, Kelly Loy Gilbert, Ayana Gray, June Hur, Jason June, M.T. Khan, Ryan La Sala, David Levithan, Margarita Longoria, Yamile Saied Mendez, Kelly Mustian, Ginny Myers Sain, Louisa Onomé, Jodi Picoult, Lev Rosen, Liselle Sambury, Adam Sass, Elizabeth Urso, Julian Winters, and Jeff Zentner. Special shoutout to Melissa See and Daniela Ramirez for being the absolute best!

I have met so many librarians, booksellers, and bloggers who have marked my journey with their kindness, enthusiasm, and support. Thank you to Brittany Bunzey,

ACKNOWLEDGMENTS

Emily Francis, Rafael Rodriguez Jr., Leyla Demirel, Yvonne Palos Vitt, Jennifer Cardenas and all the folks at the Latinx Book and Chisme Club; Simeon Tsanev, Brittany Bunzey, Tara Torres, Delia Ruiz, Sofia Rathjen, Kasee Bailey, Erik Tlaxcantitla, Astrid Pizarro, Jacob Demlow, Louis Williams, Chad Harper, Marieke du Pré, Eytan Kessler, and to everyone else who showed support for Indivisible. You are all amazing.

I am incredibly grateful to the people I met during my time in Tijuana and San Diego, who so generously shared a piece of themselves and their lives with me. Thank you especially to Pancho Parra for his invaluable insight and kindness.

And to you, if you're reading this: Thank you for being with me on this journey. I appreciate your support more than you know.

C. M. McDermott

Daniel Aleman

is the award-winning author of *Indivisible*. Born and raised in Mexico City, he has lived in various places across North America and is currently based in Toronto, where he is on a never-ending search for the best tacos in the city. *Brighter Than the Sun* is his second novel. Daniel invites you to connect with him at danielaleman.com.